"*The Journalist* is unlike any other book that you've read on the Vietnam War. Jerry—its main character, who clearly cared deeply about Vietnam and its people—is driven to tell the story of Vietnam to American readers. He fights with jaded editors back home to put a face on a war that few Americans knew or cared about at the time. This prescient memoir has the suspense of a novel that anticipates all that would eventually go wrong in Vietnam."

— Paul Mooney, Vietnam veteran and American journalist reporting on Asia

"Jerry Rose, as a young journalist in Vietnam in the early 1960s, was an intimate witness to the beginnings of the tragedy that became America's Vietnam War. This riveting memoir is a chronicle of ambition, war, love, and loss."

— Judy Bernstein, author of *They Poured Fire on Us* and *Disturbed in Their Nests*

"Two siblings. One amazing book creation. Jerry Rose's news reports of the war filled American papers and magazines. His sister, Lucy Rose, crafted a page-turner of this young man's life—all based on his journals. It is a vivid look at a world most American's never understood, one that will captivate you."

— Judith Knotts, author of *You Are My Brother: Lessons Learned Embracing a Homeless Community*

"This memoir is a must-read for those who want to see, hear, and feel Vietnam in the turbulent and secretive 1960s."

— Professor James B. Wells, Eastern Kentucky University

ssor in Vietnam when the
ist takes us into the dangerous
...of a man who went on to write the hidden stories and risked his life in the bargain, all to bring the truth to the rest of the world."

— Jack Woodville London, military historian and author of the acclaimed *French Letters* novels

"Totally engaging from the first page, *The Journalist* builds on the diaries of an acclaimed reporter for major U.S. newspapers and magazines, chronicling Vietnam's struggles just as the United States was becoming more engaged than most Americans knew or cared. His untimely death deprived us of a budding journalistic giant who knew Vietnam and presciently predicted that major U.S. involvement would be a tragedy for both parties. The photos add greatly to an exceptionally well-written story that fascinated me."

— Neal Gendler, book reviewer, American Jewish World; former staff reporter, Minneapolis *Star-Tribune*

"*The Journalist* is a compelling account of an idealistic young man reporting for major U.S. news outlets, as he resists the pressure to conform to the tidy packaging of human suffering for mass consumption. It is a hard book to put down."

— Tom Weidlinger, author of *The Restless Hungarian*

"Fischer's writing style gripped me from her very first words and carried me along a page-turning journey. I held my breath until the end. This is a do-not-miss piece of literary gold. An instant classic."

— Marni Freedman, Founder of the San Diego Writers Festival, author of *Permission to Roar*

"Destined to be a Blockbuster. I have no doubt that in a few year's time, we will see Jerry's life on the big screen. It's that good."

— Carlos de los Rios, screenwriter and producer of
Diablo and *The Da Vinci Treasure*

"I am astonished by Jerry's story of courage and truth-telling, but even more so by his sister and author Lucy Rose Fischer, who is able to bring his story to life long after his death, in a fascinating read that keeps you turning the pages until the very end."

— Elizabeth Eshoo, author of *Masai in the Mirror,*
Winds of Kilimanjaro, in *Shaking the Tree, II and III*

THE
JOURNALIST

— THE —
JOURNALIST
LIFE AND *LOSS* IN *AMERICA'S*
—*SECRET WAR*—

JERRY A. ROSE AND
LUCY ROSE FISCHER

Published by SparkPress, a BookSparks imprint,
A division of SparkPoint Studio, LLC
Phoenix, Arizona, USA, 85007
www.gosparkpress.com

Published 2020
Printed in the United States of America
ISBN: 978-1-68463-065-3 pbk
ISBN: 978-1-68463-066-0 ebk

Library of Congress Control Number: 2020903374

Formatting by Kiran Spees

To Kay, Thorina, Eric, and Nancy

North and South Vietnam in the 1960s

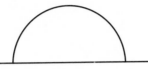

CONTENTS

Part One: 1959 to 1961. 1

Part Two: 1961 to 1962. 65

Part Three: 1962 to 1964 165

Part Four: 1965. 259

Epilogue. 313

Appendix. 323

At first, I'm not sure what I'm hearing. It sounds like a stack of lumber angrily lifting and falling. Then I understand—it's an explosion. One minute later, a second explosion punctures the air. I hurry outside and join a mass of people rushing toward the river.

"Where was it?" I ask a man on the street.

"At the My Canh Floating Restaurant," he says, pointing toward the Saigon River.

I gasp. I feel like I'm choking—as if a bone has caught in my throat. I can't breathe. I can't speak. An explosion at the My Canh Floating Restaurant? How can that be?

Less than a week ago, we were there, with our little girl, having a meal, watching the moon rise up over the river. And now . . .

I hear sirens wailing through the streets like a convoy of mourners. The evening air is hot and heavy. Though I've just showered, my shirt is already damp with sweat.

As I approach the river, I see a tight line of police and soldiers in crisp uniforms encircling the My Canh. They try to keep the crowd back. All around me, people are yelling and shoving. The scent of smoke, blood, and sweat shimmers in the hot air.

Headlights from the ambulances illuminate bodies, heaped like mounds of wet red pulp on the gangplank leading up to the floating restaurant. I taste bile on my tongue as I recognize a waiter from the restaurant—Phuong is his name—he's being hefted into an ambulance. Near me, on my side of the street, a tall man lies on his back, groaning in pain.

Then I see the girl. She's lying on the pavement, a few feet from me. She's wearing black silky pants and a flowered blouse. Her long dark hair fans out around her head. She seems to be about ten years old. A sweet little girl.

I squat down and take her arm. My hand is shaking, my body is trembling, as I feel for her pulse . . .

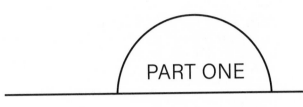

PART ONE

1959 TO 1961

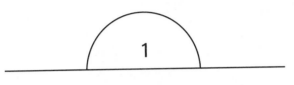

THE PHONE RINGS

Cigarettes hang from our lips, and we toss Hemingway's phrases back and forth like a basketball, dissecting his stark language. Frank's small office is warm and we're both in shirt sleeves, but Frank has on one of his signature ties, this one is Mickey Mouse. Frank Jones is my faculty advisor in the Comp Lit PhD program at the University of Washington in Seattle. He has a little of a Mickey-Mouse-as-Professor look, with large ears, smoothed-down hair, and wire-rim glasses that make his eyes look like buttons. He's young, not even thirty, hardly older than me, so he's also my friend.

When the phone rings Frank picks it up. I get up from the chair and hover in the doorway to give him privacy. He's been on the phone for a while when he fixes his eyes on me through a cloud of cigarette smoke. His look is odd, disconcerting. It's almost as if what he's hearing on the telephone has something to do with me. But I can't imagine what or why.

I'd come to his office ostensibly to talk about my credits for the coming year, what courses I should take, maybe start thinking about a thesis. But then we'd ambled into a discussion of literature and Hemingway. Dissecting literature with Frank is stimulating. But, still, I'm left restless, not quite satisfied. I want to be a writer. That's my dream, to be a Hemingway, not just talk about writing.

I'm still standing in the doorway, a little uncertain, when Frank puts the phone down and looks up at me. "Jerry, how would you like to go to Vietnam?"

"Vietnam?"

I go back into the office and sit across from Frank at his desk. "Yes, Vietnam," he says. "The Asia Foundation wants someone to teach English language and literature at the University of Huê in Vietnam. Huê is on a river, the Perfume River. They need someone fluent in French."

I'd spent my last year in college at the Sorbonne, as Frank knows.

"The thing is," Frank goes on, "the money is pretty good. And they'll pay your travel and moving. It's a two-year posting. After it's over, you can come back here and finish the PhD program."

Suddenly, just like that, I see myself in Asia. Like Conrad or Greene or Maugham, I'll write stories. I'll write exotic and magnificent novels. "Okay," I say, "I'm interested."

We chew it over, talk about what it means if I get this job. All the while blood roars through my ears, a rush of excitement fills me. I'm already in flight, on my way to the Perfume River.

Frank says, "I suppose it's safe over there now. The war's over, isn't it?"

"It's safe enough for me," I say. But as the words leave my mouth, I wonder—is the war really over? A small shiver touches the base of my spine.

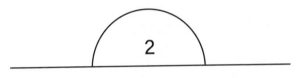

2

SORROWFUL GOOD-BYES

Six weeks later I'm at Idlewild Airport outside New York City. It's September 1959 and it seems like the whole world is here to see me off: Mother, Dad, my little sister Lucy, my aunt, uncle, and cousin. My sister Lucy, at fourteen, is not so little anymore. She's perched restlessly in a plastic chair, leaning over, with her long dark hair falling loose around her face. She's looking over the reading list I've just handed to her—twenty classic books I want her to read, from Dostoyevsky to George Eliot.

The plane is a half-hour late. I'm on edge and I think they are too. Mother doesn't feel well and keeps walking to the door for fresh air.

My father pulls me over and makes me sit with him on one of those hard airport seats. He's an immigrant from Poland, bald except for a half-ring of dark hair, and even shorter than me. Sitting next to him, I look down on his shining bald head. In his gravelly voice and gnarled Polish accent, he asks me, "Tell me again, Jerry, where are you going?"

"I'm going to teach English at a university in South Vietnam. We talked about this before."

"But you don't speak Vietnamese. How you teach there?"

"Vietnam was a French colony—so I'll teach using French."

"Where is this South Vietnam?"

I pull out a pen and a little notepad and sketch a map with North and South Vietnam. "Here, Dad, this is China and this is India and here are North Vietnam and South Vietnam, in Southeast Asia, in between China and India."

My father takes my notepad and looks at the drawing. "Why two Vietnams—North and South?"

"It's a little complicated," I say. There's no time to give him a history lesson, but speaking quickly, I explain, "The French were defeated in a big battle—that happened five years ago, in 1954. Then the country was split between the communists in the north and the noncommunists in the south—something like Korea. I'm going to be in the noncommunist south; it's called the Republic of Vietnam."

My father sits quietly for a moment. Then he says, "These two Vietnams—they have war or peace?"

"Peace," I assure him.

He shakes his head. He's worried—I can see that. He asks, "Why you going to this place? Better you stay and finish doctorate."

I wince. My spine tightens. It's a little late for this conversation. I'm about to get on a plane for a very long journey.

I love my father but there was a time, not so long ago, when we were at war. I had just finished my freshman year at MIT. I came home and announced, "I'm going to be a painter and a writer. I'm dropping out of MIT." Daddy looked as if I'd told him I was flying to the moon.

My father is a leather chemist, he owns a tannery, and he invents exotic ways to tan leather. He has a doctorate in science from a university in Eastern Europe. He thought—he expected—that I would grow up to be a scientist like him.

But I hated MIT. That summer, before I transferred to Johns Hopkins, we had fierce debates over every dinner: Science versus art. Art versus science. My father would shout, banging his fist on the table so the plates would jump, "Artist? Writer you want to be? This is hobby—this is no career for a man!"

A few years later, when I was back from my senior year at the Sorbonne and was accepted in the Master's program at the Iowa Writers' Workshop, he didn't speak to me for a month. Of course, he was worried—how would I support myself as a writer or an artist?

Now, sitting next to my father, as I'm about to get on a plane, I don't know how to explain to him that this adventure is tied to my dream—that I'm going to Vietnam for my art, for my writing. So, I just say, "Don't worry, Dad. It'll just be two years. Then I'll come back and get a PhD." A PhD is something he can understand—even if it's not in science.

The gates open at 10:30, and the rush through begins. We share hugs, kisses, and sorrowful goodbyes. My sister Lucy is smiling and crying, both at the same time, tears glistening in her hazel eyes. As we hug, I feel her thin arms holding onto me, as if she doesn't want to let me go. For her, and for me, saying good-bye for two years is a long time.

I leave hurriedly. The family goes up to the observation deck where I can wave to them. But there's a long tunnel to the plane, and I never get to see them for the "last look." I sense their disappointment and feel sad for myself—a hollow feeling as if I've silently slipped out of their lives.

At take off the jet engines feel like someone harnessed Niagara Falls. I've never felt such crushing power. This is the largest jet plane I've ever been on. And then we're flying high over the vastness of the United States. The country is beautiful. At 31,000 feet there are only patterns, like a large Mondrian, with geometric designs.

Inside the air is stale and dry. It doesn't matter. I'm on my way to the other side of the world to launch a new life. As I sit back in my seat, my breath clutches in my throat. I'm not sure what I think or feel. Exhilaration? Trepidation? This has all happened so quickly. Who knows what will be.

3

TO THE PERFUME RIVER

It seems like I've been traveling forever—from New York, where I said good-bye to my family a little over a week ago, to California to Hawaii to Japan to Hong Kong to Saigon. And now the final jaunt—from Saigon to Huê—on a small jalopy of an airplane that lurches and quivers through every cloud. Everything I know and everyone I care about I left on the other side of the world.

The airport outside of Huê is a drab concrete strip and a shack. As I walk down the clanking metal stairs, a gangly young man sprints toward me. As I step onto the tarmac, he grabs my hand and pumps it in a long and energetic handshake.

"Am I glad to see you!" he says, slightly out of breath. "I'm Paul—Paul Vogle. Welcome to Huê!" He's an American with ruddy cheeks and a friendly smile. He pronounces Huê with a double aspirated "h"—so it sounds like "who-whey." Tall and thin, Paul bends slightly when he takes my hand. I like him immediately—his horn-rimmed oversized glasses, yellow shirt, red-dotted bow tie, wrinkled brown suit, and welcoming handshake.

"I've heard all about you," I say smiling. "Howard Porter from the Asia Foundation told me you'd be here to greet me." Howard Porter, a boisterous, tall and portly man, directs the Saigon office of the Asia Foundation. I spent a couple days with Howard on my stopover in Saigon.

Everything Howard told me about Paul Vogle is impressive. Paul is one of the few Americans here who speaks fluent Vietnamese. He studied the language when he was in the army, and he came here initially as part of his army service. He became ill with a severe case of hepatitis and almost died. But he stayed on after he left the army to teach in the English Department. Howard confided that Paul cares deeply and passionately about Vietnam.

We walk out into the sun and the humidity envelopes us like a cloud of steam. The dankness stings my nostrils, in spite of the bright sun.

On the taxi ride to my new apartment, Paul gives me a quick tour: gray water buffalos with floppy ears and curled horns, rice paddies with stripes of narrow canals, and the Emperors' Tombs. Paul points to the bullet holes that riddle the beautiful marble tombs. "From the last war," he says.

I feel a quavering in my stomach, thinking of water buffalos and bullet holes. A week ago, saying good-bye to my family, I assured them that this country is at peace. But is it?

We drive by a river and Paul points, "Do you know why they call it the Perfume River?"

I shake my head. "Do you want me to guess?"

"You wouldn't get it now, but in the spring, throngs of blossoms float on the water from orchards upriver. A sweet perfumey aroma drifts over the whole town."

We arrive on the campus, which is sparse, with white-washed buildings and lines of tropical trees. My apartment is above the university library on the third floor. Its tile floors, rattan chairs, and pale beige colored sofa make it look like a scene out of a Somerset Maugham novel. They've given me a small refrigerator, an air conditioner, a desk and even a typewriter, an Olivetti. I run my hands over the Olivetti, small, black, and granular on its sides. I imagine myself sitting at this desk, with my Olivetti, composing rich and exotic stories about lovers, thieves or heartbroken artists, all set against the tropical green of Vietnam.

Paul gives me a peculiar look. "You're an artist and a writer. Howard told me all about you." He's quiet for a moment. "Be careful," he says, "This can be a dangerous place for someone with an artist's soul."

Water buffaloes

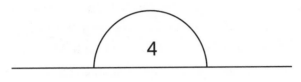

4

WE WERE THE ENEMY

I throw down my bags and wash my face, while Paul sits on the couch restlessly tapping his foot. After a short time, we clamber back down the stairs so Paul can give me a quick tour of the university campus.

He talks quickly, breathlessly, as he points to the various buildings. "This is the English department," he says, "where you and I both have our classes." He indicates a small, white building, with few windows, which looks foreboding and claustrophobic. I wonder if I'll feel trapped and imprisoned inside these stark walls. As if reading my mind, he says, "I know it doesn't look like much. The University of Huê is only a couple years old."

He's pointing out another low white building which houses the Political Science faculty when he stops abruptly and waves to a thin man emerging from the building. "Hey," he calls out, as we walk over to the building, "you two absolutely have to meet each other." He introduces me to Bui Tuong Huan and says, quickly switching to French, "You have a lot in common. You both studied at the Sorbonne."

Huan is tall for a Vietnamese man, taller than me. And he's thin. I notice his belt is wrapped around his waist one and a third times.

He has wide-spaced eyes, teeth browning at the edges, and trimmed but unkempt hair.

The three of us pass through the campus and enter a neighborhood with little shops just outside the university. We walk into the Thien Phuong Café, across the street from the signal station. We sit down at one of the scarred wood tables outdoors and each of us lights a cigarette, in unison. Leaning back in my seat, I'm aware of alien aromas all around me, mingled with our cigarette smoke—the heat of the day, the particular vegetation of the tropics, and pungent spices from Vietnamese foods being cooked inside the café.

"So you were at the Sorbonne," Huan says, looking at me through a fog of smoke.

"For a year. I spent my senior year at the Sorbonne in '54 to '55."

"Oh, I was in Paris from '47 to '52. So I'd already left when you came. That's why we didn't meet there!" he says. "I got my PhD in political science at the Sorbonne." He's quiet for a moment and smiles. "My years in Paris—that was the best time of my life."

"For me too," I say. "It was an amazing year. I was living in a tiny garret apartment. I had classes in the morning and then all afternoon and into the night, I painted."

Paul interjects, "Jerry is a writer and a painter."

Huan and I share memories—about the small cafes along the streets of the Left Bank, the wine, the art, the baguettes, the women. We were both poor students. Huan says, "There was a tiny restaurant that specialized in Vietnamese noodles. I ate there all the time. That's all I could afford."

"I remember that place—on Avenue de Choisy. I used to eat there too."

Huan is silent for a moment, leaning back, blowing smoke upward into the air. "Paris was a different world. I came home to Hanoi in '52 to fight in our war of independence."

"You came back to fight the French?"

"It was complicated," he says with a deep sigh. With his elbow on the table he spreads the fingers of his right hand over his forehead, closes his eyes, and continues, his voice almost a whisper, "We were fighting the French and also the Viet Minh, the communists. We thought when the Japanese were defeated, the French would grant independence. But the French came back."

Huan sits back in his chair and goes on. "There were many of us who wanted independence but we didn't want the communists. We wanted more freedom. So we were fighting both the French and the Viet Minh. The Viet Minh were well-organized. Their movement began a long time ago and they had been fighting against the Japanese during the occupation in World War Two. But we were many different factions. The Viet Minh were so much stronger, and they were ruthless."

"What was that time like for you?" I ask, leaning forward on my elbows. I'm intrigued by Huan and his stories of war.

"You can't imagine the chaos," he says, shaking his head. "There was fighting everywhere—in the streets, in the alleys, house-to-house—with bullets and bombs. My father was killed, standing on the porch of our house, on an ordinary street in Hanoi. He wasn't even a fighter."

"I'm sorry," I say—but I wish there were other words. Without meaning to, I shudder, looking into Huan's eyes, which are like dark pools of pain, hot and fierce. "When the French were defeated at Dien Bien Phu, were you glad?" I ask.

"No," he says quickly. "When the Viet Minh won—my friends and my family—we were terrified. You see—we were the enemy. When they decided in Geneva to split the country, with the communists in the north and the republic in the south, most of us came south. If we had stayed, we would have been killed. My mother and my sister and her husband went to live in Saigon and I got a job here in Huê. My brother and his wife were still in Paris, but later they also went to live in Saigon." Huan sighs, as if his heart overflows with painful memories. My own life so far, especially my struggle with my father, seems tame and trivial compared to what he's experienced.

"And now," I ask, "living here in this Republic in the south—is it okay here? You have freedom here?"

Paul and Huan glance at one another out of the corners of their eyes. Paul whispers, "It's not good. There are certain matters we can't speak about here. Spies are everywhere."

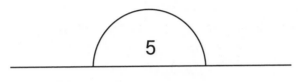

5

MONSOON SEASON

The other day Paul warned me to be careful what I write in letters. "This is not a free country," he said, "not a democracy."

The Republic of Vietnam is a dictatorship under President Ngô Đình Diệm and his brothers. They are Catholics and reign with brutality over a population that is overwhelmingly Buddhist. Paul had tossed his head when he said, with scorn, "The U.S. supports Diệm just because he's anti-communist."

I've been here for almost three months—teaching my classes, settling into a routine. We're in the Monsoon season now—winter in Huê. It's cold and wet and the dampness seeps under my skin. It seems odd that here in Huê in December the earth and skyline are seething with verdurous vegetation.

Walking the streets of Huê, I've begun to notice *security* police lurking around every corner. They have bright green shirts with darker green pants and red bands around the brims of their caps and on their epaulettes. Impossible not to spot. Their eyes are opaque and hard. When one of them looks at me, chills go running down my spine, as if their scrutiny is an accusation.

Paul also told me the government pays citizens, secret agents, to spy on other citizens. They target foreigners especially. My mail from home is often crumpled and re-taped. I assume that curious eyes in the post office go through my mail.

I'd begun to notice that a few of the students in my classes seem to have more money than the others. I wonder—are they secret agents? There's something in their faces—they look away. Do I need to be careful what I say in my classes?

The classroom where I teach is dark and shadowed, with two tiny windows and only a single light bulb hanging from the ceiling.

In my English language classes, every day is a battle of sounds. My students are not accustomed to the sounds and tones of the English language. I beg each student to stick the tip of his tongue just beyond his upper teeth, blow out air and say "thhhat" or "thhhem." They emit "tat" and "tem." I repeat "thhhat." My throat feels hoarse and raw as we repeat these exercises, over and over.

The class I teach on American literature, my afternoon class, is an overview, from Hawthorne to Hemingway. I'm rereading every-thing, as if I'm devouring the literature and learning along with my students. I can barely keep up with the reading I've assigned.

My students are bright. Their questions are interesting. When we were reading *The Scarlet Letter*, one of my students, Mai, asked, "Why are Americans so cruel?" We put the books aside and had a long discussion about how people are the same and different in our two countries. What will the student spies in my classroom report about this discussion?

I love my students—I love their eagerness to learn and their intel-ligence. But I'm frustrated too—I want to write and teaching fills up my days.

So, late at night, when all is quiet, I sit at my Olivetti and write. With a glass of whiskey on the table beside me and a cigarette clipped to my lips, I roll in pages like sandwiches: white sheet, carbon paper, white page, so each word echoes on an indelible copy. I'm working on a short story—set in Vietnam, in Huê—about a poor sampan driver who gambles his life and livelihood for a few extra piasters. Last week, Paul and I spent a night on a sampan, a small wooden fishing boat. The owner, a fisherman, by the name of Khiem, was a small man in his fifties with sinuous arms and legs. It was Khiem who inspired my story, and I think about him as I write—his muscles like rocks, his quiet manner, and the way he brushed the water with his oars.

But, even as I type, I wonder: Does the plot flow? Have I captured the character of the sampan driver? Is the dialogue rich and realistic? Why—why—do I doubt myself? A writer needs self-confidence . . .

On some nights, I work until the light of dawn seeps into the sky, over the shadows of tropical trees just outside my window. Then, I pull the sheets out of my typewriter and add them to the pile on the side of my desk.

I'm exhausted—beyond exhausted—and I lie down on my bed for an hour or two of sleep before my morning class.

As I drift into sleep, my father's words, from five years ago, dig into my heart. In his deep Polish accented voice, he challenged me, "How you know you any good? How you know you not wasting your life?"

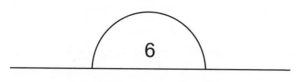

6

DR. PHAN HUY QUAT

The last few weeks I've begun to notice an uncomfortable pressure in my right side, especially when I walk. It's a tingling pain that follows me everywhere. I feel depleted, as if my energy has whooshed out of me, like air from a collapsing balloon. I've lost a lot of weight.

I decide to see my doctor—Dr. Phan Huy Quat. I've been to his clinic several times over the five months since I arrived in Huê— mostly for little things, a general check-up, a mild cold, a cut on my arm that needed a couple stitches. We've gotten to know one another. He's told me that his life is divided among doctoring, research and politics. We talk about politics while he examines me. He loves his country but so many things are wrong, he says, and he wants to help, to bring a true democracy, with real freedom.

Dr. Phan Huy Quat is about fifty or so, with a high forehead and dark hair parted neatly on the side, with only a whisper of gray. He's quite thin. He has a way of emphasizing each word so that his sentences sound like a staccato drumbeat. He's idealistic and works terribly hard both in his clinic and also on his research. His private clinic is in a small brick building on a quiet street, not far from the university campus. The room we're in has both an examining table and a work bench, which is crowded with glass beakers and bottles with hand-written labels and odd colored liquids.

Dr. Quat takes my temperature and says. "You have a high fever, well above normal, 104°F." He draws a blood sample and goes over to his work bench to run the test. When he comes back, he's shaking his head. "Hepatitis," he says.

"Really?"

"It's common," he says, "especially for foreigners. And it can be quite serious."

I shut my eyes for a moment to take in the news. Hepatitis is a disease of the liver. Paul almost died of it. I shudder, thinking what this might mean for me.

Dr. Quat refuses to let me pay him for his services. "You've come here to help our people," he says. "If you take care of yourself, you should be better in about ten days." Then he adds, "No drinking, no whiskey now—please. And you need to rest. Really take good care of yourself."

I shake Quat's hand and thank him—I feel grateful for his care. He is a good man, a truly good man.

As soon as I get back to my apartment, I carefully pick up my last bottle of foreign whiskey and put it in a high cabinet—hiding it from myself. Then I lie down on the couch. I'm staying home for the rest of the day, trying to take good care, as my doctor advises. I'm sapped of energy and feeling maudlin and homesick, a visceral feeling.

In the late afternoon, as I'm lying on my couch, I pick up the latest letter from home. It was on the coffee table. It's one of those aerograms on blue crinkly paper, not very long, just a page and a half. I've already read it, many times in fact. I read it again. Most of the letter is from Mother—it's typed. She writes that Nancy, who was married in Germany where her husband was stationed in the army, is now back home. My sister Nancy is twenty-two, four years younger than me. They're renting an apartment in Gloversville, our hometown in Upper New York State. I'm glad for Mother's sake.

On the flip side of the aerogram is a brief handwritten note from my little sister, Lucy, who is now fifteen. Just before I left for Vietnam, I typed a reading list for her—the classics, British, American, and Russian writers.

Lucy writes, "Dear Big Brother, So far, I've read a few of the books on your list. I read *Crime and Punishment* first. I found myself identifying with Raskolnikov, which made me wonder if I could ever do something horrible like him. Then I read *The Mill on the Floss* and the sister and brother in that novel made me think of us. Now I'm reading *1984*—which is why I am writing to you as 'Big Brother.' Are you watching me? Love, Lucia."

She signs her note "Lucia," the Italian-sounding nickname which I like to call her. How I miss my little sister! I've been away so long, I find it hard to keep track of how she's grown.

When she was born, I was disappointed at first—I was eleven years old and I wanted a little brother. What would I do with a baby sister? But as soon as I saw her, I was enchanted. I told Mother, "I'll take care of her." And I did. I took her for walks in her little carriage and I didn't care who saw me. I even changed her diapers.

Lucy was only seven when I went away to college. I felt like I was leaving behind my own little girl. But every time I came home, she was there. I read poetry to her. She drew little pictures for me. Sometimes I thought she worshiped me. But that was okay—who doesn't like to be worshiped?

When I think about home, I picture Lucy reading one of the books on my list. She'd be propped against double pillows on her bed, her long dark hair spread against the white pillowcase, her knees bent to hold up the book . . .

"Lucia . . .Lucia . . ." I cry out. "What are you doing now, this moment, my Lucia?" I begin humming the tune to "Santa Lucia." I must be singing loudly because I don't realize someone is at my door until I hear very loud banging. "Okay, okay," I say and get myself up to open the door.

It's Mr. Ngoc from across the hall. Ngoc works in university administration—in accounting. He's a forty-year-old man, short and broad, with thin and prim lips. I stare at him, standing in my doorway. He peaks into my room, as if he expects to find something or someone. He looks grim, his whole face bunched into a frown. "Do you have a woman in there?" he asks. "This is not allowed."

I shake my head and sigh. "I'm alone. I'm ill and I was just singing to myself."

I watch Ngoc as he walks back to his apartment. His shoulders are hunched in disapproval of me, I have no doubt.

I think, *I have to get out of Huê. When can I get a break from this place?*

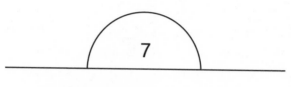

BLOOD BROTHERS

Six weeks later, when I've recovered from my bout with hepatitis, Huan and I are crisscrossing the busy streets of Saigon. As we dodge scooters, Vespas, Lambrettas, Primos, and droves of bicycles, Huan puts his arm around my shoulder to steer me through the traffic. We've come here in early February, for the Tết holiday, the Vietnamese lunar new year, while the university is on break.

Huan is older than me by four years. I've come to know his face like my own. Sometimes he's fiery, sometimes burbling with humor, sometimes full of fury about the current political miasma. And sometimes, he's just nostalgic, yearning for Paris.

We look on one another as brothers—we tell people we're "blood brothers." When Paul introduced me to Huan, just a few months ago, our meeting was like a jolt of electricity. Huan was a stranger then, but when I looked into his face, I felt I *knew* him. Maybe it was the Paris connection—that we both studied at the Sorbonne. Or that we're both foreigners. I come from the other side of the world and Huan is a refugee from Hanoi.

But I think it's something more intangible. Huan said to me once, "We are more than brothers. You are my other self." I understood

Huan

immediately. We don't look alike, not on the outside, but it's as if our souls are mirrors, reflecting one to the other.

Huan is taking me to meet his family—his mother, brother, sister and brother-in-law—they all moved from Hanoi to Saigon when the communists took over North Vietnam. I'm excited and also a little wary. Will they accept me as a "brother" or rebuff me as an interloper?

We walk into his brother's home in a quiet Saigon neighborhood. Bui Tuong Hy, his younger brother, also studied in Paris and has a French wife, Simone. Hy looks a bit like his brother but is even a little taller and not quite as thin. Simone is pixy-like and vivacious, with rapid speech and nervous gestures. I needn't have worried. Their welcome is warm and effusive, with double cheek, French style kisses.

Their home is bright and spacious with tile floors, white walls and modern furniture. The windows are large and open, so even indoors you feel encompassed by sweet green tropical foliage.

The family has gathered for a celebration of Tết, with gambling to usher in good luck for the new year and special foods. Mama is here—an impressive woman, very thin, with intelligence written all over her kind face. Carefully, she winds her way around the other family members and takes me in her arms. Her hug is all-encompassing and motherly. Mama speaks only a little French and my few words in Vietnamese don't take me very far. Even so, we're instant friends.

Also, I meet Hua, Huan and Hy's older sister, and her husband, Vu Khoan, who is a well-known writer—I'm excited to meet another writer. Khoan is in his forties. He's short, about five feet tall, with a certain solidity about his figure and some pudginess. His heavy-lidded eyes make him look rather blasé, which he is.

We're eating *bánh chưng*, sticky rice and meat, wrapped in banana leaves—delicious, sweet and tangy. Suddenly Khoan looks up, turns to Huan and me, and asks, "Tomorrow, would you like to sing the flute—*chanter la flûte?*"

Huan translates. "Opium," he says.

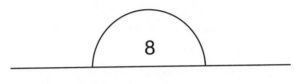

8

SINGING THE FLUTE

The next evening, Khoan, Huan, and I are at the My Canh Floating
Restaurant. This romantic restaurant, with bright white tablecloths and tuxedo-dressed waiters, is on a barge moored along the
Saigon River. The menu is Chinese. We relish a meal of bird's nest
soup, sweet and sour pork, shrimp in oyster sauce, roasted pigeon,
and Peking pressed duck. We drink Traminer wine.

All the while, with a shiver of excitement and a sliver of alarm,
I'm thinking about what's coming later this evening—opium, singing
the flute.

A mellow wind fans off the river. Beyond the lanterns of the
restaurant, a clear star-ridden sky spreads over us. On the dark river
we see several small skiffs, narrow as logs; we can hear the voices of
the people in them. We talk about politics, Vietnamese and Algerian.
"They are right," Huan says, referring to the Algerian rebels, "to kick
out the French."

After dinner, we walk down the gangplank to the shore. I'm feeling gorged from our elegant meal. But I've lost so much weight in
Huê that I don't mind.

We drive to Cholon, the Chinese district of Saigon. There's a complicated century's old history between the Vietnamese and Chinese, with intense bias on both sides. So, the Chinese have their own community, Cholon, where the residents are all ethnic Chinese.

We come to a wide, dark street in Cholon and arrive at a door with bars. It looks like a prison-door. A tall Chinese man opens the door for us, and we enter. He locks the door after us. This place, I understand, is an opium den.

Smoking opium is very illegal. I feel a tightening in my throat. To get arrested in this country would be terrifying. The government is brutal. The father of one of my students was arrested for a minor offense—I think he was selling black market cigarettes. This poor man's hands were tied, he was thrown into a dank cell, and he was beaten. His son, my student, was in tears when he told me the story. But I don't want to think about that. I look over at Huan, who doesn't say anything. I can tell he's nervous. When he lays his hand briefly on my back, I feel his hand trembling.

We are led to a small room with an elevated platform. A lantern with a small flame sits in the middle of the room, casting shadows on the walls. Khoan asks me, "Are you afraid?"

"No," I say. But I'm not being entirely honest. I feel jittery and overexcited, like a small boy about to do something very naughty.

The roller comes into the room. He's a tall and gaunt Chinese man with a sallow complexion and deeply gouged cheeks. His eyes are wide, brown, and lamblike, a vacant gentleness, softness, dreaminess.

The roller cleans the glass from the lantern and brings out a small vial. He stretches out on the table and picks up a long pipe, made of black lacquered bamboo. He takes a wire filament, heats it over the lantern, and then dips it into the vial of opium, which has the consistency of a light oil and the color of molasses. A light coat of opium clings to the end of the filament. The roller heats it, rolling the filament between his fingers and dips it again into the opium. He repeats this procedure many times. Then he hands the pipe to Khoan.

Khoan slides down on the platform, lies on his side, turns the bowl upside down so it covers the hole in the lantern, and starts sucking at the wide end of the bamboo pipe. He sucks hard and continuously and only a little smoke comes out of his mouth and nostrils. The odor is wonderful, like a combination of roasting nuts and broiling beef and good pipe tobacco. Impossible, of course, to really describe. In about a half-minute or less, Khoan smokes out the pipe.

In my head, I'm making notes—I want to get all the details right. This will go into my next short story . . .

Then the roller rolls and dips, and rolls and dips, and the pipe is soon ready—for me. I'm truly nervous now. My hand is shaking as I place the pipe on the lantern and start to inhale. A little smoke comes out. Then the pipe goes out. The roller takes it from me and taps on the opium. I light it again, and this time I smoke it through, though much smoke escapes from my mouth.

"What's supposed to happen to me?"

Khoan runs his hand through the stiff strands of his long hair. His heavy-lidded eyes don't change expression. "Like heaven," he says. "No need for women, a feeling of lightness. An insomnia without fatigue. A very good feeling."

I'm feeling nothing, except the desire for a woman. "How many pipes will it take?" I ask.

"Three for you. It's your first time." He looks over at Huan, now beginning to smoke his first pipe.

We smoke several pipes each. In between, we smoke cigarettes and we talk. Khoan admires Hemingway.

"Hemingway writes about man the way he should be," I say, "not the way he is. Take Jake in *The Sun Also Rises*. He's clean—without mushy *angst*, without self-pity, the prototype of the hard-boiled stoic. Too clean."

Huan starts to speak. He's less nervous now. "A man can be like that," he says. "When I was fighting in the war, in Hanoi, I had nine men under me. On the one hand, we were fighting the French. On the other hand, the communists. One night we were caught between them. It didn't seem that we would come out alive, but there were people in the street, and we shot over their heads and drove them toward the French, and the French stopped shooting. Then the communists attacked, but we were in a building and drove them back. They thought there were many of us. But we were only ten. We got out all right, but it was often like that. And nobody cared. We lived for today. There were many women. Now I care, and yet I'm not as alive."

We give a pipe to the roller. He smokes it complete. No smoke comes out of his mouth or nostrils. He is on the hook—addicted to opium.

"This stuff isn't working," I say to Khoan. "I still want a woman."

"Next time," Khoan murmurs, "the opium will sing for you."

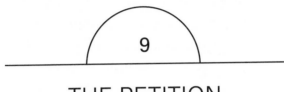

9

THE PETITION

Two days after my first opium night, I'm in a car with Arthur Dommen and Jim Wilde, speeding along Route 1. Dommen is a *UPI* correspondent and Wilde with *Time-Life*. Dommen has small, neat features, with close-set eyes and short, trim hair. Wilde, like his name, has a wilder look, with hair flopping over his eyes and an unkempt beard. The three of us are squeezed into Dommen's red Triumph convertible. I'm in the back seat, which is not really a seat at all.

Our destination is about ten kilometers outside Saigon. We're going to meet with Dr. Dan—the most famous "opposition leader." He was elected to the National Assembly last year but wasn't allowed to take his seat, on trumped charges. As we drive along, with the wind stinging our faces and whooshing through our hair, I feel a rush of excitement—I'm about to meet a remarkable politician. Ever since I've come to Vietnam, I've become fascinated with politics. I took democracy for granted when I was back in the States. But here, political issues are on a knife's edge—a matter of life and death, freedom and oppression.

My journalist friends have a question for Dr. Dan: Why didn't he sign the Petition? Eighteen Vietnamese nationalists submitted a petition demanding reforms from the brutal government of President Ngô Đình Diệm. But Dr. Dan didn't sign it.

Dommen, who is driving, turns his head 90 degrees so he can look at me sitting in the back. "What do you think, Jerry?"

"About the petition?" I shake my head. "If I were Vietnamese, I think I would have signed it. At least I hope I would be that brave. One of the signers is my doctor and friend, Phan Huy Quat. He said to me, 'I have no choice. We have to try to get more freedoms here.' I understand. I have tremendous respect for Quat and the other men who signed this petition. But what will happen? Will it change anything?"

"What will happen!" Wilde says. "They'll all get arrested—that's what'll happen."

Dommen says, "So is that why Dr. Dan didn't sign it?"

"Well, we'll ask him," I say just as our car comes to a stop next to a large, crowded marketplace. Arthur parks the car in an alley, and we walk through the market. We're all wearing dark suits, so we make a conspicuous picture.

Dommen knows the house. We come to a large doorway, which looks like the entrance of a shop. Above the entrance is a white sign written in blue letters, Dr. Dan's name in Vietnamese. Across the entrance is a green gate, which is locked. Dommen reaches through the gate and rattles the door. No response. We all try rattling the door. Finally, a servant comes and opens the gate. We walk through and enter a large waiting-room. On the left wall are three framed diplomas: one in Vietnamese from Hanoi, a diploma from France, and another, a degree in public health from Harvard.

The servant takes us toward the back where there are several chairs and a couch. We sit down and wait.

After a few minutes, Dr. Dan appears. He's a short, pudgy man with wide eyes, a nice smile, and a shock of unkempt hair. He's dressed in baggy blue pants, a white shirt, and sandals with no socks. There's something innocent about him. He doesn't strike me as the kind of man who would brave the fierce tactics of the Diệm regime. We shake hands and sit down.

Dommen, sweating badly, his eyes blinking and his nose twitching, says, "I didn't notice any black cars outside of your door. Are they letting you alone?"

He laughs at Dommen's question, and answers in fluent English, "No, the cars are no longer there, but they have motorcycles now. And they follow me day and night. They make a note of everyone who comes to see me and keep a complete record of every place I go."

I think to myself—*I suppose we're all now on Diệm's watch list. Will we be followed?*

Jim Wilde, the *Time-Life* correspondent, seems restless, nervously tapping his foot against the tile floor. He asks, "Why don't they arrest you?"

"They have," Dan answers. "Twice. But they let me go in twenty-four hours. Perhaps I'm now too well-known." Looking over at Dr. Dan, I feel a tremor of foreboding in my gut. I suppose he's too well-known, and if he disappeared, there would be reaction, both in Vietnam and in the foreign press. During the last elections, he spoke with many foreign correspondents. But, even so, I think—someday they'll assassinate him and blame it on the communists. Dan is very anti-communist.

No one has brought up the issue of the petition, so I ask, "Why didn't you sign the petition?"

"For me," he answers in a calm, matter-of-fact voice, "what's really important is having an effective opposition party."

"Doesn't the petition help promote an opposition?" I press on.

"I don't think so." He shakes his head. "I've presented such petitions before and they don't do any good. Anyway, maybe this petition will be more effective without my name on it."

At the gate, as we're leaving, Dan points to three men perched on a wooden fence that encircles the market. They're in plain clothes, sitting directly across from his door. "There they are," Dan says and smiles. "There are more too. All over the market." I notice a shiny black motorcycle to the left of his door.

What will happen to Dr. Dan? I wonder and worry.

I ask Jim Wilde what he plans to write about this. There seems to be enough here for a newsworthy article.

"Who cares back in the States?" Wilde laughs. "Everyone is reading and wondering about the marriage of Princess Margaret."

For a moment, as we walk back to the car, I imagine myself as a correspondent with *UPI* or *Time*. I'm intrigued by the story, about the oppressive treatment of Dr. Dan and the suppression of news. If I were a journalist, like my friends, I would write about Dr. Dan, his integrity, his vulnerability, and the government men perched like vultures around his home.

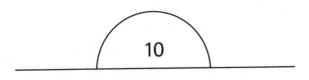

10

THE BEACH AT THUAN AN

Tropical birds of all varieties circle near the window over my desk in Huê. Summer days are hot and the light is brighter than bright, as if the sun is shooting its rays directly at me.

Over the last year I spent many late nights working on short stories—it's as if the words spewed from my fingers onto my Olivetti. But I didn't paint much. Now, the bright light of summer inspires me to paint. I set up my easel on the tile floor in the living room and the odor of oil paint suffuses the air of my apartment.

I paint what I see out the window and from my photos: a landscape of tropical trees, the Perfume River, rice fields and sky, a peasant under a conical straw cap, a woman sitting next to her market stall with assorted hanging fruit.

I paint with flecked colors to capture light in all its varieties: the white light of the sea and the clouds, the blue-green light of the sea, the blue light of water, the red light of dawns and dusks, and the red light that hovers over nightened cities, which is not merely red but many-colored.

By early afternoon, I escape to the Thuan An beach, only a few kilometers away on the South China Sea. Just about all the foreigners living in Huế come to this beach, which is reminiscent of Cape Cod, with its rolling dunes, white-as-snow sand, and scattering of beach kiosks.

I'm playing poker on the beach with Bert and Pearl Johnson and a couple of army guys. Bert has a technical job in the American Consulate in Huế. The Johnsons rent a kiosk by the year. We've got a card table and bridge chairs resting unsteadily on the sand, and the Johnsons have lugged out an ice box filled with soda and beer. We use shells as chips and play for piasters. It's not a high stakes game.

I slam my cards down, nearly capsizing the card table. "A straight flush!" I call. Pearl laughs, "Oh you, you're always winning," as she folds up her cards in her chubby fingers.

I get up to stretch and notice the Ruperts, Jeanne and George, have just arrived. George is the Consul here. They're a pleasant couple—and they're important in the foreign community in Huê. Jeanne is an attractive woman in her early forties, with blond wavy hair and a charming manner. George, who is older, in his fifties, is a little gruff but still friendly. They host lots of parties for Americans here, so I've gotten to know them a little.

They're with a younger family whom I've never seen before. They've settled into another kiosk, under the shade of their straw awning. I walk over to say hello, quickly skimming over the hot sand.

Jeanne, holding her hand up to shade her eyes, gives me a wide smile. "Jerry Rose," she says turning to the other couple, "is a professor at the university—a smart guy and lots of fun." Then shifting back to me, "Jerry, I'd like you to meet Bill and Isobel Woodman. They've just moved here. And these little ones are Joanie and Robbie." The husband, Bill, seems aloof and arrogant. He barely looks up when we're introduced. The little girl and boy are perched on their blanket, munching on sandwiches and pummeling sand with their feet. Isobel is pretty, with green eyes, burnt umber hair, and pale, freckled skin.

"Careful you don't get burnt," I say, nodding at Isobel.

"Oh, I'll slather on cream," she says with a grin. "You don't have to worry about me."

"Well, nice to meet you. I've got to get back to the Johnsons and our hot game of poker."

"I'm glad to meet you too," Isobel says. She languidly stretches out her arm. As we shake hands, I have a sense of her gentleness and charm. Her hand is warm and soft. I wave good-bye at their little group and dance over the hot sand which scorches my bare feet.

11

RUMORS OF A COUP

Hot rumors drift through the city of Saigon. Everyone is talking about a *coup d'etat*. Will the government of Ngô Đình Diệm be taken down? The American government has made a point of propping up Diệm, with monies, advice and political/military support—seeing him as a bulwark against the spread of communism. The American leadership seems blind to Diệm's brutality.

There's a short university break in October and I've come to Saigon. It's my second year teaching at the University of Huế. I expect to leave Vietnam in June 1961, at the end of this academic year. I'm not sure what I'll do then—get a PhD? Just work on my writing? I've written five short stories while I've been here—good ones, I think, I hope. But the seeds of a novel are sprouting in my head and I need to work on that.

I'm at the Continental Café, sitting at an outdoor table with my reporter friends, Wilde and Dommen. The Continental is a favorite hangout for American journalists. It has a lost-era elegance with white tablecloths and penguin-dressed waiters, a remnant of the days when Saigon was a French city.

"It's coming soon," Wilde says.

Dommen shakes his head. "It's not going to happen."

As we drink our beer, we speculate on the likelihood of a *coup d'état*. We occasionally interrupt our talk to wave off vendors of peanuts, gaudy pictures painted on silk, bawdy photographs, lacquerware, statuettes in wood, fortunes.

Wilde is optimistic. I'm not sure what to think. Like my friends, I loathe the vile, violent and corrupt regime of Ngô Đình Diệm and his cronies. But I have a sense of foreboding that's hard to shake, as if I'm in a dark room with voices whispering warnings in my ear. What if the coup fails? Who will live and who will die in the coming days?

On this visit, I'm staying upstairs in the hotel, the Hotel Continental, which is across from the National Assembly. It's an older hotel, in the center of Saigon, originally built by a French architect, one of many colonial remnants here.

At five in the morning, after I've had almost no sleep, I hear shooting. It's actually happening. The *ching-ching-ching* of distant bullets echoes the throbbing of my heart.

I throw on my clothes and make my way to the Post and Telegraph office. There, I run into Dommen and Wilde again. They're standing next to one of the leaders of the coup, Major Dong, and they introduce me. We learn that the paratroopers have joined the rebellion. But other parts of the military, most notably the sailors in Ngô Đình Diệm's navy, have stayed loyal to his government. It seems surreal—calmly talking with Major Dong, while a little way off in the city, bullets are exploding and people are dying.

I return to my hotel and enter the large dining room with its pristine white tablecloths. I'm the only patron at this hour. The bellhop puts my breakfast tray on the table when suddenly, just beyond our window, we hear guns firing loudly. The boy falls to the floor and crawls behind a chair. Instead of hiding like the bellhop, I go over to the window. Which is rash—so why do I do this? I want to watch and take mental notes. I'm a witness here.

This all seems to be happening in slow motion—my feet carrying me across the room, arriving at the window with its translucent white curtains, peering through the glass as if this were a screen to watch a gun battle, as if this were an old World War Two movie. But this is all too real and very near and frightening.

I hear the sound of bullets muffled only slightly through the window glass, which rattles and tremors. My whole body too shudders and quakes watching what's happening before me.

Three sailors with long guns are perched on the stairs of the National Assembly building, just across the street from my hotel. These sailors are supporters of the Diệm government. All three are lying on their stomachs and shooting into the archway—two have tommy-guns and the third has a sten gun. Apparently, the rebels have taken over the National Assembly building.

A small black object is thrown from the National Assembly building. The sailors look at it curiously. My first thought is, *This must be a used cartridge clip.* Then another similar object comes hurtling out of the doorway and bounces on the stairs. This time we all realize what it is—a grenade. The first was a dud. Holding my breath and clenching my teeth, I quickly duck behind the window jamb as the sailors dash across the street. The grenade explodes with a thunderous roar, shaking the dishes on my breakfast tray. For a moment, I stand with my back to the wall, feeling my heart beat a thousand times a minute. The odor of smoke and debris seeps into the dining room.

Cautiously, I glance out the window again. The sailors, who are loyal to the government, move to a corner diagonally opposite the archway. People are now beginning to gather in the streets. Occasionally a shot comes from the building. For a while, the rebels inside the National Assembly building seem reluctant to shoot. More sailors arrive. But then, as I stand at the open window, I witness a barrage of shooting back and forth. Bullets are spitting, in staccato spurts . . .pop . . .pop . . .pop . . .pop . . .pop . . .. With each pop, I wince and my insides tauten.

After a little while, I leave the hotel and hurry down Rue Catinat, toward the palace. I'm part of a gushing stream of people, all of us pouring down the street. I see a man killed. He's standing only four feet from me. I shudder . . . that could've been me. Even so, I keep on walking.

I join a crowd gathered in front of the palace. Was it just yesterday that life was normal? That we talked about the possibility of a coup? This is what a coup means—it means death. In front of me, strewn around the street, are bodies of people who have been killed, with blood spattered and pooled on the pavement. One of the dead is a man on a cyclo. His feet are upward, his head hanging limply downward. Machine gun bullets almost severed his neck. I feel the bile rise in my throat. I close my eyes for a moment to try to shut out the horror of what is all around me.

When I get back to my hotel room, I find two soldiers searching through my things. It feels like a violation, as if they were assaulting my person, my body. These men with grim faces and square fingers rifle through my things. "What are you doing?" I demand, trying to sound sharp and strong, though my hands are shaky. They look up at me, say nothing, and continue ransacking my papers. The soldiers walk off with a collection of my notes, which are in English and certainly indecipherable to them. What does this mean? Will they arrest me?

The next morning, walking across the Place Lam Son, I meet Jim Wilde. "It's over," he says, "the *coup d'état* has failed. I wanted the rebels to win. I wanted this *coup* to succeed. I really did, you know." Shaking his head, he adds in a voice damp with sarcasm, "The Americans are probably happy."

I sigh, "I suppose they didn't have the brute force or the will."

I feel despair, a sense of loss of what might have been. Grief grips my throat; I'm choking with smothered tears. And I'm worried. How will Diệm respond to this failed coup? How will he exact his vengeance?

When I return to Hué, I draft a short article about the attempted coup—not a short story—an article for a news magazine or newspaper. I list the author as Allan Esor, an alternation of my name, Jerry Allan Rose. "Esor" is "Rose," backwards.

I write, "What has happened to those billion dollars of American aid? Corruption is blatant. American funds have swollen the pockets of private individuals. Cans of cheese, clearly marked 'not for sale,' are sold in the markets . . .But this is petty theft compared to what happens in the higher echelons. The family of Ngô Đình Diệm, President of Vietnam, has become incredibly rich from American dollars . . ."

In the end, I get cold feet and put the manuscript away in a file drawer. As a representative of the Asia Foundation, I'm not supposed to engage in "political activities."

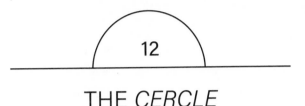

12

THE *CERCLE*

Four of us, Paul, Huan, Tran Dinh An, and I, sit in the main room of the *Cercle*, an elite clubhouse in Huế. The room is curved, with a balcony at one end, which overlooks the Perfume River.

Tran Dinh An, current club president, signed the petition last spring demanding reform at huge personal risk. Now, ever since the failed coup, An and all the other signers are in serious trouble.

An is a soft-spoken man with graying hair and wire-rim eyeglasses. We've known each other for almost a year. Huan introduced us. An and I have been playing tennis together about every other week or so. Both of us like sports, especially tennis. An is athletic, quite muscular and a little taller than me. We are a good match on the court.

An begins to speak about his small bookstore. He says, "I ordered two copies for my store of *Lady Chatterly's Lover*, translated into French. I already have two customers who want to buy this book. We need to sell it quickly before the censors find out."

Paul says, "How'd you get this book delivered, past the censors? Can't believe they didn't ferret it out at the post office."

An smiles slyly. "I have my ways. I don't put anything through the post."

Our waiter comes with our *apéritif,* Cinjaho Martini, and invites us to come to the dining room for lunch. Just as we get up, we notice two men in dark suits hovering in the doorway, at the entrance of the *Cercle.* The concierge comes out and beckons to An. With a troubled look, he follows the concierge through the doorway.

An disappears.

We wait and wait, knowing that his disappearance must be an arrest. What else could explain this sudden disappearance? As we make our way to our table, Paul, Huan, and I keep glancing over at the doorway, as if our friend might suddenly reappear.

When we sit down at the table, we all look around the room, which is filled with diners. The room resounds with the normal sounds of dining—the clatter of dishes and the din of chattering voices. But all is not normal for the three of us; our friend has disappeared.

We have a meal of cold beef broth with thin noodles, then lobster with mayonnaise. Paul begins to talk about the beauty of Chinese calligraphy. Later, he switches to an abstruse philosophical subject concerned with the reality of here and now existence. I raise some question concerning the fish in the river. If I hook a fish and present it to him, wouldn't there be one less fish in the river?

And all the time, we're wondering and worrying about An.

13

THE POLICEMAN SHRUGS

The next morning, I stop by the clinic of Dr. Phan Huy Quat, my friend and physician. I go there because I'm worried—knowing that he signed that petition for reform and caring about him.

What I see takes my breath away. Quat's clinic and his laboratory are demolished. As I walk in the door, my feet crunch on shattered glassware. The door to the refrigerator, where he had stored his precious medicines, is ajar and nothing is left. Pools of chemicals are splattered on the floor.

A young man, who is trying to sweep up the mess with a long broom, whispers to me. "He's gone. He was arrested. Some men in uniforms came to his home in the middle of the night and took him away." The young man continues to sweep, his broom pressing through congealed liquids and jangling chips of glass. I stand in the doorway shaking with anger. My doctor—this good man, too good . . . How dare they?

In the afternoon, Paul and I march over to the police station. The room is grim, with stained walls and scarred desks. We walk up to the first desk and Paul says, in his good Vietnamese, "Where is Dr. Phan Huy Quat? Where is Tran Dinh An? We demand to know!"

The policeman barely looks up at us. He shrugs and says, "There's no one here to talk with you about this matter. You can come back tomorrow." I clench my fists. I would like to hurt this man—this policeman with his callous shrug and his blasé face. But I do nothing.

We come back the next day. Same answer.

When we come back the day after that, another policeman tells us, "These prisoners are not here. There's nothing for you here." Then he goes back to reading a report on his desk and doesn't look at us at all.

Back in my apartment, I write letters—to the Chief of Police, to the Head of the Army, to the Mayor of Huê. I give the letters to Paul who translates my messages into Vietnamese.

Diệm's army has demolished five independent newspaper offices. A swarm of soldiers rushed into the buildings, ripped up masses of papers and trashed the machinery and equipment.

We hear that Dr. Dan, the opposition leader, has been arrested. I picture Dr. Dan the day that we interviewed him in his home office. He had a sweet smile and was dressed in baggy blue pants. He thought the government wouldn't harm him because he was too well-known. But now there's a rumor that he was killed, beaten to death during an interrogation.

Thinking of Dr. Dan, Tran Dinh An, Phan Huy Quat, and other friends, I am adrift in a black fog, horrified and sorrowful. I want to rush in and save my friends. But I'm helpless against this government which is like a roaring beast that crushes anyone or anything in its path.

14

THE CRACKLING OF A BRANCH

Huê is under curfew. Initially no one was supposed to be in the streets after nine o'clock in the evening. Now the curfew is moved back to midnight until six in the morning. After midnight, I walk out on the street—which is foolish, I suppose, tempting fate. I breathe in the stillness and the taut emptiness of the vacant street.

The next morning, my student Mai wants to talk with me after my class. He looks agitated and distressed. Mai is a friend, not just a student. He comes from Quang Tri Province, just north of Huê, and I've met his father, a dignified man with thin eyes and a mustache that points downward, Confucian-style.

"What is it?"

"Something happened. In my village. Just down the street. My father told me. He was crying, and now I'm crying too." Mai wipes his eyes. I've never seen him so distraught. "They killed Mr. Tuong, our neighbor. He was a simple policeman, just doing his job."

"Who killed him? Was it the government? The soldiers?"

"No, no," Mai shakes his head. "It was the Viet Minh. Two guys rode up on a motorcycle. My father heard them, the roar of their motor. Then he heard the shot—one shot and Mr.Tuong was killed.

He saw them riding away as he ran toward his neighbor. He was too late."

This is not the first such story I've heard about the communists, called the Viet Minh or Viet Cong. People warn me—don't go out alone on the country roads. The Viet Minh are known to ambush people in the countryside. There are incidents in the cities too—assassinations and bombings. A war of terror is rumbling all around us. Everyone I know is nervous. The incredible tension building up in all of us makes us afraid to cross the street…to greet our friends…to live our everyday lives.

In the evening, I invite Paul and Huan for dinner in my apartment. I've prepared American food for us—chicken, a kind of stuffing, and an Asian version of sweet potatoes—all reminiscent of a Thanksgiving dinner that my mother might prepare back home in this season. Paul eats with gusto. "Almost like my mom's cooking," he says with a grin. But Huan is not quite sure about the meal. He chews slowly and frowns a little at the unfamiliar tastes and textures.

We chatter lightly at first—about the university, the weather, our families. Then Paul says, "I've heard the communists, the Viet Cong, are planning to kill an American. They say it will happen soon." His calm pronouncement takes my breath away. I believe him. But who? It's like reaching blindly into a hat and pulling out a name.

Suddenly a door slams outside in the hall outside. It sounds like a distant explosion, reverberating. "It's a detonation," Huan says, with panic in his voice.

Ever since the coup, I jump at any little noise which resembles gunfire, and many noises seem to, even the crackling of a branch.

15

A CHERRY-RED SCOOTER

The small community of foreigners here in Huế gathers in one another's living rooms for rounds of parties, night after night. Lately, I've gone to a lot of these parties. Maybe, with all that is happening around us in Huế, our angst brings us together. The Ruperts host many of the ex-pat parties at their home, which is large and rather elegant, with carved mahogany furniture and Persian carpets.

Isobel and Bill Woodman, the couple I met last summer on the beach at Thuan An, are usually there. Bill Woodman is a career diplomat and has had positions in several Asian cities, as well as in the U.S.

Isobel Woodman is lovely. I've found myself seeking her out at dinner parties. We seem to immerse ourselves into deep conversation, as if no one else were there. I feel drawn to her sweetness, warmth and intelligence. She's told me about herself—that she comes from Minneapolis, that she studied literature in college, that she used to be a ballet dancer.

I've heard rumors that her husband is unfaithful, that he treats her badly. He's supposed to have a mistress in Saigon. I feel compassion for her—and something more. When I sit next to her and our arms touch, I feel a warm current flowing through my body as if there's a positive energy between us.

Isobel is a small woman, about five feet, with reddish-blonde hair and terribly white and delicate skin that is always slightly flushed on her cheekbones. Her lips are slender, and she has very fine lines around her gray-green eyes.

On the afternoon of March 1st, after my last class, I take a ride on my new/old red scooter. I purchased this used Italian scooter a few months ago from Sam Johnston, another American, when he was about to leave Vietnam. I suspect, but don't know for sure, that Sam is with the CIA. The price was cheap.

My new/old scooter is cherry-red and has a mass of scrapes, scratches and dents. The air this afternoon in Huê is hot and tropical as ever. I love the feeling of the wind whooshing through my hair and cooling my skin.

As I'm breezing down the street, I notice Isobel out of the corner of my eye. She waves at me with a broad sweep of her hand, and I come to an abrupt stop. "Want to hop on for a ride?" I ask.

She says, "Sure." So, I ask her to climb on the back of my scooter. There's not really an extra seat, but we make room for the two of us, and she clings to me as we jockey out into the countryside.

We whizz by rice fields and the Perfume River, marketplaces and water buffaloes. I tell her to "hold tight." Between the roar of the wind and the grumble of the scooter, we can't hear so we don't talk much. But her laughter chimes in my ear and I feel her arms encircling me. She's a little nervous. Every time we go around a curve, she grasps my waist. I'm sure she's made grooves in my body.

We ride for a long time, two hours or so. And all the time, her arms around me are holding me close, very close. It's really an embrace, under the guise of "holding tight." I love the feeling of her arms around me.

When finally I bring her back to her house, I whisper to her, "It'll take me two weeks to recover from the touch of your soft arms."

Her husband is standing in the doorway, waiting for her. Seeing his frowning face, I feel a wave of anger and indignation. I want to shout at him: *You don't deserve her!* But I say nothing. I just turn my cherry-red scooter around and drive off, leaving behind a billow of smoke and a loud roar.

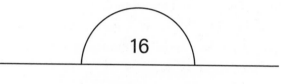

16

DO YOU WANT IT?

Huan is glum and his eyes are rimmed red. My two-year post at the University of Huế officially ended yesterday—on the first of June. I'll be leaving Vietnam soon.

Huan and I are having lunch in my apartment, which is sparse now that I've packed up some of my possessions. "Why do you leave Vietnam?" he grumbles. "You belong in Vietnam; you are one of us. Why don't you get another job here?"

I don't know how to answer his plea. Huan is dear to me; he's my brother. After two years, it's wrenching and unbearable, the good-byes to good friends—Huan, Paul, and my many other friends here.

I have my plane reservations already. After two long years I'll see my family. I miss them. We're meeting midway, in Israel, and it will be a family reunion of sorts, with my parents and my sister Lucy. We'll visit my father's sister and my cousin, who live in Tel Aviv and are Holocaust survivors.

I'll travel to Europe, with an indefinite stay in Paris. It will be a time to write, to work on my craft.

After that? I really don't know.

—

A few days later, I'm in Saigon at a small café on the Rue Catinat when Jim Wilde announces, "I'm leaving—going back to the States." He looks around at Arthur, me, and a couple other journalist friends who are smoking and drinking beer together on a hot afternoon. Then he pauses and points at me. "Do you want it?"

"What?" I say.

Jim looks at me with a squinting stare. "You could take over my position here with *Time*. With Big Daddy." All the foreign correspondents call Time Life Big Daddy because it dominates the news-making world.

"Are you serious? Do you mean it?" I'm astounded. It's like suddenly discovering a new star in the night sky.

"Damn right, I mean it. But you have to tell me right now. Then I'll put in your name." Jim bangs his empty glass on the round metal table. "It's a simple proposition. I want to get back to Chicago. I've been thinking about this for a long time, especially since that fiasco last November—that awful bloody disastrous failed coup. I want to get out of Vietnam. And there's work for me at the *Time* office in Chicago. I just need to find a replacement. So, I'm asking you—do you want it?"

With barely a blink of my eyes, I say, "Yes—okay." I don't even ask Jim the obvious question—*why me*. Jim knows that I'm a writer, I've lived in Vietnam for two years, I have a good understanding of the country, and I know everyone-who's-anyone here, both Vietnamese and foreign. Also, I don't have any other employment possibilities at the moment.

"Okay," he grins, "this is good. You'll be a stringer, doing it all freelance, at least for a while. You need to get your ass over to Hong Kong and talk to Karnow at the Bureau Office."

It's an odd feeling. A few moments ago, I was thinking that I'll be leaving Vietnam, wondering what comes next. Now I have a plan. I have a future.

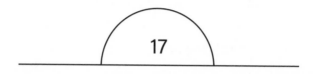

A CROSS-CONTINENTAL CALL

t's early in the morning. Back home it would be eight in the evening, one day earlier. So here it's June 5, 1961 and there it's June 4.

Over the expensive distance of a cross-continental phone call, I say, "Hello, Mother."

"Oh Jerry, how wonderful to hear your voice." I conjure an image of Mother standing in the hallway of our Gloversville home, looking at herself in the hall mirror.

I hear her calling, "Henry, Lucy, Jerry's on the phone!" And she says to me, "They're coming. They wouldn't want to miss your call. We're so excited," she starts to say, "We have our tickets and everything. We'll see you soon."

"Well, Mother, that's why I'm calling."

"Is anything wrong? Are you okay?" I hear panic in the tremor of her voice. Then there's a click, and I realize someone else has picked up the phone extension in my parents' bedroom upstairs.

"Jerry!" It's Lucy's voice.

"I'm really sorry. I can't meet you in Israel. I'm not coming home yet, not for a while anyway."

"Why?" Mother and Lucy say this at the same time.

"It's a little complicated, but it's not bad. In fact, it might be a good thing. I have a chance to take a job as a journalist here. I know a guy who's been working with Time Life in Saigon and he suddenly decided to leave. He asked me if I want to take over his position, and he said I have to tell him right away if I want to do this. So, I said yes." I'm talking fast, trying to get this all in a three-minute international phone call.

"So, how long will you stay in Vietnam?" Lucy asks me.

"I don't know. I can't say right now. It might not work out and I'll leave soon. Or it might be a long time. I'll send you a letter and tell you more about it."

"Oh, Jerry, this sounds exciting for you," Lucy says. "I haven't seen much in the news about Vietnam. But there must be interesting things to write about over there."

"We love you, Jerry," Mother says, "and of course you have to take this job." I hear a little sigh in Mother's voice. Or maybe I imagine it. I know they're disappointed, and I am too. I miss them.

My father never actually gets on the phone. He's hard of hearing, so it's difficult for him, but he'll get the news.

I wrap their voices around me as we say our good-byes. As the echoes of their voices melt away, I feel the ghostly presence of the family I love. Or am I the ghost, a distant specter in their lives?

18

GREGORIAN CHANT

A few days later I'm back in Hué. I've come here so I can submit a final report, say good-bye to friends and students, and arrange for my belongings to be stored for a while until my situation is set. My plan is to move to Saigon—if all works out with *Time*. At the moment, I'm in limbo—it looks like I'll have a new job but it's not quite sure.

I'm at a party at the Rupert's home when I see Isobel across their elegant living room. Our eyes meet and we both smile. I'd been feeling a sense of estrangement, being in Hué, as if I'm here and not here. But Isobel's smile is so warm, so welcoming, I wish I could rush over and take her in my arms.

One of the guests has brought over a record player. So, someone puts on a dance record, Benny Goodman Band music. Isobel comes over to me and invites me to dance. When the next song begins, we dance again. And again. Her feelings are obvious. I think mine are too. The Ruperts and the other guests look away, as if they don't really notice us, as we dance in the middle of the room. Bill watches us from a corner of the room. But all I want to do is nestle my cheek against Isobel's soft hair.

She used to be a ballet dancer, and she moves with a dancer's grace. Her legs are smooth and well-shaped.

At 5 o'clock the next day, I take Pearl Johnson for a scooter ride. Pearl is a huge woman, really obese. My poor little scooter sways and shudders under the weight.

The first thing Pearl says is, "You shouldn't make your feelings for Isobel so obvious. I told her the same thing this morning." Then we start discussing Bill's affairs. Pearl wants to be my confidante, to become a party to the "intrigue." Feeling her breath on my back as we ride along on my poor little scooter, I wince with an instinctive sense of foreboding and revulsion. I don't trust this woman.

At 6:30, a group of us are at another dinner party at the Ruperts' house. Bill isn't here; he's gone to Saigon for several days. Isobel and I are drawn to one another. It's as if there's a powerful magnetic force pulling us, drawing us in, even if it's wrong, even if this will come to no good.

After dinner, Isobel and I begin to dance, hardly moving. It's excruciating, just a small sway back and forth. Her lips are so close as we dance. I try to kiss her on her sweet lips. She refuses, snaps her head away, but continues to hold onto me tightly.

Everyone has gone home and finally, about 12 midnight, the Ruperts go to bed. As they walk up the stairs, they glance back at us with a troubled look on both their faces.

Isobel and I dance some more, more slowly than before, standing almost still, just holding each other. We kiss. Isobel pulls back. "It's my Scotch backbone," she whispers. "I've never done this before . . ."

We go over to the couch and talk for a long time. She starts to cry. She tells me about her husband's infidelities, how he would go off with the flimsiest of excuses. "I've never told anyone else," she said, "only you. I can talk to you because you listen. You look at me with your blue eyes and you understand my heart."

When she stops crying, we hold each other close, pressed against each other. My desire overpowers me. My heart melts for Isobel—so tender, so lovely. I know that what I'm doing is wrong—will do her no good. But I start to say over and over deliriously, "I want you. I want you. I want you. . ."

It's like a Gregorian chant or a drumbeat or like the sound of Bolero. And finally, we make love, very quickly and awkwardly on the couch, with the mosquitoes whining, and, to use Hemingway's phrase, "the earth moves," or comes near to moving.

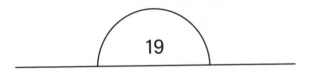

19

KEEPING UP APPEARANCES

The next night, Isobel and I sleep together until three in the morning, in my apartment, since Bill is away. Now all her moral rigidness has turned to liquid.

The day after tomorrow Bill is coming back to Huê, which will be harder on her than on me and it won't be easy on me. We talk about seeing each other at parties and keeping up pretenses. "Happy to see you again, Mrs. Woodman." "And how are you Mr. Rose?" "Just fine, thank you . . . and would you like to make love now?"

Where do we go from here? I'm just about to begin a new career—and Isobel is married, with two children.

Two nights later, we're at a party in the Ruperts' living room again and Isobel and I are all too indiscreet. An officer from Quang Tri comes up to me and says, "It's none of my business, but you're getting pretty obvious."

The next day I discover I have a flare-up of hepatitis again. I have a fever and a pain in my side—same symptoms as before. So, I can't see Isobel until next Saturday. With Paul acting as a go-between, I ask her to come to my place then.

On Saturday morning, she arrives at my door. It's a bright day with sunlight filtering through the open shutters. I show her the paintings I've been working on. She looks carefully and intently, leaning down to closely examine canvases on the floor, propped against the wall. She traces the images with her eyes; it's as if she's breathing them in.

I read one of my stories to her, "The Knife." It's about a man who trades his knife for a lottery ticket and then wins a huge sum. On his way home, robbers attack him and take all his money; without a knife he has no way to protect himself. Isobel sits with her head leaning against the back of the couch, her eyes closed, a slight smile on her lips. When I'm finished and look up at her, her eyes are bright, as if she's crying. "You are so talented," she says, "I could feel the pain of this man; all the details are alive and true."

I love her for loving my art—that she really looks, she really listens. I tell her, "The words on the paper and the paints on the canvas are what I have to live for in this world."

We're talking comfortably when, suddenly, there's a knock on the door. Isobel begins to tremble. We don't open the door, but it turns out that it isn't Bill. It's just Paul; he shoves a note under the door telling me where he's going to meet me later.

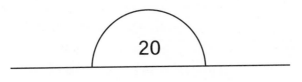

20

I'LL ALWAYS LOVE YOU

Huan knows—everyone knows—about Isobel and me. Huan doesn't approve and because he is so dear to me, his disapproval stings.

"An affair with a married woman? Why?" he says. "I know you're unhappy. I know you're lonely. I understand your angst—really, I know you. But it's not right. It's not good. You're making trouble for yourself—and, more important, you're making trouble for her. Jerry, my brother, what are you doing?"

It's early evening. From the window over my desk, a full moon ringed by mist casts lights and shadows on the walls of my apartment. We sit side by side, our shoulders touching, with lit cigarettes and glasses of whiskey. I don't answer immediately and the silence between us is like a wall of thick ice.

Finally, I begin. "You're right, of course. We should never have begun . . ." I raise my glass and take a long drink of whiskey. My head feels hollow. "Look," I say lamely, "I love Isobel. What can I do?"

"What can you do?" Huan says in his loudest voice. "You can leave her alone! You can stop—now!" He stubs out his half-smoked cigarette with such force that the ashtray slides down the coffee table and falls on the floor.

Huan has his own problem. He's fallen in love with a student—a young woman named Anh. They're working on a project together, a political study of Vietnam's war for independence against the French. Anh is ten years younger than him; she's his research assistant as well as his student. She's lovely, with dark, burnished hair and sparkling eyes, and she's very bright. I've seen them together. There's a raw tension between them. You can see the way they look at one another, glancing sideways from the corners of their eyes. A stranger would notice: he loves her; she loves him… But Huan and Anh are not dating. He won't ask her on a date because she's his student. He thinks it's not proper.

"So," I say, "I should be like you—upright, virtuous, and lovesick."

Huan leans back on the couch and smiles glumly. "Okay," he concedes. "Maybe we can't help whom we love."

Two days later, I meet Isobel and her husband by chance on the street. We're near the signal station, across from the Thien Phuong Café. The day is unusually gray and windy and a sudden rain shower batters our heads and shoulders.

Isobel's face is pale and drawn. Her voice is almost a whisper as she says, "We're leaving. Bill's been offered a post back in the States. He'll be working in the State Department—something he's always wanted. So, he's going and he insists that I go with him." She's silent for a moment, looking down at her feet, and then adds, "He knows about us. I told him."

Then Bill, who's been standing stiffly next to her with his arms crossed and his foot tapping rhythmically, begins to scream at me, his lurid voice echoing around the wet street. "Who the hell do you think you are? You son-of-a-bitch, screwing my wife." He turns to Isobel and hurls abuse at her. "You're a bitch. You're stupid. And don't think for a minute," pointing his finger at me like a weapon, "that this man will actually marry you. And if he does, I'm taking Robbie and Joanie, and you'll never see them again. The kids will be better off without you."

Isobel stands next to him, trembling and quietly sobbing. What could I say? Maybe I should insist that Isobel and her children come with me. But how would I support this family? I'm just about to try out a new job. I don't know how I could support a family. My heart breaks for Isobel, for myself.

The next morning, she comes to my apartment for the last time, to say good-bye. Her eyes are red. Last night her husband had said to her, once again, "If you leave me, the children stay with me. You go off alone." An impossible choice.

The morning light burnishes the two of us, standing in the middle of the room, clinging to each other as if to a life raft. We're both trembling. My tears fall on her hair and her tears wet my shoulder. "Oh my Isobel," I say, over and over.

But she isn't my Isobel. Not really. She's going away. Our affair has been brief, and now it's over.

"I'll always love you," she whispers in my ear.

21

CHÍ HÒA PRISON

Huan, shaking his head, tells me our friend Tran Dinh An is back. An was arrested last November, accused of participating in the attempted *coup d'etat*. Huan and I are standing in the courtyard, outside the one-story whitewashed building where I used to teach my English classes. "I just saw him," he says. "He was released from prison on the 30th of May. He was in prison for five months."

"How is he?" I ask. Huan shudders, closing his eyes.

The next day, I go to visit An in his bookstore in Huê on a busy street, with a swirl of bicycles and the shouts of hawkers selling their wares. His voice is on the edge of tears and so soft and low that I can barely hear him. He says, "You remember that lunch when I was called from the *Cercle*?"

"I'll never forget that day. One moment you were with us. And then you disappeared."

"They blindfolded me right away and tied up my hands. They put me in a car—or it might have been a small truck. They drove me a long, long distance. When they finally took off the blindfolds, I found I was in a prison—worse than a prison. It was like a dungeon. It was dark and cold. It had cement walls with ugly stains."

"Where were you?"

An shakes his head. "I'm not sure, but I suspect it was the Chí Hòa Prison in Saigon, where the French used to keep our people when we were fighting for our independence."

My hand goes automatically to my throat. "No! You were there! I've heard it's like a dungeon from medieval times."

An continues. "As soon as we got to the cell, they chained up my arms and legs with heavy manacles and put on another heavy blindfold. I couldn't move. It was the winter, monsoon season, and the wind dashed through my cell. I was always cold. I couldn't stop shivering. My arms and legs turned numb from the cold.

"I was alone. I could hear others. I could hear screams. But I was always alone, never with another prisoner.

"Once a day, they took off the blindfold and the manacles from my hands. They would make me sit in a corner of my cell, facing the wall. They gave me a bowl of food—it was white rice laden with salt. Because of the salt, I was so thirsty it was unbearable. But they gave me nothing to drink.

"After a while, I didn't want to eat anything. My throat was in pain, my thirst was so terrible. Then, they gave me water. But I could only urinate in my cell, on the floor. The stench became horrible, so I didn't want to drink."

Listening to my friend, I feel a wrenching sense of sadness and horror. "Did they interrogate you?" I ask.

An moans. "Oh yes. They took me out for interrogations in the middle of the night. I think it was always after midnight. They put electric shocks on my earlobes. It felt like knives piercing my flesh. And they hit me, over and over.

"My chief inquisitor was a square-shouldered man named Thuc. He would ask a question that I couldn't answer and then he would hit me with his large hand on my face or my neck. Sometimes he or his comrades would make an iron fist and punch me in the stomach. The interrogations went on for hours and hours.

"I kept saying, 'Take me to court. I should be tried before a court of law.' They laughed.

"One night I said to Thuc, 'You must be a communist because true nationalists would not treat their countrymen this way.'

"After a month or so, I said to them, 'If you have the slightest human feeling left in your heart, you will put a bullet through my head.' I felt such despair, I didn't think I could take any more."

When my dear friend finishes telling me all this, I'm left with a black feeling of gloom for the horror he has just described. I don't know what to say—what comfort could I offer after all he's suffered?

An has changed. His energy is drained. His buoyancy is gone; so too his spontaneous, infectious laugh. He used to have a good physique, lean, muscular and active. Now, his flesh is puffy and sallow, so he looks bloated and sickly. He also smokes now; he didn't before.

I ask, "What can I do to help you?"

"I'm still being watched," he says. "Maybe in ten days or so they'll let up and then let's go out for a meal." He sounds morose, defeated. "I am still in the throes of a *depression nerveuse.*"

He talks about the loyalty of his friends. How they cried at his release. But he also cautions me, "Don't trust Vietnamese friends." During his imprisonment, An was removed from the presidency of the *Cercle.* It was fixed. Ngoc got it. There were no other nominations.

"What can a man do for his country?" An sighs. "I've had enough."

I wish him *"Bon courage."*

An stands in the doorway and waves as I walk away from his bookstore. The narrow street is a jumble of shops, with a hodgepodge of sound, sight and smell. I pass a butcher market where slabs of meat dangle in the air, red and raw with the stench of death.

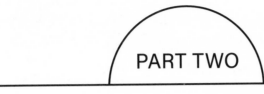

PART TWO

1961 TO 1962

22

AS A LARK

Isobel comes to me in a dream in the middle of the night. She's trying to tell me something but she speaks so softly, in a strange accent, that I can't understand what she's saying. She looks different in my dream—more fragile and vulnerable, wispy like an apparition. Waking up in my room at the Peninsula Hotel in Hong Kong, I lie in bed thinking about Isobel, remembering her smile, her voice.

I've come to Hong Kong to meet with Stan Karnow, chief Asian correspondent at the Time Life Bureau. Jim Wilde had said to me, "Get your ass over there and make your arrangements with Karnow." So, I'm here, to put my foot in the water—to launch a career as journalist.

Hong Kong is half a world away from Saigon. It's much larger, of course—a huge metropolitan complex. And it's very British, still colonial, part of their empire. Last night, when I registered, I was surrounded by servants, called "boys." And they really are boys, perhaps of seven or eight, all dressed in white uniforms. One of the boys picked up my suitcase and ran it over to the main desk. The suitcase was quite heavy, and the boy turned pale when he picked it up. But when I tried to take it from him, all the other boys snickered, not at me, but at their friend, my young porter.

The Peninsula Hotel is actually in Kowloon, a ferry ride away from Hong Kong proper. The Peninsula is a rather grand hotel, many storied, originally built in the 1920s. The building is shaped like a horseshoe surrounding a central courtyard.

Early in the morning, in my hotel room in Hong Kong, leaning against double pillows, I write to Isobel. She'll be back in the States soon. She understands my dreams and ambitions—to be a writer, to be an artist. Isobel is the one I want to tell about the confusion and uproar of my life.

> *I have many reservations about doing what I'm about to do. The primary reservation concerns my parents; you know how they've counted on seeing me this summer, and how we see-sawed back and forth on plans.*
>
> *I also wonder if I really want to become a journalist. I suppose if I don't like the job, I can always quit and go on with my writing and art.*
>
> *I'm taking the job for the experience and perhaps for the sheer novelty. I'm taking it partly as a lark, and partly because I like the idea of having a direct and effective voice to speak to the world. I'm taking it partly because I think I should take it—and yet don't understand wholly why I should (or think I should).*
>
> *I wish you were here so I could talk it all over with you. And I wish you were here for many other reasons too.*
>
> *I love you, and Hong Kong is large and lonely without you. And life is dark and lonely without you.*

23

A SMALL FAR AWAY COUNTRY

The Time Life Bureau is in a large modern building in Kowloon. As I enter the main office, brightly lit by suspended fixtures with fluorescent bulbs, I hear the click-click-click of teletype machines, news coming from around the world. I walk through rows of metal desks, with people clanging on their typewriters or talking on the phone. A few glance up as I pass and smile or wave. I feel a rush of excitement as if I'm on a high wire overlooking the globe.

Stan Karnow, the Time Life Chief for Asia, is round-faced and pudgy. I would guess he's in his late thirties, ten years or so older than me. As we face one another across his large desk, he says, "Jim Wilde tells me good things about you."

"Thanks," I say.

"He says you're a writer. Which is fine. But you don't have any experience in journalism, do you?" Karnow has the smooth, slicked-back look of a used-car salesman. He looks hard at me, sizing me up.

"Not really," I admit. "I've published short stories—fiction. I'm a really good writer. I know I can do this." I talk fast, breathless, talking myself into this career. "I've lived in Vietnam for two years and I know that country as well as anybody there. In those two years, I've schooled myself in the history and politics of Vietnam. I've gotten to know Vietnamese and Americans, journalists, diplomats, peasants, intellectuals, students..."

Karnow leans back in his chair and folds his arms across his chest. "Okay, fine," he says, "But if you come to work for us, it won't just be Vietnam. Not enough is happening there. We couldn't afford to have a reporter cover just one small far away country. You'd be working on stories all over Asia." I'm disconcerted at this announcement. I really know Vietnam; I don't have that same expertise for other countries in Asia.

"But there's a lot happening in Vietnam—a war of terror and a brutal dictator, who is, in fact, propped up by our own American government!"

He shrugs. "It's not an American problem."

Karnow is a respected journalist and is very familiar with what's happening in Vietnam. But I think he's wrong when he describes this as "not an American problem."

"Okay," I say. I suppose I'll be fine covering other stories around Asia.

Karnow continues, "You know you'd be a stringer. You'll need to find other jobs for yourself—working with other newspapers or even radio and television reporting. As a stringer, you patch together a living. If you're good, you'll get assignments and it will work out."

I wonder if I'll actually earn enough to survive. It's a little unnerving. I have money saved up from my work with the Asia Foundation and that will help for a while. Somehow I have a sense of confidence in myself—I can do this.

But what I say next almost ends the conversation. "I want to do my own photography."

Karnow shakes his head. He looks at me as if I've just told him I want to walk on the moon. "Absolutely, not," he says. "We hire professional photographers. Doing photography would get in your way.

You should spend your time getting stories and writing them up in a clear, concise way. It takes a lot of skill, more than you know. Why would you want to do both?"

How can I explain this to Karnow? It's about art. Photography, for me, is like painting. I use my artist's eyes to capture not just the surface, but something more, an essence of what I see and learn. If I'm to be a journalist, I *need* to do both. What I tell him is, "I am a professional photographer. I'm an artist, a painter, and I have a good eye. I've done a lot of photography since coming to Vietnam."

It's not technically true that I'm a professional. But I have professional equipment, and I've done a lot of photography on my own. Ironically it was my father who taught me a lot about photography. For my father, photography is a science. It's an avid interest for him—mostly the technical aspects. He subscribes to a couple of professional magazines on photography, and he always wants the latest gadget. For me, photography is art. But because of my father, I also know quite a lot about the technology and mechanics—all of which is useful. So, when I describe myself as a "professional," it's almost true.

I hold my ground. Karnow is skeptical. Reluctantly, he promises to arrange photo assignments for me.

As we talk about arrangements, Karnow leans back in his chair, looking up at the ceiling, not at me. His arms are crossed in back of his head. I'm not sure what I think about Stanley Karnow. There's something about him that I don't quite trust, but I can't explain it.

He's businesslike, rattling off the details. The pay is $25 a working day, plus expenses, but not living expenses, plus so much for each column of writing which is printed. They'll pay for photos too. It's not enough to live on. Karnow suggests I talk to other news agencies. He gives me the names of contacts at *The New York Times* and ABC.

Stan and I shake hands. As I walk out of his office, I have a strange feeling of having crossed a line into another life.

24

THE GREEN BERETS

Walking along narrow dikes

The dawn light, flat and fog-gray, barely illuminates our path. I'm following a military operation with American Special Forces. We're walking along the narrow dykes which separate one rice field from another. We've been walking since midnight, balancing step by step in the night darkness. With each of our steps, my boots slosh into mud and tall grasses swish against my thighs.

The seven Americans are distinctive in their green berets. They're here to "advise" and lead a troop of twenty-three Vietnamese Rangers. The Rangers are dressed in camouflage green with yellow and red badges on their arms. Most of them have tiger stripes on their helmets. Both the American and the Vietnamese soldiers carry heavy guns and ammunition belts draped over their shoulders, which look like glittering jewels.

I've heard that two dozen Americans have been killed here in the last few years, going out on military operations like this. But this is my first time actually following troops on a mission. I feel alert and tense, as if my muscles are on fire. I can't help wondering—are we alone on this night march, slushing through these fields? Or is the enemy watching us, crouched behind the shrubs and trees all around us?

The head of the American team is Master Sergeant Tony Duarte. He's an oversized man, in his mid-thirties, with broad shoulders and a thick neck like a wrestler. I'm walking a few steps behind him. He keeps looking around, to the left and right and in back, hyper-alert. The night has many sounds, which are not easy to distinguish from the slop and whoosh of our own feet.

Suddenly rifle fire erupts from the trees ahead. The bullets hit the water of the rice fields, raising small geysers. The soldiers around me respond with their own bullets. A maelstrom of bullets spin and hiss all around us like fierce, black flies. The night sky is flecked with dots of light as each bullet explodes.

I feel my throat tighten in tension and terror as I duck down among the soldiers. The Vietnamese soldiers are mostly young, nineteen or twenty. Fear is written all over their faces. Two of the soldiers have difficulty firing their rifles—their hands are shaking so violently. I understand; my hands are shaking too. The seven American Green Berets are older. They aim their rifles with a practiced deliberateness, focused on the job to be done.

The shooting goes on for what seems like forever. Then it stops as abruptly as it began. The night is eerily quiet. We look around. None of us was hit. I'm not sure why. When Karnow insisted this is "not an American problem," he was wrong. I've just witnessed a small troop of American soldiers under fire. Why don't Americans know about this?

I understand now—this is why I'm here, so they will know.

25

A SMALL VILLAGE

As we walk on, we come to the village of Nhuan Duc. The early morning sky is blazing red. After living through the gun battle, I have the feeling that the earth itself is on fire. The village is small, with a population of fewer than a hundred people. The village sits on the far edge of the rice fields, with tamped-down dirt pathways encircling a scattering of straw-roofed houses. The houses are simple, like small cottages, with tropical foliage in between and around the rice paddies and the homes, so it's as if the village and farm are carved out of the jungle. It's the kind of village where most Vietnamese live.

At this hour, five o'clock in the morning, the villagers are barely awake. Master Sergeant Duarte and his American team of Green Berets, take up positions on the outskirts of the village. Duarte calls over to me and says, "The Rangers will take over from here. You see this village here? This is a Viet Cong village."

"How do you know?"

"You'll see," he says and nods his head toward Commander Duc, the leader of the Vietnamese troop. Duc, a short man in his forties with a flat brush cut, looks grim and angry; his teeth are clenched. I suppose he assumes that fighters from this village are the ones who attacked us. He gestures to the Rangers and they begin to search the homes.

The Rangers tromp through every home. I follow one of them into a hut. It looks like a police raid or an invading army. The soldiers tear through their belongings, scattering clothes, dishes and cooking utensils on the dirt floor. A woman and child are crouched, quivering, in a corner.

Tony Duarte was right, it seems. The Rangers discover piles and piles of Viet Cong propaganda: song-sheets, banners, notebooks, a newspaper, printed tracts and cartoons. Every home overflows with the stuff. There's not a scrap of propaganda from the South Vietnamese government. A Vietnamese lieutenant, who speaks English, translates some of the communist propaganda for me. It has one major theme, "Down with the Americans, down with Diệm, down with the American-Diệm clique." One sign says, "The Americans will go back to America. Diệm will go back to America. Where will you go?" A small mimeographed tract reads, "Put your guns on the Americans and pull the trigger."

Seeing this Viet Cong propaganda is chilling. The Viet Cong tell the Vietnamese people that Americans are their enemy.

For Americans, communism is a global archenemy, which has spread from Russia to Eastern Europe to China. So, we—the Americans—support the Diệm government, just because it's anti-communist, never mind that the Diệm regime is despotic and brutal.

As I watch, the interrogations begin. The Rangers take over one of the huts. One by one, they bring in young villagers and question them roughly, with loud words and beatings. I hold my camera tightly in my hand, trying not cringe as the people in front of me are cruelly lashed.

The soldiers identify five young men as Viet Cong. They are poor young men—looking no different from other farmers I've met all over Vietnam. The soldiers bind their arms behind their backs and line them up. These young men look terrified, with expressions of despair and shock on their faces.

I take photos of the prisoners and the soldiers.

I ask Tony, "How do they know these men are Viet Cong?"

Tony says, "They know. Most of them confess, one way or another." Then he adds, "I don't like this. But we're not supposed to interfere."

Then there's the young woman. Her long dark hair is bound up in a bun in the back of her head. She's wearing black trousers and a blouse with light blue dots. She's thin and pretty. She looks like a sweet young woman. Commander Duc suspects her of being a VC operative. Maybe she is.

Two of the Rangers blindfold her and tie up her wrists against her back. After interrogating her for a while, he suspends her by her arms from a beam in the ceiling. She's bent over in an excruciating position as the men repeat and repeat a series of questions, all the while beating her on her back and her legs. She is silent. Tears pour down her cheeks.

As I watch from the doorway of the hut, I feel my heart breaking. Who is this young woman? I want to shout out, *Stop! Stop!* But I don't. Because I'm a journalist now, my job is to be a witness.

I take photos. What I need to do is tell the story.

When we leave the village to return to the base, we have five prisoners with us. The young woman is not one of them.

My article is published in *Time*, September 25, 1961, with the title "Night War in the Jungle." Although I submitted photos of the young woman being interrogated, the *Time* editors chose to include neither the story about her, nor the photos in the published article, which is annoying and frustrating. *Time* is a gigantic, conservative machine and controls what Americans know and don't know. I'm a tiny cog.

But they did give some press to Tony Duarte, who has become my friend.

Sergeant Duarte led his company of Rangers on a night raid against a Viet Cong village. Surprise was complete, and he returned at dawn with five Communist prisoners. Looking carefully at one, Medic Williams said, "I'm sure I've seen him right here in my daily line-up of patients. Either that, or he has an identical twin."

Next day, as Sergeant Duarte and his men were laying out red markers in a field for a supply airdrop, Viet Cong snipers fired from the bush. The first bullets whizzed by within an inch of Duarte's head...

Two of the Rangers blindfold her

26

YOU MIGHT WANT TO CHECK IT OUT

Tony Duarte nods his head and smiles when I ask him if he got any flack when my article came out in *Time* with his name. "It was fine," he says. "Didn't bother me."

We're at a small café in Saigon, having coffee and a smoke. We're sitting at one of those metal tables that wobble and squeak every time you move. We're an odd-looking pair, Tony in his fatigues and green beret, me in my casual shirt and trousers. Also, he's a head taller than me, but it doesn't seem to be as obvious when we're seated.

After trudging through jungles on military operations together—four so far—we've become good friends. I admire him immensely, his bravery and his sense of purpose. Tony served in Korea where he got a Silver Star for gallantry. I think of him as Tiger-Tony. He has a quality about him, tough, but also gentle and sensitive. I've never seen him act with arbitrary anger against anyone.

I broach a delicate subject. "What do you think about what happened in that village, Nhuan Duc? The interrogations? Especially what they did to the young woman? Were you bothered?"

Tony takes a long drag on his cigarette, blows the smoke upward, and is silent for a while. "Yeah," he says finally, "that was tough. But sometimes that's what it takes."

"Would you have tortured that woman if you were interrogating her?"

"I don't think so. But sometimes you do stuff . . . It's like you have to be a thief to catch a thief." As I look across the table at Tony, whom I admire, I wonder—what would I do if I were a soldier like him? Would I "do stuff" that I would later be ashamed to tell my family?

We start talking about the Special Forces—they're called the "Green Berets"—how they operate, who the guys are, their commitment to their country. One of the guys that was with us—Mike Bradford—is forty-four and is supposed to retire, but he doesn't want to leave the force and he's working out how he can stay on in Vietnam. I remember Mike from our night venture a couple weeks ago. He doesn't say a lot but when he does, his voice is surprisingly deep and resonant, like an opera singer's voice.

"You know my boss at *Time*, Stan Karnow, told me that Vietnam is 'not an American problem.'"

Tony shakes his head and sniggers. "That's just blind and stupid," he says. "America is in here deep. As we speak, the U.S. is upping its aid—in a big way, really big. There's a shipment coming soon, a whole mess of military supplies from the U.S. of A. I hear it's something like we've never seen before in these parts. Everything is hush-hush. But you might wanna check it out."

"Really?" I say, and we talk about the details—where and when.

Then he adds, "I hope your stories don't get you in a mess of trouble." He tilts his chin up to blow smoke high into the air.

"Same for you," I say.

Tony shrugs. "Don't worry about it."

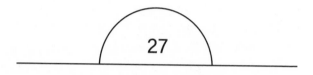

27

SITTING ON A HARD BENCH

I go out to the U.S. military base at Cam Ranh on the South China Sea two days later, on Tony's tip. This isn't exactly an assignment from *Time* or anyone else—just following my nose as a journalist.

A U.S. Marine stands guard but lets me in when I show my press pass. The Cam Ranh base is a large complex, with tin-colored buildings, landing fields, and piers for ships. Before I talk to anyone, I meander around. What I see suggests that what Tony told me must be true. Three large supply ships are docked along the piers, with men buzzing around them in droves. Huge wooden crates are everywhere—on the ground, dangling from the air, being transported across the ground.

I go up to one of the men, an American in army fatigues. I show him my journalist badge and ask, "What is all this?"

"Look," he says, "I just do what they say. You go ask someone at headquarters over there." And he gestures with his head to the largest of the tin buildings.

So, I go there, walk up to the first desk, and say, "I'm with *Time Magazine*. I'd like to talk with the base commander, please."

"Wait there," he grunts and points to a hard bench over on the side of the room.

An hour goes by. I go up to the desk again. "When can I speak to the base commander?"

"He's not available at the moment. You can wait if you like."

And so I wait. All afternoon. But the base commander never comes out. At five in the evening, when they dim the lights, I leave.

But I'm back the next morning, sitting on the same hard bench, waiting. I know there's a story here. I know it. I just have to be patient.

Finally, I get to speak to somebody. His name is Frank O'Sullivan—he's not the base commander but he's a sub-sub-lieutenant or something. And it turns out, he's a frank sort of guy. "We're helping out the Vietnamese—helping them fight the communists here," he says. He gives me details, lots of details. He just says, "Don't use my name, please." And I promise—I will just say "according to military sources."

I write up the story. I don't send it to *Time*—I don't trust them to get it right. This is important news for Americans to hear, and I'm afraid the ultra-conservative *Time* editors would bury the story. I send my article about the large mass of incoming U.S. military aid to Vietnam to *The New York Times*.

By the next day, I get a cable—my story will be published on the front page of *The New York Times*. I've scooped the world! Now, because of my words, Americans will know the truth—that the U.S. is getting deeply involved in the fighting in Vietnam.

28

THE STORY IS OUT

MAAG—the Military Assistance Advisory Group—calls me on the carpet. I'm in the office of an Air Force colonel at MAAG headquarters in Saigon. He's sitting at his oversized green metal desk with *The New York Times* spread out in front of him, and he's tapping the paper with his forefinger so hard he makes holes in the newsprint. His face red with rage, he shouts at me, "Where did you get this info? Did you just make it up? How dare you write this stuff! You must be a commie."

I'd like to kick the bastard in the teeth. But I just nod and say, "I'm a journalist and a loyal American."

Anyway, the story is out, and it's true. At first, MAAG denies everything. Then, just one day later, they confirm it, all the details.

For a follow-up story, I go out to the airbase at Bien Hoa and begin shooting pictures, both stills and film. ABC-TV hires me to do a report. This is my first time on television. It's actually a voice-over—the viewers hear my voice as they watch the film I shot. Speaking into my small microphone, I have a sense that my voice and my words are going out to the wide world, telling the truth, making an impact. It's an amazing feeling.

Then the ARVN, a unit of the Vietnamese military, arrests me. This happens shortly after my ABC-TV report. They bang on the door of my apartment on Rue Thi Sau. They rudely grab my arms, throw me into a jeep, and drive me to a Vietnamese army base just outside Saigon. A lieutenant with a pock-marked face bellows at me, in pidgin French, "I hear you a troublemaker."

"*Je sui un journaliste*," I say. But my hands are shaking and my stomach is flip-flopping almost as if I'd ingested something toxic. My Vietnamese friends have been arrested in this country—they've been beaten and tortured. What will they do to me?

The pockmarked lieutenant grunts, grabs my camera and yanks out the film. One of his buddies leads me to a small wooden chair in a corner of the station. Suddenly I'm angry—oddly not afraid—but shaking with fury, as I sit on the hard chair for two hours. Then this same lieutenant nods to me and says, "You go now." I have to find my own way back home.

Now I have three secret service police tailing me. They're pretty obvious—Vietnamese men in plain clothes who wait outside my apartment or wherever I happen to be. But I often lose them. They're not very good at their own game. It's like the theater of the absurd—sometimes funny, often irritating and also unnerving. I'm always looking over my shoulder as I walk down the street.

I hear from a friend that the Vietnamese government wants to boot me out of the country, declare me *persona non grata*. But, thus far, they haven't found a graceful way of doing this.

Anyway, I get my revenge—with words. I write a feature article for the *New Republic*. My criticism of the South Vietnamese government is derisive and sharp. I write, " . . .the political leaders are set in their ways, and their ways are clearly inadequate. The strength of South Vietnam is fading."

The Vietnamese government doesn't like it one bit, which is understandable.

When I took the job as a stringer, it was with a sense of bravado. I had no idea what this job would be like for me. That was just a few months ago. Now, I understand that what I write really matters. I have an overwhelming feeling of both strength and responsibility—like Atlas, balancing the world on my shoulders.

29

MOUNTAIN VILLAGE

My next *Time* assignment comes at me like a speeding bullet. I'm in Ban Mê Thuột, high up in the Central Highlands of Vietnam. The Green Berets, American Special Forces, are training mountain tribe soldiers. There are many different ethnic tribes living in the mountain areas of Vietnam, Cambodia and Laos. The French called them "Montagnard"—which means mountain people. It's a term of disdain, since these tribes are different from the lowland peoples and are considered primitive.

This is, I believe, an important story—about American soldiers at work and at risk in a special part of Vietnam. I've come here on another tip from Tony Duarte and have hitched a ride on an army plane.

Dave Nutting, a Sergeant with American Special Forces, meets me at a makeshift airport at their base. Dave is a short man with large blue eyes and big hands. He's a cowboy character who wears unlaced boots and blue jeans belted around his navel. He's twenty-nine.

We get into Dave's jeep. As we rumble along dirt roads, Dave says, "You won't believe what they have me doing here."

"What do you mean?"

"I'm working with this Rhadé tribe—making soldiers of them—teaching them to use guns. These men hunt with crossbows—I mean they're really primitive. And I'm making them into an army."

"Why?"

"Well, it makes sense, sort of," Dave says, pounding the steering wheel with the palm of his hand. "These mountain people don't much like the Vietnamese and the Vietnamese don't like them. The VC come to their villages and get them to fight for them. And these folks are tough. So the idea is—we get to them first and train them to work for our side, against the commies. The VC are all over the place around here." As he says this, he turns his head to the right and left, and I wonder, *Are Viet Cong lurking in the jungles all around us?*

Our jeep comes to a stop in the middle of a Rhadé village. I've visited villages of the mountain people before. I even spent two weeks on an outing in a small mountain village. It's a different world.

As we emerge from the jeep, we're surrounded by adults and children who welcome us with gestures, smiles, and chatter in their own language. The adults are short, almost a head shorter than me. Their skin is tobacco-brown and their loincloths are the color of bark. Some of the men have their ear-lobes punctured and spread wide. The women are bare-breasted and wear sarongs tied around their waists. The children, who are naked except for small loin cloths, are raucous, hopping, jumping and laughing, like children everywhere.

All the houses are long thatched huts with sides woven of bamboo. A man with a wide grin gestures for us to enter one of the huts. It's the village chief's long hut. The inside is lit by a small kerosene lantern and is dark and smoky. In one corner, three men are playing on gongs. Their notes reverberate around the long hut like murmuring ghosts. A group of older men and women sit around a large jug which has a long reed standing tall in its middle. I know what this is—it's *copia*, a sour rice wine.

The chief says a prayer over the jug. Dave Nutting and I are invited to share the drink, along with the chief and the other men and women. We all drink from the same long reed as a straw. I take several large swallows and feel the liquid roll down the length of my throat. The liquor, which is fermented from rice and leaves, tastes very sour. Being here, listening to the dissonant tones of the gongs, feels otherworldly, as if I've landed on a distant planet. I'm dizzy from the alcohol, a little drunk, and nauseous too.

30

JUNGLE WITHOUT END

Later, in the evening, Nutting insists I go with him on a hunting venture in the jungle, not far from the Rhadé village. I used to hunt, a little, with friends in the tame woods of Upstate New York. This is different. And I'm still feeling the dizzy effects of the sour rice wine.

We bump along a dirt road, through jungle without end. The open jeep has huge headlights shining the way. When you see the eyes of the animal, you're supposed to shoot.

With just two shots, Dave kills a huge deer; it must be about 450 pounds. Something odd happens. As soon as he kills the deer, Nutting begins to laugh hysterically. I'm sitting in the dark in a jeep, in an unending jungle, with an enormous dead deer in front of our headlights, and the man next to me is laughing and cackling with a booming voice which echoes in the night.

The deer is lying on its back in the jungle. Dave says, "Okay, Jerry, help me with this fellow—we've got to haul it out."

"This animal will never fit in your jeep," I say.

"Yup," he says, "we gotta gut it right here."

"Okay," I say, but this whole venture strikes me as odd and unnerving. And it gets worse.

We get out of the jeep and take out a couple of knives to try to skin and cut up the large deer that Nutting has just killed. In the raw headlights, its enormous eye stares at us as we begin to work on its body. As it happens, the animal has fallen on top of a mound of fire ants. The ants swarm all over the animal and over us, biting us ferociously. Our arms and legs are soon covered with welts.

On our way back to base camp, Nutting kills a civet cat with one shot. Nutting reminds me of a predator cat himself. He's a hunter with a code of bravery and daring, which seems to be the essence of his being. "Hey," he says, "I once did hand-to-claw combat with a leopard. You shoulda seen it!" and he guffaws, his deep voice vibrating in the hot night air.

31

THUMP AND CRACK

I'm spending the night on a thin army-requisitioned mattress, which is stiff and lumpy. My cot is in a makeshift barrack where the air is sweltering hot. I have a hard time falling asleep.

Images from this evening keep churning in my mind: the dead deer dismembered on the jungle floor, the ants, Nutting's cackling laugh . . .

Suddenly, my mind turns to Isobel. I think about the warmth of her and the loss of her. Her last letter was full of encouragement for my work as a journalist. "You have a mission"—those were her words—"Back here in the States no one knows or cares about Vietnam, but you have the talent to tell the real stories."

Thinking about Isobel is painful. She's unhappy and she feels there's nothing she can do because she's afraid of her husband. He's said over and over that he'll take the children away if she tries to leave him.

With a jolt of remorse, I understand how I have wronged her. I've made her situation much, much worse. I think about how brazen I was, holding her tight in a slow, excruciating dance, in the middle of the Ruperts' living room. I felt the eyes of the Ruperts and their other guests pressed on us. Or they were looking away, purposely trying not to see the scandal brewing in their midst. Huan berated me, but I didn't listen, and, anyway, it was too late by then.

I should have known her husband would tear her apart, which he did. Isobel is suffering now, and there's nothing I can do. There's no future for us—there never was—she knows and I know.

Lying here in the dark, in a sleepless night in the middle of god-knows-where, I feel myself blush with shame.

I get up early in the morning and go with Nutting to watch how he trains the new Rhadé soldiers. The men, who are short, with broad faces, look unnatural in their camouflage uniforms. But it's obvious they quickly understand how to use their big guns. Today they have an exercise with ambush practice. The men walk into a field in which grenades and smoke bombs explode and targets pop up from behind bushes. They're learning how to open fire quickly.

Nutting hands me an M1. "Try it," he says. I shoot six rounds and hit twice. A guerrilla would have gotten me first.

Later, Nutting introduces me to Sergeant Alex Moore, a thin, fairly tall, twenty-five-year-old man, with a lean rough-skin face. Moore is from Georgia, with a distinct Georgia twang. He wears his hat tilted over his face. When he takes his hat off, there's a mark on his crewcut hair where the back rim lies.

Moore leads me out into a field where 50mm machine gun bullets are flying overhead. I learn something interesting: First one hears the bullet breaking the sound barrier, then one hears the explosion of the bullet. Soldiers call this "thump and crack."

I take a small commercial plane back to Saigon the next morning. The plane is filled with both Vietnamese and also Americans and a lot of children. The guy sitting next to me calls it the "nursery special."

All of a sudden, we're flying through a thunderstorm. Jagged bolts of lightning surround us with brassy booms of thunder in quick succession. The plane shudders, jumps, jolts, and dips. My stomach also shudders and jumps and I grip the seat rests with my fists.

I imagine the headlines, "Plane filled with women and children goes down in thunderstorm." It would be one of those typical tragic-type headlines.

When we land, I laugh at myself, at my fears.

32

THE SOUTH CHINA SEA

My sister Lucy sends me one of her rare letters. She congratulates me on my publications. She's been showing off my articles in her high school American History class. I imagine her bringing them to school—passing them out among the boys and girls in her senior class.

There's quite a stack of articles now—a series of reports in *Time*, of course, but also a couple in *The New York Times*, as well as *The Reporter* and the *New Republic*. My little sister is excited at all I've done—so am I. I want to laugh—I began my career in journalism in July and now it's November and, only four months later, I've already published a slew of articles. I wonder if it will always be this easy.

Lucy's teacher in American History, Brad Miller, is a fellow I went to high school with. He's very bright and I'm a little surprised that he came back to Gloversville, our small hometown, when he finished college. Lucy says that he's cool and a really good teacher. She writes that when she showed him my articles, he asked if he could borrow them. He wanted to read all of them. She was reluctant to hand them over, but she did. He brought them back the next day and said to her, "Your brother is making quite a name for himself." He said it right in front of the whole class. Lucy said she blushed, but also felt proud.

It's odd to think of Lucy and the rest of my family, so far away in a small town in Upper New York State. I'm living in a country at war. I write about brave men and bullets. Do they worry when they read my stories?

Time has sent me to Nha Trang on the South China Sea as my next assignment. There's a training base just outside of Nha Trang, where American Special Forces, the Green Berets, are intensively training regular troops of Vietnamese soldiers. They want me to do both a story and photos—which is good. I want to capture what Americans are doing here, what they bring to Vietnam and how they relate to the Vietnamese people. I suspect that Americans back home don't have a clue that our American soldiers are fighting here and are in harm's way.

But that's a job for tomorrow. Today the weather is fine, and I've come to the Nha Trang beach on the South China Sea. The sea is a clear blue, dotted by fishing boats. The woven sails echo the shapes of the mountains rimming the sea.

I've brought my beach chair over to join a small group on holiday from the American Embassy in Saigon, two secretaries and an assistant consul. I sit down next to Kay Peterson, one of the secretaries. She's a pretty young woman, about my age, thin, with a floppy straw hat and long light brown hair, pulled back in a straight ponytail. With her oversized sunglasses, I can't see her eyes. She gives me a broad smile, and we talk quietly about this and that. She tells me about growing up on a farm in Minnesota.

"You're a long way from home," I say.

"Home," she laughs. "I couldn't wait to get off the farm. I left when I was sixteen and got a job in Minneapolis, the big city."

"Why?" I ask. "Why did you want to get away from the farm?" Already, I'm feeling a connection. Getting away from my small town was my experience too.

Kay thinks about my question for a moment, sitting straight up in her beach chair and sifting sand with her toes. "Bob, my brother, was already at the university in Minneapolis. He came home with stories and with lots of books from his classes. I read his books and was more interested in them than he was. My parents wouldn't think of paying for college for me, just a girl. But I knew how to type. I had a cousin living up in the cities and she invited me to share an apartment with her. I didn't think about it much. I just left."

"And then you went straight from Minneapolis to Saigon?"

"It's more complicated," she says, smiling and shaking her head. "Minneapolis got to be too small for me. I was itching to see the world. I heard about a job in D.C. in the State Department. It was just a secretary's job, but it was fascinating. I'd wake up every day and think, 'I'm here; I'm really here . . .' Then I was recommended for a job with the U.S. Embassy in Tokyo. I was there four years and I loved living there. I moved to our Embassy in Saigon about a year ago. It's been interesting. I've learned a lot."

She says all this in a calm and soft voice, as if every farm girl from Minnesota would have the fire and ambition to see the world. I tell her about Gloversville, my hometown in Upper New York State. And then I talk about art and writing and my new job as a stringer.

"So, you've joined the society of journalists. I've met some of your buddies when they stop by the embassy. It must be exciting for you."

I tell her about the stories I've been working on and my run in with the military and also the Vietnamese government.

"Uh oh," she says, "you're a troublemaker. Good for you!"

Kay has an intense way of listening. She looks at me as if she's absorbing my words. She reminds me, just a little, of Isobel. There's even the Minnesota connection. But she's single, no boyfriend even, as far as I can tell.

As I fold up my chair for the day, I ask Kay for her phone number. I take out my little red notebook and blue pen and write down her name and number.

33

A CORN-FED GIRL

"No!" I say. My voice is too loud, echoing around the white walls of my apartment. Huan, who is sitting next to me, looks startled. But I say it again, in a softer voice, "No. You can't give her up. I won't allow you to do that."

We're in my apartment on Rue Thi Sau. I've just come back from Nha Trang. I'm drafting a short piece for *Time* about Green Berets training Vietnamese soldiers there, when Huan suddenly appears at my door. He looks distraught. I pull him over to sit with me on my grungy, used sofa.

Huan has been dating Anh for half a year. They began to date as soon as she graduated. He felt it was improper to date her before that, when she was his student. But today, his face is pale and drawn, as if he hasn't slept in a long time. He announces, "I'm giving her up. She's too young for me. It's not good for her, to be with someone so old like me." Anh is ten years his junior. Huan looks like all the life has gone out of him.

Trying to be gentle, I lean over and ask him, "Did something happen—some reason to give up the woman you love?"

"Not exactly," he says. He closes his eyes for a moment and

continues. "We had dinner with her parents the other evening. I could see the way they looked at me. And when I looked across the table at them, I realized I'm not so much younger than her father. Suddenly, it didn't seem right or proper."

"What did you say to Anh?"

"That night, I told her—it wasn't to be."

"What did Anh say?"

"She didn't say anything. She just started to cry. She was crying and I was crying."

"Huan, my brother," I say, putting my arm around his shoulder, "can't you see this is all wrong—for her as well as for you? She loves you. You and Anh are meant for each other."

Huan looks at me as if I've just revealed the secret of life. And maybe I have—for him. All of a sudden he smiles and says, "Okay, I suppose you're right. I love her."

I've been thinking about the girl I met on the beach at Nha Trang— Kay. I call her and begin to explain who I am. "We met the other day on the beach…"

But she interrupts my explanation and says, "Of course I remember you, Jerry." It's as if her voice is smiling at me.

We make a date for the evening and I take her to a nightclub in the busy center of Saigon. There's a Vietnamese band playing imitation American music—from waltzes to hard rock. We come together for a slow dance, her long hair falling against my shoulder. She feels sweet in my arms.

Later that evening, when I'm leaving her apartment, with my jacket thrown over my shoulder, I ask, "Tomorrow night—do you want to go out for dinner?"

"Of course," she says. And so, it begins. We see each other every day. We're lovers.

Kay is pretty. There's a freshness about her. She's a corn-fed girl from Minnesota. Her eyes are blue, corn-flower blue. She's soft—her silken skin and her gentle voice.

We're lying in each other's arms one afternoon. It's warm in the room and we've cast off the sheets and blanket, which lie crumpled on the floor by the bed. She strokes my arms, my shoulders, my chest. "You're strong," she says, "Your muscles feel like ball bearings. I like that your chest is smooth but you're too thin. I feel your ribs."

"All of you is smooth and soft," I say and run my hands up and down the curves of her body. I like this appraisal of one another, our discovery of each other, as if we're children, playing at love.

Lying in bed, we talk leisurely. When I tell her about following troops and finding myself in the midst of a battle, she looks worried and says, "Weren't you afraid?"

"A little afraid, but also excited," I tell her with a kiss.

Suddenly a dotted gecko tumbles from the ceiling onto our bed. It swishes its long tail, looks over at us and races around frantically, trying to find its way back to the safe haven of a wall.

"Poor little thing," Kay says. "We don't want to squash it."

I joke, "Let's make squashed gecko soup, a new delicacy." Kay laughs, throwing her head back on the pillow. The little gecko scurries away.

Suddenly, Kay looks over at my small, noisy clock on the nightstand. "It's 2 p.m. already," she whispers. "I really have to get back to the embassy." This "date" began last evening. Neither of us quite expected the evening to go on past midday. She has her work at the embassy, and I have appointments late this afternoon

We get up slowly, reluctantly. We're both still naked and I watch as Kay picks up the rumpled sheets and the blue cotton blanket. She makes the bed like an artist, carefully smoothing the sheets, making neat corners, folding the blanket and gently placing it at the foot of the bed. Standing behind her, I kiss her shoulder to thank her for so sweetly making up my bed.

We each yawn while we're putting on our clothes. Kay is about to leave when her eyes fall on a photo sitting on my dresser. "Who is that?" she asks. The photo shows a Caucasian girl with dark hair wearing an *ao dai*, the traditional Vietnamese dress. Kay must think I have another girlfriend.

"That's my little sister, Lucy. I sent her that dress. She's sixteen now. I haven't seen her in two years."

"She looks like a young woman," Kay says.

"I suppose she is a young woman now. It's hard for me to be so far away when my little sister is growing up. I still think of her as a little girl. She was so full of life—she was always busy, drawing pictures or writing little poems or dancing around the room . . ." I pause for a moment, thinking about my little sister; then I add, "I hope you'll meet her someday soon."

I'm beginning to be in love with Kay. But, it's early—we've just known each other a few weeks.

As Kay walks out the door of my apartment, I say, "I'll call you in a couple of days."

She smiles and nods. "I'll be waiting by the phone."

I have an idea for a project and send a telegram to Karnow at the Time Life bureau in Hong Kong with a proposal. The concept is simple. I want to travel around villages all over Vietnam and interview peasants, really listen. Will Big Daddy buy my idea?

I've been thinking about this idea for a long time and it's been percolating in my head. So much of my work has focused on the American role—how Americans are advising, fighting and supporting South Vietnam. I suppose this is what Americans back home are interested in. This is mostly what all the reporters here write about. But if that's all Americans hear in their news media, they'll never understand what's happening and why Americans are, or should be, in Vietnam.

The peasants, I argue, are the key to understanding this difficult war. But nobody is talking with them. So, I will. What are their lives really like? How are they affected by this brutal war? What do they want? What do they think of the Viet Cong? Of the South Vietnamese government? Of Americans?

Karnow doesn't exactly leap at my proposal. Maybe he and his bosses in the New York office are apprehensive, reluctant to assume the liability of a maverick reporter wandering around in Viet Cong territory.

In his reply-telegram Karnow asks, "What's the story? Are you going fishing?"

34

PAUL VISITS

My gear is packed. It's taken a couple weeks, but Big Daddy finally okays my plan. And they're paying my expenses.

When I open the door of my apartment, my friend Paul Vogle is there, filling the doorway. We embrace. "It's so good to see you!" I say. I haven't seen Paul in a very long time, almost since I left my job at the University of Hué. And here he is. I've heard rumors—that he has been drinking a lot. But now, standing in my doorway, he looks fresh and hardy, better than I expected.

"What I hear about you," Paul says, "is that you're up to your ass in trouble. The Americans want to roast you over hot coals. The Vietnamese want to kick you out into the ocean. And meantime, every time I pick up a magazine or newspaper, American or even French, there's an article by the famous Jerry Rose. Congratulations, my friend!" If somebody else said this, it might sound sardonic or tinged with envy. But Paul really means his compliments; it's not in his bones to be sarcastic or spiteful.

"Aw shucks," I say. "I guess it's all going pretty well so far."

We sit down in my small living room. I take a couple bottles of Coke from my small refrigerator. Both of us would rather have whiskey or even wine or beer, but, knowing Paul's issues with drinking, I'm reluctant to offer alcohol. We start talking. Paul is still living in Huê, still working at the university.

Paul says, "I admire what you're doing. And it's important work—letting the world know what's happening here. But it's all pretty depressing. Every day I hear about another Viet Cong attack out in the countryside. Just two days ago there was an incident in Huê—a security guard was wounded. It was night and someone came from behind him and hit his head with a machete."

I take a drag on my cigarette. "So, it's happening in Huê as well as Saigon. There's a full-blown war of terror. You know, of course, that the Americans are supporting Diêm. Ambassador Nolting arrived in the country last week and signed an agreement with Diệm. Yesterday the first helicopters from the U.S. arrived to be flown by Americans in actual combat missions. As we both know, the Vietnamese hate Diêm. One spark could send the nation ablaze in political upheaval. Where will this end?"

"Damned if I know," Paul says glumly. For both of us, what happens to Vietnam is personal. It's all about what happens to our friends, the people we care about, the country we care about. We're quiet for a bit, sipping our soda, just being comfortable together.

Then, Paul asks, "So, what's next for you?"

"Well, there's something I'm about to do." I tell him about my next great project, which is going to begin soon, on the 19th of December.

Paul listens quietly as I tell him my plans. I expect to be traveling around the country for about a month, going everywhere in the Vietnamese countryside. My home base will be Saigon and I'll be traveling out from here.

When I describe all of this to Paul, he gasps. "You're crazy, you know? This trip is really risky, hazardous for your health. VC are all over the place, and they don't like Americans." He looks worried; his tall forehead crumples in a frown.

I nod and say, "You're right. This venture might be the most foolish thing I've ever done—or maybe the last thing I'll ever do. But I feel this is something I have to do. I really need to do this."

Paul grins at me and says, "It sounds amazing and wonderful, more power to you." This is his way of blessing my venture, that it will be tough but worth it.

One other thing I tell him—I'm going to be in disguise. I'll tell everyone I'm German. The French have a bad reputation as colonials, and VC propaganda is all about the terrible Americans. But a German would be seen as more or less neutral. I don't have to explain to Paul why I'm doing this, why I'm embarking on this perilous venture, risking everything. I believe this will be an important story for Americans to hear, maybe a whole truckload of stories.

35

A RAMSHACKLE LAMBRETTA BUS

The next day, I hit the first roadblock to my grand plan. I need to hire a driver and an interpreter and also rent a car. The hiring part isn't too hard. Bui Tuong Hy, Huan's brother, gives me the names of friends-of-friends. After a few phone calls and several meetings, I hire Tran Van Ba as a driver and Nguyen Hung Vuong as an interpreter. Ba is an older man—he's fifty-eight—and he's worked at various jobs, including as a mechanic. He was currently without a job and glad to be hired. Vuong is a man of thirty-eight, a refugee from North Vietnam and an anti-communist. He came south in 1954, when the country was split. Doing this job is an act of courage for both my companions. We're going into Viet Cong country, and who knows what will happen.

It's a job-and-a-half to get anyone to rent a vehicle for this trip. I walk into a regular car rental shop on a busy street in Saigon, and the fellow just laughs. The same happens in a couple more car rental shops. But in the last one, the assistant to the owner says, "I know someone who might help you." He sends me down a long alley where I find a very thin man with one eye. He refurbishes used vehicles. He agrees, at an exorbitant rate, to let me rent an aging Lambretta bus. It's rusted, with peeling yellow paint, and the motor makes a strange grinding noise.

It's the nineteenth of December 1961. This is the first day of our venture for the three of us: Ba, the driver, Nguyen Vuong, my interpreter, and me. We're driving down a country road in our ramshackle Lambretta bus. The landscape billows past, flat and wet, with ricefields, thatched huts, and farmers working with water buffaloes. The wetness extends in a light gray sheet from the earth to the sky in contrast to the rich green of the earth.

We're traveling northwest from Saigon. I've got my notepads and a couple of cameras. I'm also bringing a Polaroid camera and bags of candy. These were at the suggestion of an anthropologist friend, who's worked with peasants all over the world.

"Let's stop here," I say when I see a farmer working in a field, just outside a small village. All around us is shimmering green with wide-leafed plants. The farmer, in his wide brim straw hat, is bent over, intent on his work in the hot sun. He looks up when he hears us approach. "*Xin chào*," I say in greeting. Walking up to this stranger, I feel an overwhelming sense of the moment. This is really happening. The project I've been thinking about and planning is now beginning.

Vuong starts talking with the man. Gesturing toward me, he tells him I'm a journalist from Germany and we want to talk to people in the villages and learn about their lives.

The farmer is lean and handsome with good teeth, which is somewhat unusual in the countryside. He's wearing pants and no shirt. As we start talking, he puts on his shirt, to be polite I think. Vuong asks his age; he's forty-one. He's working on land that was passed down from his grandfather. He owns one hectare of land, he says, and two water buffaloes. He has two sons and a daughter.

Gingerly, we ask a question about the government. The farmer grimaces. "Taxes," he says. "They're always demanding taxes, taxes, and more taxes." Last year his rice harvest was good. But this year most of his harvest was lost because of flooding. But he still has to pay taxes. Now he's growing tobacco in his field. "I work all the time. There's no weekend for me." He gets up at four in the morning and works until dark.

His hired hand, who is standing nearby listening to our conversation, suddenly bursts out, "Americans are the richest people." It makes me wonder if they're really fooled by my German disguise, or maybe it doesn't make any difference—Germans, Americans—we're all rich compared to the people in this village.

We ask more questions about the war and about the government. He points to the west with a gesture of his head. "There's a military compound over there. They blast propaganda over their loudspeakers. They say—'Support your government. Your government in Saigon is looking out for you and wants you to be happy.' I hear what they say and then forget it." He spits out these words. I suspect the booming propaganda infuriates him.

I take out my Polaroid camera and take photos of the farmer who owns the field, then his hired hand. I hand them each his photo. They look at their likenesses and smile. I shake hands with the farmer and his helper and wave at them as we rumble by in our Lambretta bus.

We drive a little farther. I speak with other peasants in other fields.

Our final stop today is at a village where the people are Catholic refugees from the north. We're in the central square. The villagers, all wearing crosses on their necks, come over to speak with us. Five or six people are speaking at once. Vuong looks from one to the other but he has no time to translate for me. Finally, he makes a gesture with his hands for them to slow down. One older man volunteers to speak for all of them.

"We are good Catholics," he begins. "We lived in a village in the

The farmer and his hired hand

north. Then the Viet Minh took over and all of us, our whole village, moved down here. We came with our priest—his name was Le Ba Tu. He talked to the Mayor of this province who made us many promises. But then our good priest died. And nothing was done for us. We need a canal to bring water so we can grow rice—so we can support ourselves. Now we have nothing."

As Vuong translates these words, the man begins to weep. An older woman, with a checked scarf, standing next to him—I suppose she's his wife—says a few words. Vuong translates, "She asks—can we help them?"

I look over at this couple and the other villagers. I feel a lump in my throat, not knowing what I can do for them.

As we drive back to Saigon, I see a priest in a Peugot, which costs more than it would take to build a canal for the people in that village. Then I see a "high finance" man from USOM (U.S. Operations Mission) go by in a large car. What good are high finances?

That evening, back in Saigon, as I walk down the street, the richness of the city itself shocks me. I pick up a newspaper and learn that a Japanese businessman and two French priests have just been kidnapped by the Viet Cong.

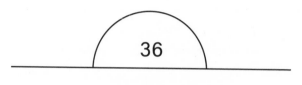

36

THE DAN-VE

It's early the next morning, with a mist hovering low in the air. I greet Vuong and Ba on Thi Sau Street, just outside my apartment. After yesterday's news about the kidnappings, we are all apprehensive, as we take our seats in the Lambretta.

We drive to Long An Province, a land of winding rivers in the Mekong delta. We stop at a café in a medium size village. People gather around us as Vuong quickly tells people why we're here—that we want to listen to them. As I look at the many faces around us, I wonder what stories I will hear today. Will there be tales of horror and suffering? I feel my jaw tightening, as if I have to steel myself, to listen with an open heart but also be objective, be a witness, to record their stories, to make their voices heard.

Vuong, Ba, and I take seats in the café and order coffees. What the people want to talk about is the Dan-Ve-Doan, a quasi-army organized by the government of Ngô Đình Diệm.

A man from the village pulls his chair next to mine and pokes me in the arm. "Just this morning," he says, "the Dan-Ve picked up one of our neighbors. He is a mat seller. He was on the road, going to another village to sell his mats. And what will happen to this poor man? His family won't hear of him for a long time. His mats will be stolen or ruined by sun and rain." I hear the timbre of his voice, loud and angry, as Vuong quickly translates his words.

Another man, leaning back in his chair at the next table, tells us, "The people are forced to work for both sides, but at least the Viet Cong don't hit people with rifle butts."

A middle-aged man wearing a stained green cap walks over to us and says, "Did you know there's a curfew every night from seven in the evening until six in the morning? It's ridiculous. We're not even supposed to have a light in our homes. Anybody out in night is shot at by the Dan-Ve-Doan. If you go out with a lantern to fetch a midwife when your wife is about to give birth, you'll be shot." His teeth are clenched as he says all this. When he's done speaking, he just stands there shaking his head.

As I listen to their stories, it's as if a chill wind blows through me on this warm day. I had expected to hear horror stories about the Viet Cong—about their brutality and violence. But these people are complaining about a military force that is part of the South Vietnamese government—the regime which my American government is supporting.

Several people glance out the door and notice our Lambretta bus. A woman says, "You know, the Dan-Ve shot at a bus just like yours and blew out the tires. It was yesterday or the day before."

As we're walking out of the café, a man grabs the sleeve of my shirt. He says, "The Viet Cong live like us, look like us, live in our homes. How can we inform on them?"

The people are all around us as we get into our bus. They warn us not to take the dirt road more than one kilometer past the village. "It's dangerous," they insist.

Even so, we drive four kilometers to a point where the road had been dug up by the Viet Cong in August and just recently filled. We were told this whole region is dominated by Viet Cong at night and about half-dominated in the day.

Vuong turns to me with a worried look and says, "Are you sure we should be here?"

"What do you think?" I ask Vuong and Ba.

Ba shrugs and Vuong says, "I guess we drive on." I notice that Ba's hands are trembling as he grasps the wheel. The bus has a tremor as we bump over potholed roads. I feel my body shuddering, from the roughness of the roads and something else . . .a sense of lurking menace around every bend.

At the next village, I speak to a man standing alone in the doorway of his thatch-roof house, with children all around. We sit at a wooden table and drink weak tea from chipped and dirty bowls. "It doesn't matter which side wins," he tells us. "We'll still be here farming the land."

The man's mother, an old lady whose face is an intricate web of wrinkles, comes into the home. She's chewing betel nut. She smiles at me, her teeth all dark from betel juice. "Are you married?" she asks me.

I take the old woman's hand and say, "Are you asking me to marry you?" When Vuong translates, the woman laughs so hard that she begins to cough—and then she laughs some more.

For our last stop today, we've come to the military post of the infamous Dan-Ve-Doan, mentioned by so many of the peasants we've interviewed. A Dan-Ve soldier, dressed in a black patched shirt and terribly worn French army pants, comes out to meet us. He's drunk. His eyes keep blinking and squinting. He tells us that only our driver, Ba, can come through in our Lambretta. Vuong and I have to walk down the long road into their military post station. It's late afternoon and the sun is hiding behind the trees as we walk down a dirt road.

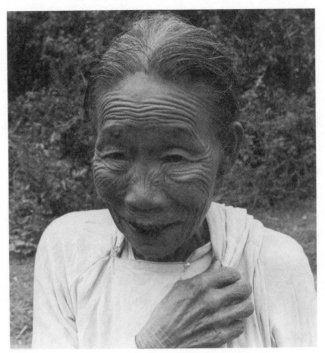

"Are you married?" she asks me.

The soldiers are all shabbily dressed and have an odd grimace around their lips. They seem to think we have connections with the central government of South Vietnam. "Tell them we need better pay and better clothes," they say.

I've heard so many stories about the Dan-Ve, about how they abuse the people in the villages, that I can't be neutral. I don't like these soldiers. But I feel sorry for them at the same time. I suppose they were themselves once poor farmers who were recruited to be soldiers. Even so, I feel a knot in my stomach as I look at these soldiers.

The Chief tells us, "Our post has not been attacked yet." But then we take a drunken Dan-Ve soldier up the road in our Lambretta. He babbles on frantically, drunkenly. "Last night they attacked us," he says. "We were scared because we're smaller than the enemy. The Viet Cong told us to surrender."

As we're leaving the post, a shot rings out from the guard tower. The Dan-Ve guard has shot over the heads of some children to scare them away from the post. I watch the children scampering away from the guard post. They might have killed a child—these drunk soldiers. I have a deep feeling of disgust that makes me nauseous.

Vuong says, "So, now they're shooting children." We look at each other and shake our heads.

37

THE SENTENCE

Vuong, Ba, and I have been traveling now for more than two weeks. Each day is amazing and exhausting. By the end of the day, when I get back to my apartment, I collapse, completely enervated—often too tired to even eat a meal.

Thoughts of Kay drift into my mind. I think of the last time we were together—how she laughed when I made a joke about gecko soup. Lying in bed, in the dark, clutching my pillow, I think, *I should call her* . . . I had promised to call her. But when I awake at dawn, there's too much to do to get ready. Another day passes and I don't call.

The dirt roads are craggy and craterous, difficult for our aging bus. Despite an occasional seizure of sweaty palms, my companions show fine courage in sticking with me.

As we drive down a dirt road, we come to a point where a bamboo tree has been bent over the road. Vuong and Ba say a few words to each other in Vietnamese. Then Vuong says to me, "This doesn't look good. This is a message from the Viet Cong—they are trying to tell us to go away, to warn us off."

"What do you think we should do?" I ask both of them.

Vuong and Ba are silent for a moment; then they speak again with each other in Vietnamese. Finally, Vuong says, "What do you think, Jerry? It's up to you."

I take a deep breath and say, "I think we should go on." But I feel a chill in my spine—I'm responsible for their lives too.

Vuong and I get out and cut the lashing on the tree. We keep going.

At a café in Ba-Ria-Vung Tau Province, we meet a Lambretta bus driver. His name is Phuong and he's at least fifty years old. He has a slight dusting of gray in his dark hair and crinkles around his eyes. We smile and chat about what it's like to drive these buses, which he's been doing for many years. Phuong leans forward on his arms on the table and begins to tell me his story, with Vuong translating as quickly as the story unfolds.

"This happened a year ago," he begins. "I was driving from Phuoc Le to Long Dien and I had six passengers. Suddenly, a group of men jumped in front of my bus and made me stop. They were dressed in black, with weapons slung over their shoulders. I knew right away they were Viet Cong. They all climbed up into my bus. They held out their hands and shouted to everyone to show their identity papers. Two of the passengers were trembling violently as they came forward with their papers.

"One of the Viet Cong men—he seemed to be their leader—looked at these men and said in a loud voice, 'We've been waiting for you. We warned you many times to resign from your job, but you didn't obey us. So now we have to carry out the sentence.'

"The Viet Cong dragged these two passengers off the bus. The other passengers and I watched from the windows of the bus, as the men cried and begged for mercy. But they got no mercy. The Viet Cong killed them; they chopped off their heads, while we on the bus saw and could do nothing. Then they pinned a sign on their clothes. I knew these two passengers; they were police agents—that was their job.

"Later, when the Viet Cong men ran off, I read the sign. It said, 'The Verdict' and it was already printed with the names of these guys."

We're quiet for a few moments. I've heard about Viet Cong killings, of course, but, even so, this gruesome and shocking story takes my breath away. "What did you do then?" I ask.

The bus driver sighs. "So, we took the bodies back onto the bus and I brought them to the police station in Long Dien. They arrested me. They accused me of being with the Viet Cong. I was in jail for a month and a half before they let me out."

That night, back home in my Saigon apartment, nightmares invade my sleep. A tangle of images float before me: A Lambretta bus with chipped yellow paint comes veering down a dirt road. Men in black garbs jump out from behind bushes. Then a parade of headless bodies dance in the air, with red flags oozing from their arms . . .

38

IN THE HIGHLANDS

We're spending a few days up in the highland areas of central Vietnam, where the mountain tribes live. This is a distinctive region, with a different culture from the rest of Vietnam. I need to explore this region and everywhere around the country so I can report a true and complete picture of the war.

Some of the roads are rough—difficult for our Lambretta bus. I try to rent horses from a highlander. He shakes his head. "Sorry, no," he says. "Viet Minh here. I not want my horses killed."

So, we go on—our poor Lambretta, spattered with mud and dust, has tremors as we bump along on dirt roads, engulfed in trees.

Our first stop is the Bien Hoa Tea Plantation. It looks peaceful enough, with undulating rows of tea plants, all the brightest green. But the Chinese director is terrified. He tells us that he and the security chief have received letters from the Viet Cong, signed by the "People's Front for Liberation of the South." The security chief's letter warns him, "You had better repent now. Those who repent are forgiven. Those who do not will be punished by the Liberation and Revolutionary Front."

We meet the security chief; he looks at us warily, glancing

sideways, as if, just talking with us places him in even more peril. Will he have the same fate as the passengers on that bus?

Leaving the plantation, we drive down the same dirt roads. We feel nervous, looking around each bend in the road. I feel my heart racing as I wonder, *Will the Viet Cong be waiting for us?*

Later that day, we push through more jungles, knowing they are heavily infiltrated by Viet Cong. We come to a narrow jungle path on route to a village which the Viet Cong attacked and burned down just last week.

We look at one another, each of us gauging what we should do. Finally, Vuong says, "We need to turn back." Ba doesn't say anything, but he nods and begins to turn the Lambretta around. I'm disappointed, but relieved at the same time. Going down this path would be foolhardy. It would be truly dangerous to travel here. There would be no hope of escape in the event of ambush on a small jungle path.

But the next day, we are again risking our necks, driving down back roads in our Lambretta. We are on our way to a tribal village. The Viet Cong make special efforts to recruit the mountain tribe people. I need to meet with these people, to listen to them and understand their story.

We're sure the Viet Cong know we're here but choose not to bother us. Why, we don't know. Two men run across the road and disappear into the brush. They must be Viet Cong. The people we've spoken to in this area have a saying, "Those who travel fast don't get killed." We travel as fast as we can go.

In the afternoon, we meet in a mountain tribe village.

The people live in longhouses woven from bamboo and straw and set on stilts, about three or four feet off the ground. Each family has a separate compartment. As we enter the village, we are greeted by goats, chickens, and pigs that wander freely around the dirt pathways.

We visit with the village chief in his longhouse. The house is smoky—it's hard to breathe—they cook on open hearths with no chimneys. The chief, whose name is Leej, is a man in his forties—short and broad shouldered, with a friendly grin. Once we're settled, sitting cross-legged on the dirt floor of his longhouse, we begin to talk in a sort of pidgin French. "They came here to visit us—the Viet Minh," he says. "It was a while ago, maybe one month before now."

As we talk, he offers us fermented rice alcohol. We take long swallows of this sour drink, even though we know it will make us ill—it will give us the trots.

"It was at night they came," he says. "There were many of them—a hundred Vietnamese people, not our people. Now, they were here in our village. There was one man who spoke in our language, just like me. He told us we should all come to the middle of our village. We made a big bonfire and we sat around the fire while the man who spoke in our language made a speech. This is what he said: 'When the French people went away, they left the country to us, to the Viet Minh. Soon we will be masters here of all Vietnam. And when we are masters, you can have everything in the jungle—all the fish, all the meat. You will be happy when we are the masters of all Vietnam.'"

I ask, "Do you believe him?"

Leej is quiet for a moment, languidly nodding his head. "*Moi pas vu, moi pas croire,*" he answers in pidgin French. "Me no see, me no believe."

39

A PLAGUE OF RATS

Vinh Hy hamlet is beautiful. Nestled on a bay, overlooking the South China Sea, it is surrounded by rocky mountains and luscious green forests. The people earn their livelihood from fishing and rice farming.

We've come to the village of Vinh Hy to see an example of the Strategic Hamlet Program, which is touted by the South Vietnamese government. With this program, peasants are induced to leave their regular villages and come to these special hamlets. They're offered protection, economic support and all sorts of aid. The idea is to isolate villagers from the Viet Cong and create loyalty to the South Vietnamese government of Ngô Đình Diệm. All the funding comes from U.S. dollars.

I've come here to ferret out what is really happening and how American monies are used. The only way I can do this is by talking to people and listening to their stories.

What I quickly learn is that, instead of being a beacon of light for the people of Vietnam, it is a place of despair. It is a place where corruption is rampant.

The people are plagued by rats. A farmer says, "The rats are the size of a man's leg from knee to foot." He points to his own leg, demonstrating the length of these creatures. "They eat up our rice crop. They attack our chickens. They eat bark off the trees and even the straw roofs of our houses. In past years we could buy raticide and it was good. It killed the rats. This year, we go to buy the same raticide and it doesn't work. So, this powder isn't really poison, but just something fake."

Another man interjects, "Every month we've protested the situation. We've begged for help. Nothing has been done to help us." I look at the two farmers who are talking with us—their faces are open and honest. My heart goes out to them. I imagine them, with their families, sitting in their huts and listening to rats gnawing on their straw roofs. It makes me angry, a helpless rage, when I think of the government officials growing fat over the money that ought to be used to help these poor farmers.

This is not the first time we've heard about the rat problem. The rats and corruption plague all the villages around here.

One other villager says, "We're always for the government, no matter which government is in control. But our heart is for the government that takes the least from the people and brings happiness and abundance."

"We're always for the government."

40

CREATIVE WRITING

We've been traveling for a month. In Tu Tri, a village in Quang Ngai province, a poor farmer and his wife invite us into their home and give us sweet potatoes to eat. He is about forty or so, very lean. The wife is tiny, fragile looking. Their home is clean and sparse—wooden walls, a straw roof, a table, a couple of chairs, a bed.

"We're tired of potatoes," the man says, "but the rats have eaten up our rice harvest. They eat the potatoes, too."

On our journey, we've often been treated to such warm hospitality. We've had lunches of boiled potatoes. We've drunk innumerable cups of tea. I often wonder and worry—are we taking their last food? But I don't want to offend our hosts.

Later that day, we return to the poor farmer's home in Quang Ngai province. We bring them two bags of rice. The wife says, "We were very happy to receive you and you came from so far. Your presence makes us happy. There's no need to give us rice."

Over this month-long journey, I've seen suffering and I've experienced kindness. I've been to regions where the Viet Cong are always "just around the corner." I've often wondered—are some of the people I've met farmers by day and Viet Cong by night?

I've talked with at least three hundred people. I'd start talking to one person and others would gather around, so it's hard to calculate the exact number. I've learned so much, and yet it's hard to take it all in. I've listened to visceral stories about corruption, suffering, and danger. I've filled over a hundred pages in my logbook with these stories.

So now, I am writing up my report, fifty-three pages, which I'm sending to Karnow at the Time-Life bureau in Hong Kong. I keep writing and writing—I even write an appendix to my report. My mind is racing, as if I can't stop. As I write, the faces of all the people float in front of me. Their stories have become part of me and I have an obligation to tell what I've learned. I know *Time* won't publish anything close to that length. But I have so much I want to say, so much that Americans need to hear.

The response from Stan Karnow is swift and mortifying. He cables that my report contains "much good information" but is "creative writing."

My hand is trembling as I write my return-cable:

> Of course your cable came as a shock and stung. I worked hard to get the information that went into the story, and I risked my neck daily.
>
> I sense in your cable that you think my writing does not strictly follow the truth, the reality of what I saw and heard among the peasants. Let me assure you I haven't embellished any facts. If the manuscript is too lyrical for journalistic purposes in parts, it's only because I wanted, and needed, to express the whole being of these peasants, not only their political condition, but also the condition of their skin and teeth, fingernails, and minds. There was no

other way to express all that I experienced, so I wrote it in rich detail.

What is considered "good color" in journalism and what is considered too lyrical? I'm confused and shaken.

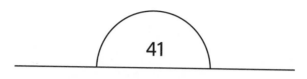

41

MY NEIGHBORS WILL GOSSIP

knock on her door, 27 Rue Gia Long in Saigon. A long time has passed since I've seen her, more than a month. I've missed her. But my travels around the countryside have consumed every moment and all my energy. I'm worried, wondering—will she be angry? Will she want nothing to do with me?

As Kay opens the door, her look is puzzled. She doesn't say anything for a long moment and then her voice is quiet, almost a whisper. "I didn't think I'd ever see you again."

"I'm here now," I say, "and I'm sorry. I've been on a journey—it's been amazing and sometimes terrible. I'll tell you about it. I know it's no excuse. I've been thinking of you, wanting you. I'm sorry I was so preoccupied." I take her in my arms. I feel her trembling. The two of us stand in her doorway as I gently stroke her long, sand-brown hair. She pulls away and smiles, her blue eyes sparkling.

"Come in," Kay says. "My neighbors will gossip about me." We're inside for a long embrace. I feel as if the room is filled with bright air—it's okay, she hasn't sent me away.

Then I say, "Let's go out for a little stroll and stop for a drink at the Imperial Café."

So, we go out. The evening is warm but not too humid. Kay links her hand in my arm. She leans over to me. "You look pale and your face looks gaunt. Are you ill?"

I assure her, "I'm okay," but it's not entirely true. I've suffered yet another bout of dysentery, the aftermath of my travels around the countryside.

We go into the café which is lit by soft hanging lights and has only a few other customers. As we sit down at a small table, she says, "I thought I'd lost you. I had given up hope you'd return." Her eyes glisten with tears. It's her confession, that she loves me, that she was crushed when I disappeared from her life.

I close my eyes for a moment, realizing what I've done to her. "I'm sorry. I'm sorry," I say, wanting to make it up to her, to ask her forgiveness. With a jolt of contrition, I realize I might have lost her. She might have given up on me.

I begin to tell her about my month-long journey through the Vietnamese countryside. She listens and then she peppers me with questions. "How did you know whom to trust? How did you protect yourself? What would you do if you were attacked?" I try to answer but I can't deny that what we were doing was possibly dangerous, maybe even reckless.

Finally, she says, "If I'd known what you were doing, I would have been terrified, afraid that I would truly lose you."

"But Kay," I say, "that's my life as a journalist." I take her hand and kiss each finger. "Do you think you could stomach a guy like me—a reckless, foolish journalist?"

Kay looks at me across the table. Her eyes are clear and blue, like a lake, like an ocean; I'm swimming in the deep pools of her blue eyes. "I could," she says. She looks down at her lap for a moment and adds, "But call me. Don't go away without a word and leave me wondering and worrying."

"I won't do that to you again—not ever again," I promise.

Our arms reach one another, leaning on the surface of the table. I hold her hands, which are warm and supple. It's as if I can't let go; I don't want to let go.

I had forgotten how sweet she is, how comfortable to be with. I joke around with our waiter and Kay laughs and says, "You're a nut, Jerry." And I know she loves me for being nutty, for being myself. Her laughter is spontaneous, bright as her fine teeth, bright as her eyes, brightening her face, brightening my life. Her love is soothing. Her sweetness and honesty create a haven where I can relax, where I don't have to prove anything, where I can just be me.

And suddenly I know—I love Kay. I love her. What I feel for Kay is different from previous tumultuous affairs. It's not a wild passion. Not a frenzy. I've had enough of the wild fires, the burning, the anointing of scars. The why and wherefore of these things is impossible to define. I look across the table at Kay, sweet Kay, and I feel enveloped in love.

When I leave her at her door, I say "I'll see you tomorrow." I mean for all our tomorrows.

Kay

42

THIS IS HIS REPORT

Everything happens all at once. My life is a whirlwind. Stan Karnow, with his blue pencil, edits the first article about my odyssey through the treacherous countryside. The story is published in *Time* on February 9, 1962, with several of my photos. It doesn't have a byline (*Time* never gives a byline) but it has my name in the text: "To hear something of the people's feelings, Time Correspondent Jerry Rose traveled through farms and villages, from the canal-laced Mekong delta to the lowland jungles of Darlac to the sagebrush plains of Pleiku. This is his report . . ."

But that's just the beginning. My logbook overflows with material, and I dip in it over and over again.

Kay and I are together just about every day. She's my comfort, my love, my lover. I meet her after work at the American Embassy in Saigon on 39 Hàm Nghi Boulevard. The Embassy is a large and imposing building encompassing a whole corner of the street. From a certain angle, it looks like the hull of a ship. As Kay hurries over to take my hand, I feel like the sun is shining on me, even though the sky is almost dark at twilight.

I'm writing frantically, story after story, selecting photos, meeting deadlines. Kay offers to help. "I can type clean copies of your manuscripts," she says one evening. We're at my apartment and she sees the piles of papers, different versions of each story.

"You'd do that for me?"

"Easy," she laughs. "I'm a professional secretary."

So, we fall into a pattern—when a manuscript is ready, I hand it over to Kay, and she creates a word-perfect copy, ready for submission. Kay is my partner. For the first time in my life, I feel like I have a helpmate, which is amazing and liberating.

I have a surge of long articles published in *Time Magazine*, *Life Magazine*, *The New York Times Magazine*, *New Republic*, *The Reporter*. I feel a thrill, deep in my gut, that millions of people are reading my words and that somehow my writings might help shape the destiny of Vietnam and America.

I do more television broadcasts for the American Broadcasting Company—sometimes from the studio, but more often out in the field. I wonder if my family back home ever catches any of my broadcasts.

There seems to be no end of stuff to write about. Someday it will all go into a book—a novel, a political book about Vietnam, or both. I've just started to outline a new novel, a story set in Huê. My next fiction writing will be different, because I'm different now.

43

A DONE DEAL

Ambassador Frederick Nolting, the new American representative to Vietnam, invites me for a private meeting. He's heard about my travels through the countryside and my hundreds of interviews with villagers. I come to meet him at the Embassy to share what I've learned. I really want him to listen to me—not just *pro forma*. This is a chance for me to have a direct impact on American policy—and they really need to hear what I have to say.

Nolting is a tall man, with hair parted on the side. He reminds me a little of old photos of Herbert Hoover, and he seems just as misguided and befuddled. We sit facing one another in his office—he's in a wing-backed chair with gold-colored studs; I'm on a dark brown leather couch. A large framed photo of President Kennedy looks down on us from over his large, mahogany desk. An American flag sits in a corner of the room. The setting makes me feel that I'm somehow back in the States.

I share the essence of what I have learned—the problem with rats infesting crops, the corruption in the distribution of raticide, the corruption in the resettlement centers. I tell him, "You have to realize that most of the aid America sends here never reaches the people. There's a huge amount of corruption. So, all the money the U.S. invests doesn't do any good." This is an important conclusion from all my travels.

"Of course, of course, I understand," Nolting says, and nods his head. He makes a few notes. But I'm not convinced that what I'm telling him actually is getting through. I feel like the moment is slipping through my fingers. I want to shout—*Listen! Listen to me!* But, of course, I do nothing of the sort—I just politely shake the hand of this powerful but inept American bureaucrat and thank him for meeting with me.

Nolting has come to Vietnam with virtually no understanding of Asia. Just recently, he signed an agreement with Ngô Đình Diệm, promising to bring substantial amounts of American aid. This is a done deal. It's pretty clear that he doesn't want to hear what I have to tell him.

After I leave Nolting, I stop by Kay's cubicle at the embassy. Her back is to me and she startles when I say, "Hi, Kay-nik."

"Oh, Jerry," she says, smiling at my new nickname for her—so her name sounds like a Russian submarine. "Did you see the Ambassador?"

"Yes," I say, "I saw him, but I don't think he saw me—or heard me. I tried to warn him but the man is pretty dense. It's damned annoying, and all too typical of what the American leadership is like around here."

Kay looks around to see if anyone might overhear us. "I know what you mean," she says.

44

A MEETING OF SOULS

A couple days later, Kay and I have dinner with Huan in the My Canh Floating Restaurant on the Saigon River. The evening sky is clear and studded with bright stars. I've told Kay a lot about my close friendship with Huan and about the Bui Tuong family, my adopted family. Huan also knows about Kay. I wonder, *Will they like each other, these two people who are most dear to me?*

We converse in English, which is difficult for Huan, but Kay knows almost no French. We talk about politics, family, art. Kay listens. She's not glib or pretentious, but she understands everything. And when she speaks, she has something important to say. When we discuss politics, she asks intelligent questions. When the topic is art, she has more to say, but always in her quiet, deferent way. She goes to museums and art workshops. She's read extensively on Asian art and has become something of an expert on Vietnamese woodblocks and also Vietnamese lacquerware, although, in her modesty, she would deny this. I sense right away this is a meeting of souls.

We talk for hours. Our dinner, with all the many dishes, is long since over. Huan and I have smoked a dozen cigarettes. Kay doesn't smoke. As we're about to leave, Huan says to her, "I was worried. Jerry need good woman. Now I meet you, I know he be happy."

Late one afternoon, Kay and I are in bed together at my apartment. We're looking up at the ceiling, watching the geckos do their little scurrying dance. Kay is nestled on my shoulder, her long hair spread out on my pillow.

"Let's get married," I say, just like that.

"Okay," she says. And we both start to laugh, to giggle, like little children, like what we're doing is silly—getting married. But it's serious, and good and easy and natural. Of course, we're going to get married.

45

THE HONG KONG BUREAU

Richard Clurman is the Foreign News Editor of *Time Magazine*. I catch a rumor that Clurman is coming for a brief visit to the Time Life bureau in Hong Kong. I write to Stan Karnow and suggest that it might be good for me to meet Clurman while he's in Asia. Karnow sends me a quick cable in reply—telling me to go ahead and arranging a meeting time.

This is a chance to meet my boss's boss, to see if I can secure a more permanent and stable position at *Time*, with regular assignments and maybe even a regular salary. I've been successful as a stringer—but still, there's this gnawing insecurity—the money flows only if and when I can catch another assignment. And now I'm about to get married, with a new wife to support.

The next week, I fly out to Hong Kong and find myself once again entering the Time Life Hong Kong bureau. As I walk through row after row of clacking teletype machines, I reflect on how much has changed since I walked through this room last July, only eight months ago. Then I was only exploring the idea of becoming a journalist. Now I am a journalist, with a slew of publications. It's happened so fast I can hardly believe it myself. So, I'm wondering—what's next? This could me an important meeting for me. I feel hopeful, excited and jittery, as if jumping beans are leaping and skipping inside my belly.

Clurman shakes my hand as I enter his temporary office. He's a man in his late thirties, with tortoiseshell glasses and dark hair swept to the side. He has a kind and intelligent face. "I've seen your work," he says. "It's impressive."

We talk about my interviews with Vietnamese peasants. Clurman has a sharp mind and understands the significance of all this material and the insights I'm offering. I'm even getting a byline in the next issue, which is unheard of with Big Daddy.

"Okay," I say to him, "isn't it time for me to get a permanent staff position with *Time*?" I might as well come to the point and press my case. Clurman sits across his desk, puffing on his pipe, while I wait, wondering what the hell he's thinking.

"The work you've done is really fine," he says, finally, "but you're still pretty new as a journalist. Everything you've done is in one small country, Vietnam. Maybe we need to take a step back."

I'm deflated, as if the air just rushed out of my dreams. But I try not to show my disappointment with his less than enthusiastic response. I ask, "What do you mean?"

"Let's have you move to the Hong Kong desk," he says. "This will accomplish several things at once. It will give us a chance to see how you work on a variety of stories, not just Vietnam. You'll get a much broader knowledge of Asia. You'll also get familiar with the operations of a foreign bureau."

I think, with relief—okay, that's not so bad.

Then we talk about the details, moving to Hong Kong, and money. The money is better than being a stringer; it's a real salary, even with a housing allowance. The plan we discuss is for me to work for a few months in the Hong Kong bureau, then maybe New York and Washington, then somewhere else. It means more security. It could mean a true career path for me as a journalist.

I'm impatient. It's not exactly a permanent staff position yet, but I'll have to wait. I'm now working full time for Big Daddy.

46

DOUBLE GOOD NEWS

"What do you think?" I ask Kay. We're having lunch at a café near the Embassy in Saigon. My new position at *Time* affects her as much as me—mostly in good ways, I hope. It means I'll have a steady salary to support us. But it also means we'll be separated for a couple of months. I'll be moving to Hong Kong within the week. Kay will join me later and we'll get married in Hong Kong. It will mean she'll no longer have her job at the embassy here.

"I'm happy for you and for us," she says and clasps my hand across the table. "But I'll miss you—I'll cry for you every night."

"And I'll be crying for you," I say, "but it won't be for too long. Anyway, for now, we need to tell our parents about us. I know someone with a two-way radio set up. His name is Mike Aberman—he works for the Foreign Service—and he told me we can come any time and make an international call for free."

So, later that same day, Kay and I squeeze together on a single chair in Mike's tiny office, speaking into a silver mike. I can hear the staccato of radio-static, as I say, "I have news for you, Mother."

Her voice sounds like she's underwater. "Oh Jerry, is it good news?"

"Very," I say. "Double good news. I'm getting married and I have a new job."

Mother says something which is garbled over the tetchy two-way radio line.

Then I say, "I want you to meet my Kay." I hand the mike to her. Kay says a few words in her soft voice and Mother says something. It sounds like a nice greeting, though we can't really understand most of the words. I take the mike again. "I'll write a letter," I shout into the mike.

We send long letters to her parents and mine. We tell them we're in love, and we're getting married. Her parents live on a farm in a tiny town in Minnesota. Letters don't even need a street address, just her father's name, Walter Peterson and the town, Dundee, Minnesota. I don't know how her family will feel about her marrying a Jew.

Kay is a Catholic, like her mother, but she's not a really strong Catholic. Her father is Lutheran. I suspect my own parents would have liked me to marry a Jewish woman. They're not particularly religious. Kay and I talk about this.

"I don't want a church wedding—is that okay?" I say.

"Really, I don't care," she says. "Do you want our children raised in the Jewish faith?"

"Absolutely not—no religion, no baptism, no indoctrination in any religion."

Kay laughs. "I guess you're religious about your anti-religion."

In my letter to my parents, I tell them about a "revolution in my life," both Kay and my new job. About Kay, I write, "As American women go in this modern era, Kay is direct, loyal, and loving." And I tell them about my new staff job at *Time.*

To both Kay's parents and mine, we write, "We're coming home soon, maybe this summer."

I know my parents will be pleased at my new job. I can just imagine my father's relief—after all his worries that I would never be able to support myself as a writer. Now I have a paid job with a major American publication.

But I wonder—what will it really be like to work for Big Daddy?

47

BIG DADDY

Kay-nik my love,

I miss you terribly. I see many things and want your eyes to share them with me. I have your picture on my desk, the one with your warm eyes and smile. I look at it and long for you . . .long do I long longingly for you who's a long distance away.

Did you see the Time *article with my byline? . . .big success and all that . . .shucks and gee whizz . . .it embarrasses me and I love it. Who wouldn't . . .?*

I'm working on a design for your wedding ring. I've found a good jeweler here to fabricate it. The design is very modern, asymmetrical and abstract, with a diamond and two pearls. While I'm working on it, I imagine seeing it on your sweet hand, with your delicate long fingers that I want to kiss at this moment.

Still no apartment for us, but I keep looking. For now, I'm camping out at the Schecter's place . . .

Working for Big Daddy in the Time Life Hong Kong office is not hard, not strenuous, not risky, nothing like what I've been doing up to now, going out in the field, hunting up stories, following troops, interviewing all sorts of people from peasants to politicians.

At the Time Life office, Monday is an easy day. We rummage through newspapers and wire services for possible stories. For example, there might be little human-interest stories (an animal rescuing a child) or there might be reports of battles or kidnappings in Asia or anywhere around the world. It's a game and a quest, just eyeballing stuff to see what pops out. By Tuesday afternoon, I get a little busier, writing up a list of suggestions and cabling them to the New York office. Wednesday, there's a little activity. We notify the journalists who are out in the field what stories are scheduled. That used to be me. Before I came here, while I was working as a stringer, I never knew which stories actually would be published. It's only when you get this notice that you know if your story is accepted.

Every now and then, there's a story to do in Hong Kong itself, or a story to research, and I get busy. Mostly, however, the story is occurring in some other country and there's little for me to do on Wednesday.

About Thursday afternoon the files from our correspondents in the field begin drifting in. Then the work starts fast and furious, as we rewrite the stories, add and subtract bits and pieces, and send them on to New York by cable. Thursday sometimes goes on well into two or three o'clock Friday morning.

Friday again grows idle until late afternoon when we begin clearing up odds and ends of questions from New York, and Saturday is much the same. At times, however, there may be a very late query on Saturday, or even on Sunday morning, as happens this Sunday. At just before seven the cable boy comes with a frantic question from New York. Sleepily I answer it and dash through the rain to the cable office. With the twelve-hour difference between here and New York, it arrives just in time to make the magazine.

—

I need to find an apartment for us by the time Kay comes here to join me. This is an impossible task in overcrowded, overflowing Hong Kong. When the communists took over China in 1949, two million refugees flooded from the mainland to Hong Kong, a British colony.

So, finding a decent apartment is a relentless mission. When, after many weeks, I find a place, I write to Kay:

> *Kay-nik my love,*
>
> *I've found an apartment—at last. I hope you're okay with it—there wasn't much choice, and I wanted to have a home for us by the time you arrive. It's a little shabby and more expensive than I wanted to pay. The landlord kept telling me he's a good Christian, and like any Jew, I was impressed. A few moments later, I realized he was telling me this so he could swindle me with overcharges.*
>
> *We have a living-dining room, one bedroom, a maid's room, a study, a hall, a kitchen, a bathroom for us, and one for a maid. I found this place through Takashi Oka—I think you've met him—he works for the Christian Science Monitor. He and his wife, Hiro, and daughter live in the same building. They'll be our neighbors, just down the hall from us.*
>
> *I've grown to hate this office work. I'm not made for it. I sit on my rear the whole day and look at wire service reports, which are fantastically confusing. I read a report from Reuter's, "column of 34 Vietnamese government soldiers ambushed, 15 killed, 18 wounded, 1 captured, and the rest resisted bravely." What am I supposed to do with this "news?" How am I supposed to write a cohesive story out of that? It's no wonder that newspaper reporting is 95% fiction, and bad fiction to boot.*
>
> *How are you bearing up? I suppose you've been busy*

packing, sorting through stuff and saying your good-byes. Do you miss me a little?

I miss you so much—but you'll be here next week. I'll have you in my arms. We'll be married and all will be well.

48

A CHINESE BANQUET

Today is our wedding day: Friday, May 18, 1962. The ceremony will be later this afternoon.

It's a quiet morning—a usual Friday. The New York office has cabled two questions about a story we submitted—simple stuff, the location of an incident and the age of someone mentioned in the story. Even so, it takes a little running around to ferret out the exact information and cable these bits back to the New York office.

Suddenly, a secretary comes to my desk and hands me an envelope. The address is my old postal address in Saigon. It was dated three months ago and has just been forwarded here. The envelope is small and pink, with round blue handwriting. I know this handwriting.

Isobel and I have been out of touch. I haven't written to her in a long time. In part, I've been preoccupied with work. But also—what could I say? I didn't know how to tell her that I have another love. I haven't heard from Isobel in a long time either.

Then, today of all days, I get this letter from Isobel. Sitting in my office at *Time* and reading her long letter on pink sheets of stationery, I feel a lump in my throat as large as a water buffalo.

Isobel writes, "We're moving to Bangkok. Bill has taken a position

146

in the American Embassy there. It will be good to be in Southeast Asia again—I always feel a special affinity for Asia, and Bangkok is beautiful. Bill is the same—sometimes he's almost kind. A lot of the time, he's just silent, as if I'm not there. This is the way he is. We're sticking it out together. We have our family. I'm pregnant. The baby is due in September—so this will be an Asia child."

When I think about Isobel, my heart aches. If I'm honest with myself, my feelings about Isobel are different now. I care about her. She is dear to me, as a friend, more than a friend. If things had been different, we might have married. I wonder—if I had asked her, would she have come to me, willingly, lovingly?

But it was not to be.

Instead, I write a long letter to Isobel to tell her that today I'm getting married. I tell her about Kay, that she reminds me of her, a little—and maybe that's why I was drawn to her. I tell her about my work with Big Daddy. I say that I'm sorry for hurting her.

When I drop my letter in the mail slot, I feel like I'm sending a poison dart to someone I care about. Even so, I can't allow myself to think how our joy will cause Isobel pain.

At four in the afternoon, Kay and I are married at the Hong Kong Marriage Bureau. The room is stark, with dark wood furniture, and a few red-gold oriental embellishments—the décor is a combination colonial British and generic Chinese. The Justice of the Peace conducting the ceremony is old and bald, very British; he never smiles.

A few journalist friends and their wives are the witnesses. Kay looks lovely in an elegant blue silk dress with a silver and pearl necklace, which I designed and had crafted for her in Hong Kong. I'm in a white dinner jacket and black bow tie. As the somber Justice of the Peace makes his pronouncements, I look over at my Kay. She's smiling, a sly, happy, triumphant smile. I'm smiling too.

We bring our friends to a favorite restaurant in Kowloon. As soon as we enter, we're greeted by that special blend of delicious aromas in Chinese cuisine. We have a many-course Chinese banquet, with eight main dishes—eight for luck—whole roasted chicken with head, soya glazed prawns, Ying Yang fried rice, quail, sea cucumber with seared vegetables, roasted suckling pig, deep fried crab claws, and steamed rock cod, ending with shark fin soup, a delicacy. We're celebrating just as if this were a traditional Chinese wedding banquet. Our friends drink toast after toast with glasses of *baijiu*, a Chinese whiskey. "*Ganbei!*" they shout, as we down our drinks to the bottom.

But my bride isn't drinking with us. Kay is pregnant.

Jerry and Kay

49

NUMBER ONE *AMAH*

On a cloudy summer afternoon, Cheong Jun comes to our apartment for an interview. We had put an ad in the paper for an *amah*—this is the term for household maid in Asia. With no supermarkets here or modern laundry and with the water sometimes turned off for several hours each day, we need help. And hiring someone like this is inexpensive here, really cheap on my American salary base.

Cheong Jun is a small woman—no more than five feet tall. She tells us, "Speak little English but Number One *amah*, cook girl, house clean . . ." She's forty-five and thin with her dark hair pulled back in a bun. She has a nice smile. We hire her on the spot.

At last, Big Daddy gives me a real assignment—to hop off to Burma for a story about General Ne Win, the military strongman who has just taken over Burma in a *coup d'etat*. Ne Win quickly suspended the constitution, dissolved the legislature, and declared that "democracy is not suitable" for his country. I'm eager to go there and report about the character of this Asian dictator. This is the work I like—something real, something I can sink my teeth into.

But, when I come home to our new apartment, excited about my new assignment, Kay looks crestfallen. We've been married just two weeks, and now I'm leaving and will probably be away for a week or more.

"We were separated for more than two months and now we're finally together," she says. "We're not even unpacked and our apartment needs all sorts of work." She says all of this in a quiet voice, but she's angry and hurt. Her face looks drawn and pale.

"What do you want me to do?" I ask.

"Stay home with me for a few minutes!" she grumbles.

"Should I turn down the assignment and stay home? I will if you tell me to."

Kay is quiet for a moment. Then she sighs. "I know this is what you really want—to be out in the field, to be chasing stories. It's just that I'm tired and irritable—and I want to be with you."

"And I want to be with you," I say. I take Kay in my arms and she settles into my shoulder as I stroke her hair and her soft arms. She's tired, from the pregnancy and the move, and what she says is reasonable. "I'm sorry, my love," I whisper into her long hair. "It's not fair, I know, I know."

The truth is—I'm in a quandary. I can't stand office work—I'm no good at that. I need to get involved in a story, to be out with people and see and hear what's really going on. But this is so soon, and Kay's right—we're finally together and now I'm leaving again.

The next day when I leave for Burma, Kay is left home with our Cheong Jun. If I want to be any good as a journalist, I need to be out in the field. I can't stay home.

50

LEAPFROGGING

My story about Burma fills 95 lines in the July 20, 1962 issue of *Time Magazine*:

> *. . .Once they have attained wealth or fame, most alumni like to do something nice for their alma mater. Not so General Ne Win, Burma's military strongman, an alumnus of Rangoon University, who last week handed his old school a painful surprise. On his orders, an army demolition team marched on campus and blew up the two-story Student Union building. . .*

Now, Big Daddy gives me assignments, so I'm leapfrogging from one place to another. I go to Burma, to the Philippines, to Thailand, back to the Philippines, then to Laos and Vietnam, working on a variety of stories.

I'm in Saigon one hot afternoon when I meet with Don Schanche, Managing Editor at *The Saturday Evening Post*. My friend Art Dommen pulls me over when I'm at the Caravelle and introduces us. Dommen says, "You should meet Jerry Rose. You might have seen some of his articles."

"Oh yes," Don nods his head and smiles warmly, "I've heard about you. You were one of the people I wanted to meet here." Don is tall and blond, in his mid-thirties—an imposing man with a strong voice and a cigarette perpetually hanging on his lip.

As we shake hands, my first thought is about the short stories I've drafted since I've come to Asia. *The Post* is famous for publishing short fiction. I'm still eager to publish my fiction—that continues to be my dream and my ambition. Maybe they would be interested.

But that's not what Don Schanche wants to talk about. As we take our seats on the terrace café, he says, "I've seen your articles in *Time* and other places, too. I'd like to see you write stuff for us."

I'm surprised. "I didn't think *The Post* was interested in international news." *The Post* with their Norman Rockwell covers doesn't seem like a news magazine. "You publish short fiction, don't you? I'd love to send you some of my short stories."

"We're changing," he says, "trying to have a really different focus, to keep up with important news—switching to photography on the cover. I'll tell you something in confidence—Otto Friedrich, our Foreign Editor, knows Stan Karnow and would like to recruit him for *The Post*. And you're another one whose name has popped up."

"I'm flattered," I say, "but I have a contract with Time Life—so this wouldn't work for now. I'd like to send you some short stories. I have several about Vietnam—if *The Post* is still publishing fiction."

"Sure," he says, "Send me your stories—but think about what I'm saying—about writing for us instead of *Time*. It could be a whole different world for you."

I tuck this invitation in the back of my mind. Maybe someday.

Kay is my partner, more than a wife—her work is professional. She types my manuscripts, manages my correspondence, and keeps my files in order. But I've been leapfrogging around Asia for almost all of the three months since our wedding. She's lonely and alone, with only our No.1 amah to keep her company when I'm away. I miss her too and ache for her—but I'm doing the work I love.

One morning, as I'm going off for one more assignment, I see Kay standing in the hallway. She's about four months now—her pregnancy just barely showing. She's leaning against the wall, one hand on her small belly, the other bunched by her mouth, as if she would like to scream but is holding herself back. Instead, she whispers, "So, you're leaving again."

I put down my suitcase and take Kay in my arms, holding her tight for a few moments, my nose buried in her hair, breathing in the scent of her citrusy shampoo. "Kay-nik, my love," I sigh in her ear, "my love, my love . . ."

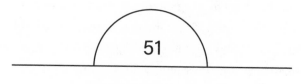

51

TIGER'S MILK

For once, I have story assignment based in Hong Kong. Now, I come home every night. The story is about the Kadoorie brothers, two Iraqi-Jewish brothers who are the wealthiest businessmen in Hong Kong. The story intrigues me because of their unique position in Hong Kong. The Kadoorie brothers have a vast empire, owning huge hotels and major transportation systems. How did it happen that the wealthiest businessmen in this Chinese-British colony are Jews from the Middle East?

I meet Lawrence and Horace Kadoorie in their elegant office, with its enormous windows overlooking Hong Kong harbor. My first statement is a joke, that turns out to be a serious mis-statement.

I ask them, "How did a couple of Yids end up in the Far East?"

Lawrence Kadoorie starts to laugh and guffaw. "You may be a Yid," he says, "but we're not. Our family came to the Far East from Bagdad. We're from a rich tradition of Sephardic Jews—we speak Ladino, not Yiddish. We have lots of friends here who are Yids—lots of them came here during the war." In fact, I've heard that they were responsible for supporting many Jewish refugees in Hong Kong from England and Europe during and after World War Two.

Lawrence, sixty, is gray-haired, broad-chested, and slightly bald. His brother, Horace is a few years older and has hair parted in the middle, which may or may not be a toupee. They are generous men— active in philanthropy as well as in their businesses.

I spend five weeks researching and writing the story on the many facets of the Kadoorie empire. When I submit my story, it is swallowed into the mysterious labyrinth of the New York bureau of Time Life. It looks like it's all a waste, never to be seen in print.

Over dinner one evening, Kay notices my sagging mood. "What's wrong?" she asks.

"Nothing and everything," I say, "working for *Time* is like entering Dante's purgatory. You never know what will see the light of print. They turn down stuff that's really good. And then they rewrite stories so they're muddled and full of errors. Sorry, my love, I'm just annoyed and frustrated."

My dark mood dissipates a couple days later when I start working on a story that intrigues me. I get the idea from a brief report in one of the Asia newspapers. A plane flown by a Frenchman is forced down in Thailand. The Thais accuse the pilot of being a spy. He denies it and says he is just "an honest opium smuggler."

I drop by Karnow's office and propose doing a story about the opium trade. "It's a big deal in Asia," I say, "and opium flushes into the States and Europe, too. I'd like to research how it's grown, processed, and smuggled across borders."

Karnow is skeptical but finally he nods and says, "Okay, but don't get too involved in this. It's pretty exotic." What I don't quite admit to Karnow is my personal interest—I've smoked opium many times. Huan and his brother-in-law, Khoan, and I smoke together whenever I'm in Saigon.

I go to Laos and track down the owner of the plane whose pilot was the "honest opium smuggler." The guy in charge of the whole business is a shady character by the name of Francisci, who is rumored to have murdered four people and maimed at least one other. I saw the maimed man. His car was blown up with *plastique*; he was missing his leg from the knee down, and his wife and child were killed in the explosion.

Francisci is a short man with broad-shoulders, age fifty or so. When I interview him at a plain-looking office in the center of Vientiane, the capitol of Laos, I have an eerie feeling of talking to a monster in the costume of a normal person. It's not a productive interview. He evades answering my questions, looks down at the papers on his desk, and after a short time abruptly says, "I have no time now."

But then I go on an all-day drunk with one of his pilots, wandering from one dirt-floored bar to the next in Vientiane. The pilot, by the name of Lai, is short and dark-skinned. He's 45 and appears to be strong—at one point he sets his elbow on the bar and flexes his large and sinewy muscle.

We're drinking *pernod*, which Lai calls "tiger's milk." The pilot and I are both getting drunker and drunker until he begins to relate the ins and outs of his profession. He tells me, "We wrap opium like so," and he moves the flat of his hands in a zigzag fashion to show how the stuff is stacked. "This job dangerous but I fast—so fast. I fly over Vietnam and see jet planes—they Vietnam army planes and they chase me. But I get away. Up to now, I always get away. I fast and I smart, smarter than those big jet army pilots." He grins proudly, drunkenly, as he tells me all this. The only thing that keeps me sober is what he's telling me, and even then I'm pretty smashed.

When I get back to Hong Kong, I do more research on the opium trade, how opium is refined into heroin and morphine and various techniques for smuggling the stuff, in dolls, hollow logs, and cashew nuts. One morning I visit a prison for drug addicts. The prisoners are all Chinese and are sad looking characters, terribly emaciated. Only half of them manage to recuperate from their addiction.

I've smoked opium more than a dozen times. *Be careful*, I tell myself, *don't get addicted.*

I write and write until my fingers are blue. But my opium story is a no-go at *Time*. The editors in New York send me a terse cable—this stuff is not what we want. Our American readers don't smoke opium and don't care. I'm at the office, when the yellow piece of cable paper is delivered into my hand. I whisper obscenities under my breath.

But then, out of the blue, I get another cable from the New York office, "Never say die. Rose's Kadoorie runs 90 lines." It's in the November 16, 1962 issue.

> *Seldom has Hong Kong's business been better. Big hotels such as the fustily genteel Peninsula and Repulse Bay are packed with tourists. The repair yards of the Hong Kong & Whampoa Dock Co. hum with ships coming and going. Passengers crowd the Star Ferry Co. boats and the Peak Tramways' cable cars, which provide the most spectacular 10¢ rides in the world. China Light & Power Co. is adding four 60-megawatt turbines at a total cost of $34 million.*
>
> *This bustle brings a special glow to a remarkable pair of brothers named Lawrence and Horace Kadoorie, for they control all those profitable enterprises, as well as 30 others. With a personal worth of $30 million and yearly dividend earnings estimated at $2,000,000, the Kadoories, rather than the wealthy Chinese in the colony, are the richest businessmen in Hong Kong . . .*

The walls of my study in our Hong Kong apartment cast long shadows in the middle of the night. I sit at my desk looking through the latest issue of *Time*—all the stuff they consider news, including my piece with its 90 lines on the Kadoorie brothers. I've had three good stories turned down, in addition to the opium piece. I'm so frustrated, I feel gall rising in my throat.

Suddenly I see Kay in the doorway. She's in her nightgown, looking barely awake. "What's wrong?" she says. "The Kadoorie piece is fine, isn't it?"

I sigh. "It's not really how I wrote it. They rewrite everything."

Kay comes over to my chair and runs her cool fingers through my hair. I look up into her blue eyes. "What's the point of working for Big Daddy?" I say. "I'm a writer. I should be working on my novel. If I'm going to be a journalist, I want it to be real stuff—something important. *Time* is a factory, which churns out columns of news reports like an assembly-line. I just don't fit there."

52

THE WAY TO THE TEMPLE

It's three in the morning, two nights later. I'm sitting in my study, at my new Olivetti, working on my novel, a Vietnam story set in Huê. "The Way to the Temple" is my working title.

The story is deeply personal. The characters, Vietnamese and American, are composites of several people; so they're fictional. The political events are not fictional and grow from my experience as a journalist. The politics of South Vietnam strike deep into the souls of every individual living in the country, both citizen and foreigner. The back story of my novel is the failure of American involvement in Vietnam, diplomatic, financial and military. It's a story that's burning inside me—a story I need to tell.

For me, writing my novel is like a birthing process. I have so little time to write fiction now, so it has to be at odd hours, when the rest of the world sleeps.

The key protagonist, "Michel Dobret," is an American medical doctor teaching at the Faculty of Medicine at the University of Huê. He speaks French fluently. Dobret has a scorching love affair with the wife of the American Consul.

I have a huge and daunting problem with this novel—many of the incidents are both true and painful. What keeps me up at night is my anxiety about how to protect the people in my story, both Vietnamese and Americans. Of course, I disguise the names; but is that enough?

For the Vietnamese, the danger, and it's quite real, is intimidation and persecution by the South Vietnamese government. I don't want to put my friends' lives at risk. For the Americans, my concern is their recognition by other Americans, especially wives by husbands, husbands by wives. I would hate to be the cause of misery and mutual destruction among these people, should they ever read my book, which most likely they will.

A sheet of onion skin is flapping in my typewriter, a page from chapter seven of "The Way to the Temple." Kay stumbles into my study. She's wearing her thin blue nightgown with the strap falling over her shoulder and her hair in disarray, sleep-hair. "What are you doing? Why are you up and working at this hour?" She looks at the page rolled in my typewriter and reads a few lines, nodding and silently mouthing the text. Kay understands that I need to write words of fiction, to work on my craft and my art. She knows me, knows that it's my angst and my life of words.

She runs her cool fingers through my hair, which is beginning to recede at the corners just a little. Kay is very pregnant, though not huge and still thin. She's carrying this baby like a Chinese mother, perhaps because of all the counseling from our No.1 *amah*, Cheong Jun—a small bump protruding from her slim torso.

I place my hand on Kay's round belly and feel a few tiny jolts. Who is this person-to-be? A boy? A girl? Will this baby be like my little sister when she was a baby whom I loved so much? For a moment, I imagine myself walking down the street holding the sweet hand of a small child.

I stand up and wrap Kay in my arms. I love the shape of her, the softness of her, even the swelling of her body. A time for love. Enough writing for this early hour.

53

LUCY IS A COLLEGE GIRL

ucy, my little sister, is a college freshman now. We write letters back and forth. I'm excited for her, and I want to share her new experience of learning. So, I send her an expanded reading list, telling her about my favorite novelists and poets.

> . . .I'll mention a few of the writers with whom I hope you soon become acquainted. . .that warbling, whistling, wooing Welshman, Dylan Thomas . . .T. S. Eliott who can plot your walks through the winding narrow streets of Boston and point out the sights that only eyes with feeling can see; there is Carl Sandburg and Walt Whitman for brute Americana, and Robert Frost for the profound gentle side; and Wallace Stevens and Amy Lowell for images from Italy . . .

She sends me poems she's written—asking for my critique. I write to her, "I like the imagery in your poem on dancing by the sea; try to do more of that. Read Archibald MacLeash, 'Ars Poetica.'"

She even asks me, her big brother, for advice on sex. "Does love have to be physical?" she writes. "Can't one have a spiritual connection, without going to bed together?" In my reply, I write,

*Sex is not necessarily love. The pure unadulterated liquor
of sex is of the senses and the sensualities in a person wherever
they grow raw and burn. This liquor is frequently not beautiful. You partake of it to escape or to soothe the burning. And
then you are left with a grubby hangover. Love is necessarily
sex in my opinion. Love doesn't exist without the burning to be
as close to someone as the laws of nature permit.*

Lucy has a new boyfriend, her first love. His name is Mark and he
is Jewish and religious. When she writes that she's keeping Kosher,
like her boyfriend, I write back about my own theory about Jewish
dietary laws—they were about health and these restrictions are no
longer relevant today.

I haven't seen my little sister in three years. I'm about to become a
new father now, but I feel like I've been a quasi-father to her all these
years. I wonder and worry—I don't really approve of her keeping
Kosher. I don't want her to be too Jewish, too narrow. My hope and
dream for her is that she will explore the world. Maybe she'll be an
artist or a poet—the actual career doesn't matter—I want her to have
a life of rich and full experiences.

But how much can I influence my sister when I'm so far away?

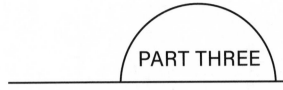

PART THREE

1962 TO 1964

54

CHEONG JUN'S APPLE PIE

I sit in my cubby in the Hong Kong Time Life bureau, listening to the clacking of the teletype machines bringing news from around the globe. It all feels stale. *Time* muzzles the news—so truth gets filtered and softened, like Pablum, until it's no longer recognizable as truth.

I'm restless. I feel like screaming and running out of this office.

Last summer, when I met Don Schanche, Managing Editor of *The Saturday Evening Post*, I wasn't ready to switch from my salaried position at *Time*. My feelings are different now.

The Post is changing, dropping its Norman Rockwell covers and becoming more of a monthly news magazine. This could be an opportunity for me.

So, I send ideas to Schanche for feature news stories about Vietnam. One proposed story is about U.S. Medics in Vietnam. Another is about the U.S. Special Forces in Vietnam, especially those working with the mountain tribes. Either story would reveal what's really happening in Vietnam—how Americans are deep into it.

Schanche writes back a friendly warning. "I shouldn't do this, but rather than cause you economic ruin, I'd better. Time Inc. has a rigid policy against allowing its correspondents to write non-fiction articles for *The Saturday Evening Post*. If, however, you are back to freelancing and merely using up your pirated supply of Time Life stationery, I'd be delighted to see your story ideas."

My correspondence with *The Post* is not a secret. I've talked about it with Stan Karnow, who knows Otto Friedrich, the Foreign Editor at *The Post*. Friedrich would really like to woo Karnow to *The Post*. I don't think that's likely to happen. At least, I hope not. Anyway, in my letters to *The Post*, I include regards from Karnow.

Friedrich has his own ideas. He suggests I interview American soldiers about "America's forgotten war." He'd like me to write a "heart-wrenching" piece with soldiers "blasting" our Vietnamese-American policy.

I respond, "I've personally been one of the first and primary blasters at the regime since the whole mess started popping, as you well-know. And I've plenty of buddies among the U.S. army there who out-blast me with ease. But any soldier who sounds-off in *attributed* quotes about Vietnam is likely to end up in the stockade."

Kay and I eat dinner late, European style, after 8 p.m. We have a folding table set up in my studio, which has ample space and tile floors. Cheong Jun cooks both Chinese and western food. Tonight, we're eating a western style dinner and Cheong Jun has baked an apple pie for dessert, with a sculptured flower on top. Her cooking is okay and her artistry is impressive. It would have been better if I had not once wandered into the kitchen when she was sculpting her pie-dough-flower. I stood in the doorway and watched her blowing on the dough, with her cheeks puffed and her salty breath and spit hovering over our pie.

Kay knows about my correspondence with *The Post*. But we haven't talked much about what this means for me or for us. That is, until tonight, over dinner.

We talk in quiet voices about our future. Kay is very pregnant now. The baby is due in a little over a month.

"Are you sure, Jerry?" she asks, looking at me across the table. "Is this really what you want?"

"I don't have a choice, my love," I say, which is true and not true. "I can't bear it any more at *Time*. It's stultifying and too damned conservative. They change my stories or they don't like my stories. I can't take all the garbage that goes on in that organization. I'm fed up with working my ass off on stories that don't run or stories which don't run the way I wrote them. Or maybe it's that I'm restless, ambitious, and impatient. So, I'd like to quit, which means giving up our salary. What do you think?"

I wonder and worry—*Am I asking too much of my very pregnant wife?*

We chew on our slices of apple pie. The crust is leathery. Kay takes another bite and looks down at her plate. She doesn't say anything for a few moments. Finally, she looks up at me. "We have savings," she says.

I reach across the table and stroke Kay's hand. "I know you're worried," I say. "I guess I'm a little worried too. Do you regret marrying a crazy guy who wants to quit a salaried job just before our baby is due?"

Kay smiles at me and says quietly. "You warned me that this would be our life. It's not like I didn't know."

In mid-December, I get a cable from Schanche. "If you're serious about breaking loose from Big Daddy, there's a possibility of doing articles for *The Post*. Personally, I'm eager to see you break the mold of anonymity." But he also warns, "If you do quit Time Inc. on the basis of a single *Post* assignment, I must, in honesty, say that there's some risk involved. Although in your case, I don't think it's very great. The risk, of course, is that the piece would not come off."

He says both he and Friedrich like my story idea about U.S.

Special Forces working with the mountain tribes up in the highlands of Vietnam, training them to be soldiers. I show the cable to Kay. As she reads it, a frown wrinkles her forehead. She says, "You're really going to be in the thick of it—following troops again."

"Yes, my love," I say. "I'm on my way back to Vietnam."

We're standing in the hallway of our apartment. Kay leans against the wall and, unconsciously, rubs her large belly. The baby is due in mid-January—about a month from now. With luck, I'll be home before the baby comes, but such things are not perfectly knowable. I bend down, kiss her hand on her belly and say in a loud voice directed toward her belly, "Hold on there! You wait for me—wait 'til I get back. I want to be here to greet you!"

55

PLEIKU

My lovely, pregnant Kay is standing on the watch-roof of the Hong Kong air terminal. She's chewing her handkerchief, wringing her hands, and biting her lips, with her eyes full of tears. I look up and wave at her as I walk up the clanking metal stairway into the plane. It wrenches my heart, seeing her so miserable.

Entering the airplane, I stow my bag in the overhead compartment. Suddenly, I feel a rush of excitement about this new venture—for me, this is a chance to do important work. I have a new energy. And I'm not afraid, not for myself.

But, as I sit back in my seat, I think about Kay, what it's like for her. She's left behind and sees me going off to a war zone. Kay is like a soldier's wife who sees her loved one leave for far-off battles and wonders, *Will he return? Will I ever see him again?*

The moment I arrive in Saigon, I begin making arrangements to join up with Special Forces units. I have a telephone conversation with a transport info officer. "Don't worry, Jerry," he says. "We'll take care of everything!"

I'm thinking, *I'll believe it when I see it. I know about the military's promises.*

I have a day in Saigon before heading off to follow the troops. It's good to be back in Saigon—I have a sense of home here, even in the wild traffic with flocks of bicycles swerving in and around me as I cross a busy street.

I drop by to see Huan, who's staying with Hy and Simone, his brother and sister-in-law, in their roomy and airy home, with red tile floors. As soon as I walk in the door, Huan runs over to me. "I'm getting married!" he shouts, with a broad grin. "You see, I'm following in your footsteps. I have a good woman too."

"*Félicitation à toi!*" I say, basking in his joy. I'm delighted but not entirely surprised. Huan has been dating Anh for a year and they've known each other much longer. Their relationship has been complicated. He wouldn't date her when she was his student. And even later, he worried about the age difference—she's about ten years younger. But now—it's all resolved and happy.

Hy, Simone, Huan and I are circled around the coffee table in Hy and Simone's living room, with bright sunlight floating through the windows. And, though it's still morning, I say, "Champagne! We need to make a toast!" And that's what we do, all of us smiling, reveling with Huan in his happiness.

A little while later, I have lunch with John Mecklin on the terrace of the Hotel Continental on Rue Catinat, sitting outdoors at a small table, trying to hear one another above the noise of street traffic. Mecklin is Public Affairs Officer at the U.S. Embassy in Saigon. He's in his mid-forties now and has spent most of his career as a journalist. He's an impressive man, with dark eyes that have a way of looking through you. I tell him about my assignment with *The Post*, that I'll be following the troops up in the boondocks, in the Central

Highlands of Vietnam. Mecklin leans forward and speaks in a low voice, as if we're conspiring. "I want to know what you see and hear out there," he says, "even if there's stuff going wrong, especially if there's bad stuff, I want to know about it."

Dinner that same day is with Mal Browne and his fiancée, Le Lieu. Browne is chief correspondent for the Associated Press in Indochina; he's a brilliant guy and a fine journalist who does deep investigative reporting. We talk about my assignment and he wishes me luck. We're drinking wine and I raise my glass in honor of their upcoming marriage. This is my second toast of the day.

Before the crack of dawn the next morning, I'm at the airport, which has the blank look of an empty saloon—there's no one around. The military is taking care of things for me. Sort of. They've arranged for a 5:30 a.m. military plane to Ban Mê Thuột, but the flight is cancelled. I would have been the only passenger; so it's no wonder they cancel it. Instead, a couple hours later, I get on a plane to Pleiku.

Pleiku, in Gia Lai Province, is on a plateau up in the central highlands, not far from the Laotian and Cambodian borders. It was a strategic location in the war with the French and it's a major center of the current conflict. As I get off the plane, I see soldiers everywhere— Vietnamese and lots of Americans, their green uniforms stark against the dusty runways. Each soldier's face has a dour look, with steely eyes and downturned mouths, as they walk briskly around the maze of dirt pathways. The Viet Cong have a stronghold all over this region. You can feel the tension in the air. Although we're up high, in a mountain region, all I see around me is flat land and low metal buildings.

I have a sense of mission—to explore deeply what's happening in this war. The Viet Cong, the communists, are winning. They have a sense of brotherhood, which is often brutal, but it seems to be effective. What are the Americans doing in this complex and dangerous place? I need to see it all with my own eyes.

Kaynik my love,

I'm in Pleiku and I'm missing you . . .

I thought I'd see my buddy Tony Duarte here because that's where he's supposed to be. He was here. Just today, Tony left for Okinawa. But he's coming back next week.

Tony has talked about me so much that his Special Forces buddies greet me like a long-lost friend. I went out with these guys on an all-day operation through jungles, the likes of which I've never seen and hope never to see again. We sludged for miles and miles through tall grass laced with thorns and briars and mucky water where your foot slips and twists with each step. My arms and legs are scratched and gashed. The muscles in my legs are tangled in knots so tight that even Houdini couldn't untie them.

Don't worry, my love—all is quiet here. Just hold on to that baby until I get home.

A couple days later, my muscles still aching, I'm on a two-engine plane, called a "Caribou," traveling from Pleiku to Ban Mê Thuột, which was my original destination. I'm on my way to a Camp Plei Mrong, where American Special forces are training Jarai tribesmen. The core of my story will be if or how American forces are changing the course of the war in Vietnam. Americans back home know nothing about what's happening here—and they don't care. But American soldiers are here, in harm's way. I want them to know about this and I want them to care.

There are seven of us passengers sitting on scratched wooden benches which line the sides of the plane, plus the pilot and co-pilot.

I'm the only non-soldier. Captain Tiller, the pilot, age about forty, is a tall man with oversized red hands, and Sergeant Beaumont, his copilot, is a broad-shouldered man in his late twenties with almost albino features and very light blond hair.

Suddenly the plane starts to leak oil. You can hear a swishing sound and, as we all look out the windows, we see black drops descending into the clouds.

Captain Tiller looks at Beaumont, who apparently was in charge of getting the plane ready for take-off. He turns to the rest of us and growls, "The Sergeant forgot to put on the goddamn fuckin sonsbitchin oil cap." Then he looks over at Beaumont, whose face has gone from white to bright red. "You're not supposed to forget things like that, Sergeant. An' if we'd been flyin' from Juneau to Greenland, I'd have had you out on that wing screwin' in that cap."

All of this is unnerving. We're flying over sharp, cragged mountains. I grasp the edge of the bench—as if this would help.

When our little plane finally skids to a stop onto a dusty runway at Ban Mê Thuột, I let out a long breath. I think I've been holding my breath for an hour—ever since the oil started leaking.

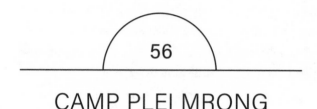

56

CAMP PLEI MRONG

It takes two more days and a bumpy and jerky ride in an army jeep for me to actually arrive at Camp Plei Mrong. It's now the day of New Year's Eve.

We're up in the Highlands though the surrounding area is relatively flat—we're on a plateau. It looks like a native village with nine neat longhouses of newly woven straw. But it's really a military training center, encircled by 900 yards of barbed-wire fence, 15 feet wide, with a trench running parallel to the length. The camp even has electricity, supplied by a hefty 10-kilowatt generator.

I'm surprised to find Tony Duarte here. "Hey, man!" he exclaims as soon as he sees me and gives me a bear hug. Tony introduces me to Captain William Grace, of Arlington, Virginia, a gaunt West Pointer, whose crew-cut hair is prematurely gray at 29. Tony, pointing to the Captain, says, "This camp is all his doing. He came here about three months ago with a bunch of Special Forces and they've been busy training Jarai tribesmen to be soldiers with us." The Jarai are another of the many tribes of mountain people. Then Tony puts his arm around me and, with a wide grin, says to the Captain, "It's an honor to have this Jerry Rose with us. Whatever he writes about us will be the truth."

We're standing in the middle of the camp and I can't help noticing the odd assortment of "uniforms" surrounding us. The Special Forces soldiers are in their usual army-olive fatigues and green berets. But most of the Jarai "soldiers" are nearly naked, wearing only loin cloths—many of them with guns strapped over their shoulders.

I want to really understand what our American Special Forces units are doing here. How do they train these Jarai men to make them into a modern fighting force? What are the challenges of their tasks here? What are the dangers?

On New Year's Eve, the American troops at Camp Plei Mrong drink small cups of champagne that Captain Grace brought back on his last reconnaissance flight. The Strike Force is ready to go on patrol. Captain Grace chooses the Special Forces men: Tony Duarte; Lou Woelfel, a thirty-two-year-old sergeant who came "once upon a time from Brooklyn"; Sergeant George Hoagland III, twenty-seven, of Phoenix, Arizona, and himself. The five American soldiers will be going out on patrol with about a dozen or so of the Jarai troops.

"Sure am disappointed I'm not going," says young Private Mike Boyd, one of those left behind.

I had planned to go out with them on this patrol. That's why I'm here—to follow the troops when they're actually on a mission. But Captain Grace shakes his head—he can't permit me to go along with the patrol. I clench my fists from disappointment and frustration. Tony brings it up and tries to argue my case. "He's a good guy," he says, "and what he writes is important for the folks back home to read."

"I'm really sorry, but there's no extra space on the 'copters," Captain Grace says.

Tony looks over at me and shrugs. "Damn it," he says under his breath.

At supper, meals are always the same, with cabbage salad, tough buffalo meat, greasy potatoes, and canned milk. Talk naturally turns to the imminent patrol. Some of the talk is light, but some is edged with a faint note of tension.

"If there are three thousand Viet Cong across that river," Sergeant Lou Woelfel says, "and they decide to attack the patrol, then it would be another Dunkirk." Dunkirk, of course, was the famous Allied defeat and evacuation at the beginning of World War Two. It's a grim reminder of the seriousness of our current war.

"Except without boats to get out," notes Captain Grace wryly.

Lieutenant Leary will be in charge of both the American and Jarai troops that are left behind in the camp. With one cheek bulging with a wad of chewing tobacco, he comments, "Wouldn't it be funny if we got hacked instead of you guys?"

57

THE ELECTRIC GENERATOR

On New Year's Day, we all get up in the dawn grayness. The morning air is cool and moist. I can't say I'm hung over from my tiny paper cup of champagne last night. But my disappointment hangs over me like a gray fog. I wanted to follow the soldiers on patrol—to see and hear what they confront, how they deal with this strange, amorphous guerrilla war. But I'm not. Instead, I'm plonked back in the base camp, fortified with a wire fence. What's the point of my being here?

Captain Grace and the other Americans that are going on the patrol are packing their gear. Their olive-green packs look like camel humps on their backs.

"Got cigarettes, transistor radio, razor. I'm ready," says Lou Woefel.

The selected Jarai troops stand in line to get their food and ammunition. The Jarai troops have guns but without ammunition most of the time. The fact is—some of them might be Viet Cong infiltrating the camp. So, the American Special Forces are cautious—they don't entirely trust these troops even while they train and work closely with them.

At eight in the morning, the artillery support, two mammoth 155-mm howitzers, lumber clumsily through Plei Mrong. These tanks will be trawling through the jungles, like giant beetles, following the same route as the helicopters, which will carry the troops.

At a quarter to nine, Grace and his troops move out to the airstrip. The two large helicopters arrive, swirling gigantic, blinding clouds of brown dust. The Jarai troops, broken into 10-man units, run forward, weapons in their left hands. The crew chief grabs them by their right hands and yanks them into the choppers. The process of loading the troops is swift and efficient and then the helicopters take off. I stand under the noisily rising helicopters and wave until they're out of sight.

I think—*There goes the story I was supposed to write.*

Late in the afternoon, I walk around with my cameras, but there isn't much to shoot with the main force out on patrol. Lieutenant Leary is in charge of the camp while the others are on patrol. He is working with the Jarai trainees, who are assigned trench positions around the west side of the camp. Leary, at age 32, is six feet tall, slim and muscular. I take a few shots of Leary instructing his trainees.

I'm standing next to Leary when Lieutenant Till, a young Jarai tribesman, who speaks excellent French, comes to see him. Till, who is about five feet tall, broad-shouldered and soft-spoken, requests, hesitantly, that some of the camp defenders be given ammunition. He knows it's against regulations for the Jarai trainees to have ammunition during the night, a precautionary measure because some of the soldiers might actually be VC. "Our camp doesn't have much strength now with so many out on patrol. Wouldn't it be wise to have a few more defenders?" He adds that he's personally selected eleven men whom he's sure are good loyal men.

Leary listens and thinks about it and, after a moment, nods. "Okay."

—

As night falls, Camp Plei Mrong grows quiet. The moon sinks below the horizon. Most of us are in bed in our barracks.

Suddenly there's an explosion, then frenzied screams and staccato gunfire. I feel the sounds rippling in my gut, as if my body is echoing the artillery. I'm hyper-alert, breathless.

Sergeant Marvin Compton, who's just gone on guard duty, runs outside and fires three pistol shots, the signal for alert. "Attack!" he hollers.

I jump off my cot, pull on my clothes as quickly as I can with my hands shaking. Around me, all the American troops are already up and pulling on clothes and boots. Leary is sitting on the edge of his cot, yanking on his boots, when a fragment of a recoilless-rifle shell slams through his footlocker. If he'd been lying in bed, it would've hit him in the chest. I grab my notebook and pen and slip a camera bag over my shoulder. Leary hands me an M1-carbine and I run out, following the other men. As a journalist, I'm not supposed to be a combatant, and for a fraction of a second, I think about handing it back to him. But, hell, we're under attack. I'll only fire the carbine if I really have to.

The darkness is alive with moving figures and specks of shooting weapons. I trail after Mike Boyd and some of the other men, headed toward the mortar, which is surrounded by sandbags. Sergeant Compton is already there. He swears under his breath—the sights are completely out of line. "Sabotage," he mumbles. In a flash of fear, I sense the peril—not just from the outside, but from all around us, inside our camp.

I see Compton swinging the mortar around toward the west, toward the main siege of fire. He looks like he's straining, trying to adjust and re-adjust the mortar's sights.

Boyd and the others begin shooting flares and high-explosive shells. I crouch behind the sandbags frantically writing notes. I keep talking to myself—*it will be okay . . .it will be okay.* I concentrate on describing what I see and hear.

Bullets hammer into the sandbags surrounding the emplacement, and hand grenades burst in front of us. The flashing lights are beautiful and terrifying. Each flicker is an attack. I've never felt so small and vulnerable.

In the light of the flares, we see guerrillas huddled around the ammunition stored inside the fort. Most of them wear the black calico uniform of the Viet Cong. One man is passing out ammunition. *Who is this man?* I wonder, with a sense of foreboding. *He must be one of ours—maybe someone I nodded to as I walked through the camp.*

Lieutenant Leary rushes in to join us. All the soldiers around me are throwing grenades and firing at the guerrillas near the ammunition crates. My heart is galloping, as explosion after explosion tears at the darkness in bright flashes. I think about sticking my notebook in my pack and firing off a few rounds—but I don't. Not yet.

Behind us, we hear a tap-tap-tapping. One of the men, sitting in the bunker, is rapidly tapping at a Morse-code key. We know what message he's sending: "Zulu Foxtrot need air strike, Zulu Foxtrot need air strike." Under heavy attack, need reinforcements, need air strike.

No response. No one hears us. No one will come to rescue us.

The ground quakes; gargantuan explosions suddenly shred the night; the air is filled with acrid smoke. The Viet Cong grenades land closer and closer to us.

"It's getting too hot here!" Lieutenant Leary shouts. We're short of ammunition.

We all get out, running in a half-crouch to the left rear corner of the barracks for extra ammunition. Two of the men wrench the lids off the boxes, and we all scoop out grenades and boxes of ammunition.

All I can do now is keep up with the soldiers; my throat tightens in the rush and the fear.

I help the soldiers gather up as much ammo as we can carry. We run over to the electric generator, which is the biggest and most solid structure on the base. All of us hover behind the generator, using it as our shield. Mike Boyd holds a 60-mm mortar in his hand and fires round after round. The beating of my heart echoes the staccato of each round.

We take our stand on this small island behind the generator. There's nowhere else to go. I'm crouched behind the soldiers; I wonder and worry, *What will happen to all of us? We are so few . . .*But there's no time to really reflect on the enormity of what's happening, what might happen. I quickly jot down notes, frantic notes, in my little notebook in the light of flares and a pale moon.

"Don't shoot weapons," Leary orders tersely. "Throw grenades." The flame of weapons would pinpoint our position. Still, the mortar in Boyd's hands continues to flash over and over again until there's no more ammunition. Then the silence of our mortar is like the sound of doom.

Mike Boyd runs forward into the barracks for boxes of ammunition. As he bends over to open a lid, a grenade bursts near him. We hear him mumble, "Damn! I'm hit! I'm hit!" And then quiet—he must be taking out his medic kit from his ammunition belt. *How badly was he hit?* I wonder, *Should I dash back to see?* But only a few minutes later, he races back to rejoin us behind the generator, balancing a large box of mortar shells. His left hand is bandaged.

The hell at Plei Mrong goes on and on. I look around at my buddies—we all have the same thought—*Will we see tomorrow?*

For a moment, I see Kay's face hovering before me. *Is she giving birth to our baby now?* I wonder. Her visage quickly melts away, leaving me lonely and bereft.

At 3:15 in the morning there's a sudden lull.

We hear rain falling and then realize it's water dripping from the barrels of the shower stall, which was shot full of holes. We're all still crouched behind the generator. I have piercing cramps in my knees from being in this position so long, but there's nothing to do.

"Lieutenant Leary," Mike Boyd says softly. "Do you think we'll make it?" I'm wondering the same. This battle seems less like Dunkirk and more like Custer's Last Stand.

Before he can answer, the battle erupts around us again and goes on and on. To keep up my courage, I think about the story that I'll write—it will be an amazing story . . .if only I get out of this alive.

At 4 a.m., there's another lull. The lull shrouds the camp in a funereal silence, lengthening from seconds into minutes. There's an acrid smell in the air, sulfur, and something else, an animal-like stench of raw flesh.

No plane arrives.

"I'll sure be glad when that sun comes up," Lieutenant Leary whispers. We're all famished for light.

At 5 a.m., flares bring an artificial dawn over the battle scene. Cautiously and slowly we leave our position by the generator and move toward the center of the camp.

Under the flare light, we survey the camp. A 100-yard arc of trench from the south gate to the western point of the fence is a long and narrow tomb for grotesquely maimed men, arms and legs sheared off, necks without heads, open abdomens revealing coiled intestines. These are Jarai tribesmen, our soldiers, along with Viet Cong guerrillas in their shredded calico uniforms. Eyes closed in mock-slumber . . .Eyes and mouths caught in a scream . . .Brown torsos and limbs mangled and tangled in death . . .. None of the half dozen Americans here were killed—I'm not sure why.

I can't begin to describe the sense of horror I feel, and the realization—this could have been me . . .this might have been me. It's all I can do to hold back my nausea as bile rises to my throat.

There's a large hole cut through the western sector of the barbed-wire fence. The wounded, some as badly maimed as the dead, are collected and laid in a line in the center of camp. The acrid scents of blood and dust choke the air. I take out my camera and begin shooting, quick snaps, one after another. Mike Boyd, who's had a little medical training, treats the wounded.

One man, found near the crates of ammunition, was shot four times through his body. Having bandaged his wounds, Boyd stands up and is about to move on when the man suddenly opens one eye. The eye glints in the flare light as the wounded man states proudly in English, "Me Number One VC." This must have been the man who was distributing ammunition to the Viet Cong from the crates in front of the mortar position. I have a sense of Kafka-esque unreality. How many more among the camp defenders belong to the enemy? Are guerrillas still inside the camp?

And what we don't know—is the nightmare over? Or will we be hit again?

The answer comes at six a.m. The Viet Cong hits the camp again, from the outside. Once more, the uproar of weapons starts. Those of us still standing dash behind the generator again. But the shooting stops abruptly. The guerrillas are just saying good-bye.

In the gray morning light, I stand in the midst of this scene of horror. I'm exhausted, beyond exhausted. My body feels wrenched, like I've been stretched on a rack. My head is heavy, as if it would fall off. I guess I'm shell-shocked—I think that's the word for it . . .like the soldiers in World War Two. But for me, as a journalist, the work is not over. I walk over to Lieutenant Leary and say, "I'd like to ask you some questions about what just happened . . .what you saw . . .what you felt . . .." I have a story to write.

—

A few days later, I'm on my way back to Saigon. It's January 5, 1963. My head's buzzing with all I've seen and experienced. Plei Mrong was terrifying and I still feel the fear echoing in my bones. I remember Huan telling me about fighting the French and the communists in the early '50s—how he felt intensely alive during that time, along with the terror. I understand that now. I'm in awe of the soldiers. I'm also itching to write it down, to get the story on paper, to tell it all.

I call Huan from the airport in Ban Mê Thuột. "Any messages for me?"

"A telegram for you," he answers, "it came three days ago, from 'Thorina H.'" We have a little girl, born on the second of January.

She didn't wait for me! I'm a little disappointed but mostly excited, and also in a daze and dizzy with emotion.

Leaning against a stained cement wall in a dark corner of the airport, all I can think to say is, "Well, I'll be damn . . ."

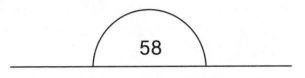

58

THE RIGHT FORMULA

A shaft of white sunlight illumines my wife as she sits on her bed at the Queen Mary Hospital. She's leaning over a small bundle in a fuzzy yellow blanket. I stand for a moment in the doorway and take in this quiet maternal scene, Madonna and child, against a modern, hospital background. Kay's face lights up when she sees me. "Jerry!" But she can't say anything more because I'm closing her lips with kisses.

She unfolds the blanket so I can get a good look at our baby, who looks like all newborns. After what I've just lived through on the battlefields in the jungles of Vietnam, war and death, it's all too amazing—being here, with this new life, our daughter.

"I should've been here to greet you," I say to our little one.

"You're with us now," Kay says with a bright smile.

Kay has lived through her own battle; her fifteen hours of birthing was grueling. Even before that was the ordeal of being in labor and making her way to the hospital in a cab with Cheong Jun. Of course, Kay couldn't understand what the driver and Jun were saying. With her labor pains hitting like thunderbolts, she crouched in a back corner of the taxicab wondering and worrying, *when will we get there?*

Our baby's name, Thorina H. Rose, is written in blue letters on a white plastic band on her tiny wrist. Thorina is a feminine adaptation of Thor, the Norwegian god of thunder and strength, to reflect Kay's Minnesota-Norwegian heritage. The H is only an initial and is in honor of my mother, Helen. In the Jewish tradition, we don't usually name a child after a living relative. Even so, I want our daughter to carry a token of her Rose grandmother.

We're all back home in our apartment now, with baby Thorina. It's a time of frenzied work.

All day and into the night, I pound out words on my new and improved Olivetti. I have a story to write—a story about danger and courage, a story for Americans to hear, about their own soldiers fighting in Vietnam. No one else has told this story yet.

I've promised *The Post* 4000 words and photos to be delivered by the 15th of January. I send the photos off first, full color shots of men at war, along with captions. Like a madman in a fever, I write and write and write. When I reach 4000 words, I keep on going and going, 15,000 unique and well-chosen words, four times too long, long enough to be a bloody book. Despite baby wails, whines, whimpers, whistles, and wheezes, I send off my story in the mail by the 15th of the month, with incredibly rich material.

When that's done, I start writing another article, which I promised to *The Reporter*. And so, more writing, banging away at my Olivetti. Now that's done, and the tips of my fingers are chapped raw. My head is spinning.

Kay's work is as frenzied as mine. She is changing baby, holding baby, feeding baby . . . up all night with baby . . .. And when little Thorina sleeps, she retypes my manuscripts. Her swift secretary's fingers create clean copies of my edited, crossed-out, layered-over words.

—

One afternoon, as she's typing, I hear an intake of her breath now and again. I'm carrying baby Thorina, who is nibbling at my shoulder, and I walk over to her typing desk.

"Is something wrong?" I ask. "Does something need more editing?"

She looks up at me. "You were really there? During that battle?" she says. "You almost got yourself killed!"

"But it turned out okay," is all the reassurance I can give.

The next morning, Kay comes into the study holding little Thorina against her arm like a small, very small, sack of potatoes. She's pacing, back and forth, back and forth. Kay is usually calm and confident. I've never seen her so frantic.

She's in tears. "It's not working. I'm trying and trying to nurse, and I don't know how much she's getting. And then nothing stays in her. She's either spitting up or she has the runs. My shoulder is permanently stained with sour milk. Her diaper looks like mushy soup. What's wrong with this baby? What's wrong with *me*?"

"Let me hold her," I say, and Kay puts the baby in my arms. Her tiny head rests on my elbow and I look into her miniature gray eyes that seem to be looking right back at me.

"What's wrong, little Thorina?" I play with her tiny fingers.

She doesn't say anything but has a crooked grin on her lips and then I hear a small explosion as something liquid pours from her other end.

Kay sighs. "What are we going to do?"

I'm worried too. Thorina weighed less than 5½ pounds when we brought her home from the hospital, so this rapid two-way evacuation could be serious.

"What we're going to do is find a good doctor."

And that's what we do. The good doctor is Dr. Yu, who shakes his head and says, with doctorly authority, "Really, not big problem. Your little baby probably hungry—not get enough milk. So not breastfeed, give baby formula. Then you know she get enough."

Formula. My father used to talk about formulas, chemicals for tanning leather. Now we begin to experiment with baby milk formulas—combinations of evaporated milk and sugar as well as various commercial brands available in Hong Kong markets. This is easier said than done. We, in consultation with Cheong Jun try more experiments on formula than my father tests on leather.

After several long and very messy days, we find the right formula. Little Thorina starts gobbling down SMA infant milk like it's going out of business.

Kay is calm and smiling now. "Look," she says, pointing to the baby's round cheeks, "she's getting fat." And Cheong Jun smiles too and adds, "Like good China baby."

59

WHO THE HELL IS THIS JERRY ROSE?

Three long weeks have gone by since I sent in the article and film to *The Post*, and I've heard no word from them. Now I wait and worry. I'm beginning to suspect that their editors are somewhat less enthusiastic about the article than I am. Will my article ever be published?

Then, finally, a month after I submitted my manuscript, I get a long cable from Otto Friedrich, my editor at *The Post*. My story is accepted. I breathe a sigh of deep relief—it wasn't all for nothing! Friedrich explains the delay:

> *Nothing was done about your piece while I was away in Europe. When I got back, first I got it accepted, then took it home to edit over the weekend. Everybody was flipping over it. There was talk about the "best war reporting ever done," which I trust won't unduly turn your head, and one dramatic demand, "Who the hell is this Jerry Rose?"*

I'm standing in the hallway, by the front door, reading the cable. I shout out, "Kay, you have to see this!" She races over to me, with the baby in her arms.

"What is it? What's happened?"

I hand her the cable on its pale-yellow paper, which she quickly reads, then reads it again. Kay doesn't get excited easily or often. But we're both electrified at this moment. I put my arms around Kay and little Thorina and the three of us do a jig together. We dance all over our tile floors. Singing and whooping, we whirl down the hall, around my study, and into the living room. The walls shake from the flurry of our dance. Even our baby, sings and screams in ecstasy, or something.

I don't make any pretense at being blasé about this. There's joy in the Rose household!

The Post sends us a box of copies of the March 23, 1963 issue of *The Saturday Evening Post*. As I unwrap the package, I feel my face flush—one of my full color photographs is the cover of the magazine! My article, titled "I'm Hit! I'm Hit!" fills fourteen large magazine-size pages, with many of my color photographs.

I send individual photos, autographed copies of *The Post* article, and personal letters to Tony Duarte and a number of the other guys in the Special Forces. I've been nervous that my *Post* article might have gotten these guys into trouble. Last year, my story in *Time* created a stir. One of the generals called in a few guys and read them the riot act. The higher-ups seem to be fine about this story. Which is a relief.

I get a friendly letter from Bill, Captain William Grace. He says all the guys are thrilled to see themselves in print.

The Post editors write an introduction on the table-of-contents page:

Now and then our editors see a manuscript which is so jarring and so compelling that no one can put it down. Such was the case with Jerry Rose's "I'm Hit! I'm Hit!" which begins on page 34. This is war reporting that ranks with the best of Ernest Hemingway and Ernie Pyle. Rose's powerful story, constructed with all the grace and suspense of a novel, conveys the feeling of Americans in actual combat so brilliantly that, after reading it, you will feel as if you have faced the same fire with the brave men he portrays.

60

A NEW ASSIGNMENT

The Post quickly gives me a new assignment. I'm going to Indonesia. The leader of this nation of islands is charismatic and erratic—Sukarno—who led the struggle for independence from the Netherlands following World War Two. He seems to be veering toward communism. I want to find out what's really happening. Is Sukarno pro-communist? Anti-American? Is he an effective leader for his people or not? This is most important.

Indonesia is new territory for me. My desk is littered with a pile of books on Indonesia, with jotted notes and slips of paper. I make my way over to the Time Life building in Kowloon. Sitting at a long table, I study all their files on Indonesia.

Then I go to speak with Bernie Kalb, a friend and colleague at *Time*, who knows Indonesia upside down and inside out. Over drinks and lunch, Kalb generously gives me a tutorial. "The country is horribly poor" he says, "and yet Sukarno builds towering and sumptuous edifices, all for the sake of his glory." Bernie goes on to describe Sukarno's particular brand of autocratic rule, called "Guided Democracy." I wonder what this means. Is he simply a dictator, out for himself? I'm intrigued by the possibilities of this story.

Indonesia is a country made up of islands and the population is now mostly Muslim. In an earlier era, the people were Buddhist or Hindu, and even now one of the islands, Bali, remains a Hindu enclave.

"Sukarno," Bernie says, taking his pipe out of his mouth, "is an interesting, colorful, and difficult character. You absolutely must go hear him give a speech. He's charismatic. He enthralls his audience. He's also famous for his wild extravagances."

"I'll interview Sukarno," I say. "Any ideas how I can arrange that?" This seems like the most direct way of understanding this leader—let him tell me in his own words about his plans, his ambitions.

But Bernie shakes his head and chuckles. "Sukarno never gives interviews. And he hates western journalists." Then he adds, "More power to you if you can manage that!"

I go to the Indonesian Consulate in Hong Kong and get a visa. I have my "jungle suit" restitched; these are army-colored clothes I'll need if I do any work in Indonesian jungles or find myself on battlefields. My clothes need serious repair after my last assignment in Vietnam. I get maps of all the islands and also a phrasebook in *Behasa Indonesia*, the Indonesian language. And I check the five cameras I'm carrying with me. I make sure all my equipment is in good working order. *The Post* insists on hiring their own photographer. But I'm taking my equipment, just in case.

Kay and I have been talking and talking about when and how we can go back to the States for a visit. Our plan is to go there this summer. We both miss our families and we want to meet one another's parents. More than that, our families are anxious and eager to meet baby Thorina.

We're eating dinner in my study. It's a large room with tile floors. We don't have a regular dining room and the living room is cluttered with other furniture and baby stuff.

Kay is unusually quiet. "Are you okay?" I ask.

"I'm thinking," she says, "of going to Minnesota to visit my parents—leaving in May. Your folks and mine want to meet the baby."

"I thought we'd go in the summer."

"Yes, but I'd like to take Thorina and go to the States ahead of you. I'd visit my parents in Minnesota and then meet up with you when you come to see your family in Gloversville."

I nod and say, "If that's what you want to do, I guess it makes sense. I'll probably be away some of that time anyway. But I'll hate not having both of you here. I'll be so lonely without you."

"So, then you'll know what it's like," she says with a sigh. "I'm lonely for you all the time."

61

ASSALAM ALAIKUM!

Jakarta, the capitol of Indonesia, on the island of Java, is a mass of people. I'm besieged by the jumble of sounds and huge crowds. As soon as I step off the plane, I feel a torrent of heat and humidity. The straps of my camera bag stick to my shoulder. My shirt is already damp from my perspiration.

Yusef "Joe" Amin, my interpreter-assistant, meets me at the airport. We shake hands politely and, as we wind our way through the airport crowds, he tells me a little about himself—that he comes from a village on Java, not far from Jakarta. Like most Indonesians, he's short, about my height. He has a gargantuan shag mustache that slogs over his lips. He speaks English tolerably well.

Yusef-Joe has a car and drives me through the streets of Jakarta, where the traffic is dense and scary. He has to maneuver among cars, smoke-emitting trucks with vegetables falling out their open backs, bicycles, motorcycles, pedicabs, and ox-drawn small carts. It's a small miracle that we don't hit anything or anyone along the way.

Only a few hours after my plane lands, we make our way to an outdoor arena to hear Sukarno give a speech. Bernie Kalb had insisted this is a must-do. I want not only to hear Sukarno's words but also watch his people as they listen to him.

Even without understanding the language, I sense the emotion—powerful. Seventy thousand people, standing under the tropical sun, lean forward to listen, their faces intent. His voice is resonant and deep, "*Assalam alaikum warachmatulahi!* Greetings to you with God's blessings!"

The crowd shouts back: "*Wa'alaikum salaam!* The same greetings to you!"

Then he shouts "*Merdeka!* Freedom!"

And the declaration "*Merdeka*" explodes from 70,000 voices.

Using no notes, he speaks in whispers, then in shouts. He clenches his teeth and his fist. He laughs and 70,000 people laugh with him. Then he weeps and this huge crowd weeps together with him. Even as a foreigner, I find myself swept into the feelings of the crowd around me. My face, like the faces around me, is flushed with feeling, looking up at Sukarno.

All this while, Yusef-Joe rapidly whispers a translation in my ear and, just as rapidly, I write in my little notebook. Sukarno speaks about his plans. "We are going to build the world anew. We will change this damn world to a new world of happiness." Sukarno sees himself as the savior of his people. "Here I am, I, Indonesia."

The photographer *The Post* was supposed to hire doesn't show up. I had argued with them that I wanted to do my own photography. Now I'm sorry. I've got too damn much to do, and I can't do everything.

I interview everyone I see: pedicab drivers, farmers, politicians. I ask about their daily lives, their beliefs, their politics. I want to understand what's happening with the people, not just the leadership on top.

People tell me stories. A pedicab driver, fifty years old, tells me that his wife left him to raise their five children by himself. The muscles

Assignment—Indonesia

on his legs look like ball bearings—so hard and strong. But he says he doesn't earn enough to feed his family. A farmer has high praise for his wife, who sells their produce in the markets—she's the one who understands money. I meet a Chinese businessman who runs a successful taxi company, hiring local Muslim drivers, but he's afraid for his life—the Indonesian people don't like the Chinese.

Each day we do dozens of interviews, some lengthy, some brief. I feel like a farmer harvesting his crop. The personal stories I hear are coming together to create a larger story about Sukarno and the people of Indonesia. Yusuf-Joe says, "Mesterr RRose, I cen nott worrk soooo harrd. It mmaakes mee seeeck."

We get on a plane to the island Bali. Bali is a Hindu conclave, distinct from the rest of Indonesia. I need to understand the diversity of experiences to capture the life of the people.

Yusef-Joe warns me that he always gets sick on planes. But I tell him it's all in his mind. He doesn't believe me. He says it's all in his stomach. By the time our two-hour flight ends, it's all out of his stomach.

In Bali, our pace is a little less frenetic. Bali is completely different from Jakarta. Bali is an artists' haven, with art everywhere—batik, paintings, wood sculptures, dance, and music. Balinese are Hindus. You see little offerings everywhere, in private and public spaces. When I talk to people here, Sukarno and the leadership back in Jakarta seem distant, not very important. Their lives are focused on their gods and the many festivals to celebrate.

When we return to Jakarta, we stay in the Hotel Indonesia. They make delicious whiskey sours, of which I deliciously consume a great number.

My story is more or less shaping up, but I still need more material and more perspectives. I interview America's Ambassador Howard Jones, a balding soft-spoken man in his sixties. Jones tells me, "Don't believe everything you hear about Sukarno. Some of my American colleagues don't like him because he allies himself with the PKI, the communist party here. But Sukarno is a nationalist. He's a fine leader here." I wonder if Jones is wise in his pro-Sukarno stance or is he, like many of the citizens here, emotionally swayed by this charismatic dictator.

Then I interview General Nasution, Minister of Defense in Sukarno's government. This is my chance to understand the politics of the country from a key insider. At age forty-five, Nasution seems calm and gentle, belying his role as a warrior—he is one of Indonesia's heroes in the fight for independence. He tells me that his country, in its post-colonial independence, is young and the world should be patient.

I send a letter to Sukarno, requesting an interview—no response. I try contacting him at the Presidential palace; nothing happens.

Then I go to another of his public speeches. Sukarno is standing on the podium, talking with the mayor of Jakarta, a tall reedy man. I push my way through the crowds and rush up to him just as he's walking down the steps of the podium. "Mr. President," I say, speaking as quickly as I can, "I'm an American journalist working for *The Saturday Evening Post* and I've been in Indonesia three weeks trying to see you."

"And you want an interview!" he says, with a big smile, clapping me on both shoulders. "Noooo!" And he walks on. Sukarno has not given an interview since 1956.

Back home in Hong Kong, I have another frenzied stretch of writing. The working title for my article is "Behind the Batik Curtain: Indonesia." The story is about economic and political turmoil under Sukarno. I've come away from my exploration of Indonesia with mixed feelings about this erratic ruler. His one major accomplishment is education. Elementary schools have sprouted up like mushrooms in the fall. Under Dutch colonial rule, only about 10 percent of the people could read and write; now about 90 percent can. This is an impressive accomplishment.

But the economy is in ruins. So, the teachers are paid barely enough for subsistence. I write about Sukarno's extravagance. He has built a $17 million stadium while his people are starving. My heart breaks for the people . . .

Like every article I write, it's much too long.

About a week later, I get a letter from Friedrich. *The Post* will buy my Indonesia story. Friedrich writes, "Let me say at the start that your article has what I now recognize as the Rose touch, which conveys the sense that you are there and you bring the reader with you. The reporting is good, the details are rich, and I like it. Let me also say, though, that length is a problem again."

It's a warning. My articles are long and rich, too long for this magazine.

He doesn't have another assignment for me at the moment. "You'll have to wait a bit," he writes. But he mentions Laos for my next assignment.

62

INCIDENT

Kay is packing for her trip to the States. This is, apparently, a major enterprise with a baby. She will be visiting her parents in Dundee, Minnesota for two months.

I have a cold that hangs on and on. My ears hurt, my chest too. I go to the doctor but nothing seems to help. I find myself in the throes of a terrible mood. I can't seem to shake the blackness. I don't really know why.

Kay and Thorina are ready to leave. Their bags are piled high near the door. Out of the blue, I launch an argument.

"You can't wait to get out of here and leave me," I growl. "Don't you love me anymore?"

"What are you talking about?" Kay is already in her travel clothes, about to leave for the airport. She looks stunned by my attack.

"If you loved me, you wouldn't be running off to Minnesota, abandoning me."

Kay stands there for a moment, her face flushed, her eyes narrowed into slits. She shouts back, with a fury I haven't heard before, "You're the one who's always running off!"

"But when I go away, it's to earn our livelihood. We wouldn't have any money if I didn't do that."

"Well, that's because you *chose* this career that takes you away from me. And now I want to see my family."

"But you could've waited for me—waited until the summer and we'd go together. You're just going so you'll have a vacation away from me."

Our quarrel goes on, with our voices climbing. I suspect our neighbors can hear every word. Kay's eyes are red, with tears dotting her cheeks. It's time to leave; they need to catch their plane. We drive to the airport in silence.

They are about to depart. We're standing at the foot of the narrow silver stairway leading up to the plane. I lean forward and kiss Kay on the lips and our baby on her little forehead.

As I step into our Hong Kong apartment, I feel overwhelmed with remorse. Why was I so bad-tempered? I can't even remember what our quarrel was about. The apartment feels barren and bereft, empty as a church tower, without Kay and baby Thorina. I ache for their touch, for their presence, and for their noise in this echoing apartment.

"Kaynik my love," I write, "Can you forgive me? Our quarrel was all my fault—my dark mood, taking it out on you. It was unfair. I love you. Kiss our little girl for me. We'll be together soon." I mail the letter to Kay, c/o Walter Peterson, Dundee, Minnesota—no street address needed.

I'm going to Laos—*The Post* gives me the go-ahead. It's another kind of war front. There are no great battles here, but 'incidents' and more 'incidents' as the communists take over a hapless Asian kingdom, bit by bit. It will be a good story—an important story, just because Americans don't know anything about Laos and it's a strategic place for the battles going on in Asia.

But I'm tired, burnt out from all the work and the traipsing around from one country to another. I need a vacation, but anyway—I'm going to Laos. I'll leave the day after tomorrow.

Two weeks later, when I return from Laos to an empty, echoing apartment, I find two cables waiting for me—good news and disturbing news. One is from the Arora Agency—an agent, by the name of Mike Handler, is taking me on. This is on the strength of my work so far, especially on my article "I'm Hit! I'm Hit!" I lay the cable on the desk for a moment and breathe in the good news.

Then I reread the content—more good news. Mike has already sold a Vietnam piece to *Candide*, a French magazine, and is close to selling *Newsweek* a photo for their cover. So, he's really going to work for me. He's pressing *The Post* for a more definite commitment. He takes a 10 percent slice but it's still okay. And he'll try to sell my fiction, too. I'm elated; even in this depressingly empty apartment, I feel like celebrating.

But the other cable is not so good. It's from Otto Friedrich. He tells me that Stan Karnow is going with *The Post*. I know they've been trying to recruit him for a long time. I'm not sure why he finally said yes.

Will there still be work for me at *The Post*? Will all the good stories go to Karnow, who's more experienced, more famous? I wonder, *How much should I worry?*

63

BAKER STREET

"Kay, Kay, Kay," I sigh, holding her in my arms, breathing in the smell of her, the feel of her.

Mother and Daddy have driven with Kay to greet me at the forlorn little airport in Albany, in Upper New York State. We're all standing around on the tarmac, next to the airplane, blocking the way as other passengers push around us.

Kay and the baby have been with my parents for about a week. But it's taken me more than a week to get here, traveling around the globe—a westward route, from Hong Kong to New Delhi, Moscow, and Rome.

I stop in Philadelphia for a meeting at *The Post* headquarters at Curtis Publishing. I've latched my career as a journalist to this company and their magazine—so this can be an important meeting for me with my editors. I'm hoping for a good meeting—maybe an actual contract? The Curtis building is enormous—it fills a whole city block— and when you walk in, the interior is magnificent, with a waterfall and huge glass mosaic in the atrium.

Otto Friedrich and Don Schanche greet me like a long-lost friend and introduce me around to other staff. "This is Jerry Rose who wrote that amazing piece on Vietnam." I sign a contract with them, four stories over the next year, and they give me an advance.

Then I go to New Haven, Connecticut for a whimsical story about Good Humor trucks that go clinging and ringing through suburban neighborhoods enticing children out of their homes like the Pied Piper.

Finally, I board a small propjet from New Haven to Albany.

Mother holds me in a long embrace. She looks a little rounder, a little older. Her hair is salt-and-pepper, black with strokes of gray—I don't recall seeing the gray before. I embrace Daddy, too. He seems to have aged a bit—his face is thinner, making his oversized ears and nose more prominent and he has more lines in his forehead. What did I expect? It's been four long years.

The airport is not quite an hour's drive from home. Mother is driving. Her hands shake a little. She's not a good driver, too hesitant, puts on the brakes too often. It doesn't help that my father keeps giving unhelpful advice and warnings. He sucks in his breath and cries "Watch it!" as she's trying to merge onto the highway.

When we walk into the house, my eighteen-year-old sister Lucy rushes into my arms. She feels small and warm as we hold onto each other. Then, I pull her away so I can look at her. "You look different somehow," I say, "more filled in and grown up." Lucy is a college girl now—she's just finished her freshman year. Her dark hair is still long—so that's the same. She's wearing a light green cotton skirt and white blouse and has a diaper draped over her shoulder. She's been taking care of little Thorina.

"The baby's asleep upstairs," she says. When I tiptoe into my old bedroom, I see the crib in a corner. The venetian blinds are pulled so the room is in shadow. Little Thorina is lying on her back, her eyes closed. Her face is so familiar and sweet. She makes little baby snores in her sleep.

I walk around the house which used to be home for me—19

Baker Street. I lived here from the time I was eleven years old until I went off to college: the long mirror in the hall, next to the telephone, so you look at yourself while you're speaking on the phone, the wooden banister and stairs leading up to our bedrooms, the assortment of flowered wall papers in each room. Even the smells are familiar: Mother's cooking, household cleansers, and dust buried deep in the carpets and woodwork of an old house. I'm awash with memories.

My paintings are here. My oil paintings that were in a gallery in Seattle were sent here after the show. I had asked my parents not to store them in a hot attic or garage, where they would be damaged. So, they've hung them all around the house. Copies of the magazines with my articles are strewn around the house too.

On my first night home, Mother invites my sister Nancy, her husband Simon and David, their little boy, to come for dinner. It feels like a festival—like Thanksgiving. Mother at one end of the dining room table, Daddy at the other, and the whole family gathered together. Mother smiles at each of us—her children and grandchildren. Our reunion is bittersweet—will all of us ever be around one table like this again?

Nancy is four years younger than me. She's pretty as a young woman, with blue-green eyes and metallic blond hair that I presume comes from a bottle. Their little David is two years old. He wants to play with baby Thorina but doesn't quite know how. He rushes over to her as she's sitting in Kay's lap and shouts "Boo!" Thorina is frightened and starts to cry.

They all want to know about Vietnam. "So," Daddy says, "What is this war?"

I try to explain about North and South Vietnam and the communists in the North wanting to take over the whole country. But then I stop myself and say, "This is my first night home—let's not talk about that. Tell me about Gloversville. What's happening with you?"

But Daddy persists. "I read your story in *Saturday Evening Post*. Where were you when there was so much fighting?"

"I was fine. Don't worry, Daddy." My father is a worrier. He looks at me with a deep frown on his bald head. I can't stop him from worrying, but I change the subject again, "What do you think of President Kennedy?"

Mother says, "Daddy voted for Nixon. I like Kennedy." Then she adds, her blue green eyes sparkling, "He's so handsome—and Jackie—so lovely."

I'm surprised my father voted Republican. He always used to be a Democrat. "Why?" I ask him. "Why Nixon?"

"Nixon would have been better for this country. I don't trust the Kennedys. You know his father is anti-Semite. In the war, he was pro-Nazi."

Kay and I have enormous respect for Kennedy. But there's no point trying to debate with Daddy.

Later, over dessert of chocolate cream pie, Mother says, "I wrote to you about your friend Morrow Solomon."

"Is he very ill?"

"He's dying," she says. "He has brain cancer." Mother gently shakes her head. I can imagine what's in her heart, thinking about the pain of another mother. Then she adds, "He's at Nathan Littauer Hospital. You should go visit him there."

When I was in Gloversville High School, I had a coterie of friends. Morrow Solomon was the brightest of us, an interesting character, and the most arrogant. When he was sixteen, he seemed like a man of forty, with his round face, slight paunch and his argyle sweater vests. He went to Yale Medical School, and he became a doctor. Brain cancer is the worst fate for a young man of his brilliance.

The next morning, I go to the hospital to visit Morrow. Nathan Littauer Hospital is a large red brick edifice on a quiet tree-lined street just up the hill from my old high school and downtown Gloversville.

From the outside, it looks like a hotel with a manicured lawn, an arch of trees, and a broad staircase leading up to a polished wooden doorway. But as soon as I walk in, I'm greeted by medicinal smells.

Mrs. Solomon is sitting on a plastic chair in the hallway outside his room. She's bent over with her head in her hands. Hearing my footsteps, she jumps up and hugs me. She's trembling and tears are streaming down her face.

Morrow has a private room. The shades are pulled, so the room is dark despite the bright sun outdoors. He's lying on his back, surrounded by rumpled sheets with hospital equipment looming over his head. He looks wasted, nothing like the round and boisterous boy I knew so well. I feel a lump, like a rock, in my throat, so I can't breathe. My eyes sting with tears. But Morrow shakes his head, groans, points his finger at the door; he doesn't want me there. I suppose he doesn't want to be seen like this, ravished by his illness. I back away and quietly exit his room—respecting his privacy—but wishing he would let me stay and hold his hand.

Someday I'll write about Morrow and also my writer friend Ted Cumming, who had a strange and awful death after eating a plate of poisoned chicken livers. And there were others whom death swallowed young. They are all part of me as much as my youth, which is no more.

On the following Sunday, Nancy, Simon, Kay, and I drive out to the country, where Simon's parents have a dairy farm, about an hour from Gloversville by car. We leave the children with Mother, who adores her grandchildren. Simon and I have been talking about guns. We want to do some shooting out in the woods near the farm. I still have an old hunting rifle at home and Simon's gun is at the farm.

The family farm is small, with a modest white-painted wood house, red barn and a couple dozen cows. It's a dairy farm but Simon's mother has a garden stretching around the side of the house where she grows vegetables for the family.

It's a sunny afternoon, as Simon and I trudge out into the woods, our guns slung over our shoulders, pointing downwards. Simon is a little taller than me, with wavy dark hair and very thick glasses that make his eyes look like large bubbles. The air is fresh, with a scent of green grass, trees and dirt.

"Grouse or pheasants," Simon looks over his shoulder and points at birds pecking on the ground ahead of us. We find a good place to stand and raise our rifles to get a good sighting. Suddenly we're attacked by a swarm of wasps, whirring and buzzing all around us. Simon jumps out of the way, but I'm the main target. They're all over me. Angry stings puncture my arms, hands, ears, cheeks, and nose. We race back to the farmhouse.

Nancy appoints herself as my nurse; she pulls out stingers and takes ice from the small freezer to make ice packs, which she applies everywhere there's a welt. She finds a bottle of calamine lotion in the medicine chest and rubs it on my hot red skin. It turns out I'm allergic to wasp stings. I'm covered with bright red hives.

So, the irony. I venture through the jungles in Vietnam, through clawing vegetation with bullets whirling in the air, and I walk away fine. I come home and get injured in the tame woods of Upper New York State.

While I'm here, I have a story to write. Mother has an old typewriter— so I set myself up at her small metal desk to write up the Good Humor story. But I'm having a hard time with this piece. Where's the story? Where the drama? After my intense work in Vietnam, this seems like a bit of fluff. With a page sitting in the typewriter, I get up, stretch, and take little Thorina out for a walk in a borrowed baby carriage.

The next day, I get a call from Don Schanche. "Did you know," he says, "the *Herald Tribune* published an ice cream truck story in yesterday's paper. It sounds a lot like what you were working on."

I've been scooped!

Baker Street is only one block long, arched by large maple trees. Late one afternoon, I sit on the side porch of our house with my sister Lucy. The porch, at this time of day, is in pastel-shade. It's warm but not too warm. Everything around us is vivid green—bushes, grass, and Mother's garden.

We sit together on the old glider and rock gently. Lucy sits with her knees pressed to her chest; her dark hair is in a ponytail that trails on her back. She's not a beautiful girl. Her features are plain, but her face is animated, so she exudes intelligence and vitality. Lucy has just finished her freshman year in college.

"Well," I say, "have you thought about what you want to do when you grow up?"

"I am grown up," she laughs.

"I mean, after college."

She doesn't say anything for a moment. "I don't know anymore," she says. "When I was younger, I thought I wanted to be an English professor, like you, or like you used to be. Now I'm thinking about Jewish studies."

"Are you sure you want to limit yourself like that?" She doesn't answer, and we sit silently for a while. The rusty glider creaks, as we slide gently back and forth.

I've been away from my little sister too long. It feels like she's slipping through my fingers. I used to think she idolized me, and I could guide her. Now I'm not so sure.

"Look," I say suddenly, "why don't you come visit us in Hong Kong next year. You get the summer off. It's a chance you shouldn't miss while we're still in Asia."

Her eyes light up and she jumps off the glider. "Could I really come?"

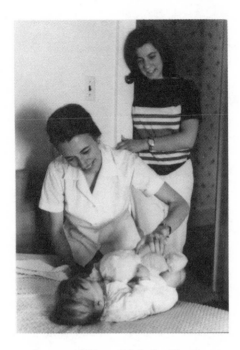

Lucy and Kay with baby Thorina

Vietnam is a distant world. A lot is happening while I'm here, spending the summer away from the ongoing tumult and terror. The Buddhists, who have long hated their treatment by the Ngô Đình Diệm regime, launch huge and wild protests. A Buddhist monk sets fire to himself on a busy street in Saigon. The photo and story by Malcolm Browne, on the front cover of *The New York Times*, creates an outcry in the U.S. and around the world. Vietnam is exploding, with more protests by crowds of Buddhists and other monks following the path of self-immolation.

And here I am, isolated in a little town, on a quiet street, with my family. We're stopping in Minnesota at Kay's family farm before returning to Asia. So, it will be more than a month before I can get back to where the action is.

Was it a mistake to come home?

TURMOIL

Finally, I'm back in Saigon with its mayhem of motor noises: cars, scooters, Vespas, Lambrettas, Primos…along with flocks of bicycles. The intersections of streets are crammed, as always. At one intersection a Vietnamese army private in a white helmet is desperately trying to start his stalled motorcycle. His face is red. A heavy-throated C-123 rumbles overhead.

The Vietnam I've come home to is in turmoil. I hear about battles in the countryside and bombs in the cities. More monks are setting themselves on fire in the streets.

The Buddhists in Huê and all over Vietnam are in uproar, with massive marches protesting the government. Diệm's brother, Ngô Đình Nhu, who heads the dreaded Secret Police, arrests scores of protestors. His wife, Madame Nhu, considered the First Lady of Vietnam since President Diệm is unmarried, scorns the protestors. I read in the papers that she calls the self-immolation a "Buddhist barbecue" and says, "Let them burn and we shall clap our hands." Her words make my blood boil. This woman, with her lacquered glamour and kohl-blackened eyes, is beyond cruel—she is sinister; she is evil.

—

I go to visit Hy and Simone at their home. When Simone opens the door, she's crying. "Huan is in jail," she says.

"What!" I stand there, my mouth open, stunned. We all sit down together in the living room. Each of us lights a cigarette. As we inhale the smoke, it's as if we're sighing in unison.

Hy, speaking slowly as if carefully measuring each word, says, "He joined the An Quang Buddhist Circle. You know my brother was always interested in them. Some of his comrades from the War of Independence are active in An Quang. They had protests and marches in Huê and down here too."

Simone, with her usual rapid speech and expressive hands, breaks in. "Huan came down here to stay with us. As soon as he came here, we were worried. They were arresting many people—many of his friends. Then it was the middle of the night—I think it was three in the morning . . ."

"Yes," Hy says, "it was three o'clock in the morning. We all woke up from the banging on the door. That was two weeks ago."

Simone continues. "It was the police—five of them burst into our living room. One man in a dark suit announced, 'We are here for Mr. Bui Tuong Huan.' They didn't even let him get dressed. He went off in his robe and pajamas and slippers. We were half asleep, dazed, didn't know what to do . . ."

"And yet," Hy says, "It wasn't exactly a surprise. Lots of people were being arrested. And we knew Huan was at risk because he was doing things with the An Quang."

Simone is shaking, tears in her eyes, saying, "I'm so worried."

"What can we do?" I immediately start thinking about whom I know—John Mecklin from the American Embassy, some of my contacts in the US military. . .

Suddenly the front door opens and Huan walks in. "They released me. I don't know why," he says in a soft voice, almost a whisper. "It's okay. *Je vais bien.*" He looks tired and limp, and he has raw bruises on his arms. Huan seems, at the same time, tough and vulnerable.

We all rush up to him and take turns embracing him. Simone brings Huan a glass of water. He collapses into the armchair. The rest of us sit around him.

"It was difficult," Huan says. He speaks with long pauses between his words. "I was held in a large room underground with a dozen other men—some my friends, some I didn't know."

"Were they all from the An Quang Buddhist Circle?" I ask.

"Five of them were my An Quang friends—the rest, I don't know. They would interrogate us at night. At least, I think it was night. We were held in a basement with no windows. I heard other men scream when they were interrogated in other rooms. They kept asking about names. They would read a list of names. What did this person do? Do you know this person? When I kept silent, they would raise their voices and sometimes shake their fists at me. They beat me once and they threatened a lot. 'You must know him or him or her.' And then a day went by and nothing happened. A man came by in a suit and he said I can go now. I don't know what's happened to my friends." When he stops speaking, he leans his head into his hands, with his elbows pressed against his thin torso.

We're all quiet for a long time. What is there to say? Then Huan sighs, "All I want to do now is take a shower"

Hot tears stream down my cheeks, but also, I feel relief—at least for now, Huan is okay.

I have work to do. I have an assignment from *Newsweek* to take a photo of Henry Cabot Lodge, the new U.S. Ambassador to Saigon; they want a photo for their cover. And then there's another story assignment on Lodge for *The New York Times Magazine*. Then an article for the *New Republic*. All of this work comes because I'm on the spot, I know the country and am known.

Vietnam is now overflowing with American and other foreign journalists. They arrive here like bees to honey. Most of them have no specific knowledge of the country, but they've heard there's exciting stuff and they've come to sniff out stories.

Some journalists, like Malcolm Browne and like me, go out in the field and do our own investigations. We travel into the countryside and out to military bases and report on the unrest throughout the country and the huge increase in American military involvement, which the U.S. administration still tries to hide. But many of the reporters hang around the U.S. Embassy or MAAG and report just what the administration tells them.

It's annoying what passes for the truth.

The Diệm regime is as brutal as ever. Huan has been unable to find out what's happened to his colleagues and he's very worried. The U.S. continues to bolster Diệm but rumors are flying about that the CIA is urging the Vietnamese military to stage a *coup d'etat*. I've seen a confidential report that Kennedy has called for a phased withdrawal from Vietnam—to begin soon.

The country is seething. What will happen next?

65

ASSASSINATION

"Not like this!" Huan says. His face is pale, and he can't stop shaking his head. "Diệm had to go, and his brother too . . . But like this???"

Huan and I are sitting in his brother's living room. It's a day after a *coup d'etat*, engineered by General Duong Van Minh. This happened on November 1, 1963. Unlike other attempts, this one was successful. Ngô Đình Diệm and his younger brother Ngô Đình Nhu, the head of the secret police, knew it was coming.

It's evening, dark outside, but we haven't bothered to turn on the lights. We're sitting across from one another, in silhouette, with a slight glow on our faces from the flame of our cigarettes. "I heard the Americans were offering asylum to Diệm and Nhu," I say. "There was an arrangement—they were supposed to stay in Gia Long Palace and surrender. They were promised to be given safe exile. But that's not what happened."

Huan says, "Maybe the brothers didn't trust the deal. I don't know if they didn't believe the Americans or their own generals. They managed to escape the Palace during the chaos of the coup, and they went to hide out in a restaurant in Cholon."

"It sounds like they had this scheme all worked out."

"But someone betrayed them, I suppose. I don't know how they were discovered. But what happened next was horrible. It was horrible even though Diệm and Nhu did worse to thousands of people."

"I heard they were arrested, and the brothers committed suicide."

"That was a lie," Huan says. "They were executed. They were driven to a remote railroad crossing, told to get out of the truck, and then sprayed with machine gun bullets. It was done probably by General Minh's bodyguards, on his order. There was a photograph of the bodies, with their hands tied behind their backs, covered with blood—so they had to stop pretending it was suicide."

"Everyone says the Americans just let it happen."

"I think even the Americans were disgusted with the Diệm regime, especially their treatment of the Buddhist protests. The irony is that Madame Nhu, who is probably more hated than the brothers, is on tour in the United States. So, she's escaped."

It was assassination—that's what it was; there was no jury, no judge, no legal proceeding. Huan and I are both troubled. "These men were dangerous, worse in some ways than the communists," Huan says. "But what does it mean for our country, to begin our new government washed in blood?" Huan sits on the couch with his fists clenched, his foot tapping on the floor.

I'm a journalist. I'm supposed to look at this objectively. I start to say, "Diệm and his brother weren't going to go quietly." But I don't say anything more. I agree with Huan, and I'm worried.

I come home to Hong Kong the next week. When I walk into little Thorina's room, she looks at me as if we've never, ever met before. "Hello, Thorina," I say. But she looks and looks with her round blue eyes, all serious and sober. I think she doesn't understand; maybe I need to talk baby-talk. "Goo-goo-gitchy-goo," I say. She stares, with a slight frown. Now she probably thinks I'm a babbling idiot. And I do feel like something of an idiot—being away from my lovely daughter for so long that she sees me as a stranger.

Ten minutes later, after I've put down my baggage and talked with Kay and had a few sips of an *aperitif*, I walk over to Thorina's crib. Now she smiles, showing off her pink gums.

Thorina has two tiny bottom teeth. You can hear them when she clicks against something she has in her mouth, like a comb, a piece of bamboo, an ink bottle, or an electrical cord. For some reason, this child doesn't believe what her eyes behold until she tastes it. So far, we've been able to prevent her from "tasting" the neighbor's dog.

It's been three weeks since Ngô Đình Diệm and his brother were assassinated. Kay comes into my study with the Asia edition of the *New York Times* dangling from her hands and with tears running down her cheeks. "President Kennedy was assassinated in Dallas! How can this be? How can this happen in America?"

I feel like I can't breathe. Kennedy assassinated! Both of us are crying. We're in shock. Kay hands me the newspaper and I feel myself trembling as I read the story. "How can this be?" I whisper.

"I just didn't expect such violence back in the States," she says. "I don't know what to think."

We were impressed with Kennedy, especially Kay. We both appreciated his liberal values and his global perspective. I think she was secretly pleased that a Catholic had been elected President. Kennedy offered hope for America's future. Now—who knows?

I take Kay in my arms, and we comfort one another.

66

MOTHER GOOSE

It's been more than a year since I received a letter from Isobel saying that she and Bill were moving to Bangkok. I got that letter on my wedding day and I wrote a long letter to her telling her about Kay.

I have an assignment for *The Post* in Bangkok. I write to Isobel asking if she would like to meet for a drink while I'm there.

Kay knows. When I tell Kay that I want to write to Isobel and maybe see her while I'm in Bangkok, she says, "I think you should." I look at her, surprised, and she continues, "You should see her because she's your friend. You owe it to her. She's suffered enough because of you." Then she thumps my chest and adds in a sharp voice, "But don't you go on with your affair. Friendship is fine. But you're mine!"

Sometimes Kay, my love, astounds me.

In the quiet lobby of the Erawan Hotel, I greet Isobel. It's been over two years. Seeing her walk through the door brings a rush of feelings. She's still lovely, still so appealing with her green eyes and delicate skin brushed with light freckles. Her hair, which is the color of burnt umber, is shorter now, creating an arc just below her ears.

"Let's get a drink in the bar."

"That would be nice." She smiles shyly.

"How are you?" I ask, as soon as we sit down at a small table. It's midday and the hotel lounge, a room with small yellow lights and no windows, is dusky and almost empty. Isobel looks the same, petite and still quite thin.

"I'm okay. Really. Bill and I have a life together of sorts. He doesn't love me." For a moment, I think she's going to cry. But the waiter comes, and we order our whiskeys, mine straight up, Isobel's over ice. "What happened between us—that was so not like me. It was wrong what we did. But I loved you. And I still do. There, I've said it."

"Things are different now for both of us," I say, cautiously.

Being here with Isobel, I'm overwhelmed by a sense of awkwardness, a fear of hurting her even more. If I took her in my arms and kissed her, I think she would melt. But it's not to be. It would only make it harder for her.

I light a cigarette and we're quiet for a few moments. We sip our whiskeys slowly as the moments tick by. "I want you to be happy, Isobel."

"I've been reading your articles. They're wonderful, always. What's next for you?"

I tell her that I'm in Bangkok to do research on Thai boxing—my next assignment for *The Saturday Evening Post*. I mention my meeting with Otto Friedrichs at *The Post* when I was in the States this summer. "I suggested doing a story about Thai boxing, which has old roots in Thailand, with special rules and distinctive body moves. That's why I'm here now—for that story. Have you seen any Thai boxing?"

"Oh yes," she says, "we went to watch a performance once—it was completely different from American boxing, almost like a dance."

We talk a little more about my work. Isobel nods, listening carefully to my words, looking at my eyes, my face, my hands. I feel her warmth and her love. But I also sense a profound sadness in her and there's nothing I can do. I glance at my watch. "I have to go." As we hug good-bye, I feel her quavering in my arms, like a wounded bird, fragile, delicate and vulnerable.

The next morning, I'm the one who gets beaten up. I get into the ring with the Thai-style boxing champion of Thailand. This is my research! His legs, feet and arms are flying at me in ways I didn't think possible. He quickly lands two blows, one on my ear and another on my face, which knocks me off my feet, all this with his left foot. I try to get up but, feeling dizzy and woozy, I decide I've had enough and crawl out of the ring with as much dignity as I can muster. After less than a minute in the ring, my cheek has a three-inch gash, my lips are puffy and bleeding, and my ear is swollen.

At least I now have a close-up idea of what this business of Thai boxing is all about. I wonder what Americans will think when they read my article in *The Post*. Will this story be worth getting beaten and battered, just for my research?

I hope the dizziness will go away.

When I get back home in Hong Kong, I'm in a strange mood . . . burnt out, I suppose. I've been working like a crazy man, taking flights to anywhere and everywhere, chasing stories, writing and writing and writing. I feel like I'm a rat on a wheel that goes round and round.

Maybe my Thai boxing research left me with a concussion.

I owe *The Post* two stories, the one about Thai boxing and the Good Humor story. I do them both with tongue-in-cheek.

I write the Thai boxing story as if I were a broadcaster at ringside, " . . .sponsored by Guillotine Red Blades, guaranteed to give you the closest shave of your life, no lather needed. Guillotine has been solving men's shaving problems since 1789."

Then I work on the Good Humor story. Because the *Herald Tribune* just published a similar story, I try something different, with a little flair. I write the Good Humor story like a Mother Goose rhyme, a sort of child-fantasy.

Friedrich hates both stories. "That *boom-ah* tone poem effect—stop it," he writes by return-cable.

I feel lost and disoriented, wondering if I'll ever get things right again. I have just had two articles rejected by *The Post*. This has never happened before.

I'm reading his letter and just outside my window, on the street, I hear a bell ringing. It sounds exactly like a Good Humor bell, but it's a garbage truck. That ominous Good Humor bell on a garbage truck rings in my ears.

An evil omen?

67

VIETNAM'D TO DEATH

Another glitch. I propose going back to Indonesia to do a story about a famine on the island Bali. The editors at *The Post* say—go ahead. But I can't get a visa.

I apply to the Indonesian Consulate in Hong Kong for a visa as a journalist. Rejected. My colleagues had warned me—if you write an article that is critical of Sukarno, he'll never let you return to Indonesia. Sukarno must have been fuming about my last Indonesia article in *The Post*, which was indeed critical.

I'm back in Vietnam doing a story for *The Post* on Westmoreland as chief of the US forces here. I fly to Da Nang in Westy's plane and spend much of the time interviewing him. William Westmoreland is a tall, striking man with slicked back gray hair. He's friendly to me and willing to talk. But I'm wary of his approach. His strategy is to make this as a war of attrition. So, he counts bodies—if more Viet Cong are killed than "our" troops, that's supposed to mean we're winning the war. But I don't think we are winning. Not even close.

When I'm in Saigon, I go to the Indonesian Consulate there and put in another visa application, this time presenting myself as a professor, which I used to be. It doesn't work—rejected again.

Damn—they're more efficient than I thought. They've distributed a blacklist among their embassies.

I have a new editor at *The Post*. Otto Friedrich has just been promoted; he's now Editor of Articles. Dave Lyle has taken his place as Foreign Editor.

I'm itching to do another major Vietnam story. I cable Dave Lyle with a proposal about the American air war in Vietnam. It's really an important story. American pilots are involved in combat day after day and they're suffering the heaviest casualties. Nobody else is really covering this story. There are "eagle flights" of Marine and army detachments of helicopters, Air Force 0-123 units flying into dirt airstrips of jungle outposts with pigs and ammunition, jet units flying daily bombing missions in South Vietnam and into North Vietnam from Da Nang air base and from 7th Fleet carriers.

Lyle nixes the idea. I respond:

> *What perplexes me, Dave, is that in Vietnam we have one of the most dramatic American stories going in the world today, yet The Post has steadfastly refused to do a single 'American in Vietnam' piece since my long article last year. And I simply can't fathom this editorial policy. It's something like running one piece on GI's during the whole Korean War, and calling it quits. Or so it seems to me. Could you explain the thinking of your editors back in the States?*

And this is what Lyle writes back.

> *Our thinking goes something like this: Vietnam is one of about 115 nations in the world. It happens to be one where we are letting our people get shot at, where we are pouring in a jillion dollars every day, but it is still one of many. We also*

are concerned with other parts of the world—Algeria, Cuba,
Germany, Brazil, and a few others like that. And we publish
45—count 'em—45 times a year. That means 40 to 50 foreign
stories, max. And we can't let ourselves be Vietnam'd to death.
Your piece on the Special Forces war was good enough, solid
enough, to hold us for a while. Nothing better has since been
published anywhere, to my knowledge.

Vietnam'd to death??? So, this is their thinking. It's a mistake. A
big mistake. I have a bitter taste in my mouth. The American administration and American soldiers are deeply immersed in Vietnam.
It's just that back home, in Pennsylvania and Kansas and California,
they don't know it yet.

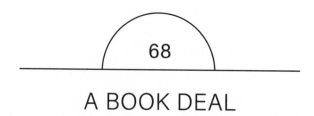

68

A BOOK DEAL

"I think I should talk with Karnow," I tell Kay over breakfast one morning. "Now that Karnow is writing for *The Post*, I don't know where I stand."

"What do you think will happen if you talk with him?"

"Honestly, I don't know," I say, "but we can talk about the situation. Is there room for both of us to write about Asia? As you know, I've been anxious, with a nagging worry chewing away in the back of my mind."

"I suppose it can't hurt to talk with him," Kay says. Then my sweet Kay does something unusual for her—she starts to giggle.

"What is it?" I ask. "What's so funny?"

"It's not something funny—just something fun I want to tell you—and you're so serious…"

"So, what do you want to tell me?"

"I'm pregnant—well, just a little pregnant," she says. "I just found out. I'm due in late October or early November."

The next moment, I jump up, run around the breakfast table, and sweep her up in my arms. "Oh, my love," I say, "I'm thrilled! Maybe we'll have a boy this time!"

—

Two days later, I meet with Karnow at the Hong Kong Hilton, in their large and echoing cafeteria. I've been wondering if I'll be out of a job or if all the important stories for *The Post* will go to him. I say bluntly, "Is there really room at *The Post* for two Asia correspondents?"

Sitting across from me with his plump arms folded on the table and leaning slightly forward, Karnow chortles and says, "Not to worry—there's enough work for both of us."

We chat for a while about the situation in Vietnam. We agree about a lot—the deteriorating conditions, the incompetence of the American leadership. Karnow is quiet for a moment. Then he says, "I think I might have something for you, if you're interested."

"A story for *The Post*?"

"No. It's a book deal. You probably heard of Grant Wolfkill. He's the NBC cameraman who was shot down in a helicopter in Laos. It was all over the papers when he was released a couple years ago."

"I remember," I say. "His helicopter was shot down and he was held captive in Laos by the communist Pathet Lao for a long time— more than a year, I think. It was a big deal when he was released."

"He was held for fifteen months in the most horrible conditions. Anyway, he came to me a while ago asking me to write his book for him, to be a ghost writer for his memoir. I said okay, and we started working on it. But I've been tied up, too much on my plate, and we haven't gotten anywhere."

"Is this really a book deal or just an idea?" I ask.

"It's a book deal," he says. "He even has a contract with Simon and Schuster. Do you want to take this thing over? I think this would be a good project for you and you would be good for Wolfkill. If you want it, it's yours." He writes Wolfkill's phone number on a slightly used napkin and hands it to me.

Laos and Vietnam are neighboring countries, with similar

experiences. Both were French colonies and in both there is an ongoing war with communist guerrillas. In Laos, the communists are called Pathet Lao. I've been to Laos many times and have written stories about the complex situation there.

So, I'm interested.

But I'm wary, a little suspicious. Is Karnow being generous—helping me by handing me a book project? Or is this just a clever method for pushing me out of his way?

I meet Wolfkill over a lunch at a small noodle restaurant in an alley in Kowloon. Grant Wolfkill is a tall, lanky man and he bends his head when he walks through the door of the restaurant. His hair is the color of white sand and is brushed back on his high forehead. He has a bright smile as we shake hands. You wouldn't think, from a first meeting, that he had endured fifteen months in the dark, in a brutal communist-Pathet Lao prison.

"I've read some of your stories," he says with a smile. "I'd be pleased to work with you."

"That's kind of you," I say, "but we need to talk about your story."

"What do you want to know?"

"Everything."

"That will take a long time." Wolfkill is quiet for a moment. He lights his pipe, takes a couple draws, and begins, "You never think this will really happen to you. I mean I was a cameraman in a war zone. I was flying over battlefields. I was a witness to tragedy. But when our 'copter crashed in a remote mountain area of Laos, I just wasn't prepared for being captured." Wolfkill goes on to tell me a little of his story—how he was marched through deep jungles, along with two American soldiers, with their hands tied behind their backs. Then they were kept in solitary cells, with little food, and no idea if or when they would be released or shot.

I like this man. I'm impressed by his story and also by his courage. If I decide to write his book, it will be a serious commitment and a major change in my life. It's like deciding to climb a mountain—it's not the same as a casual stroll. It will be a mountain of work.

And yet, I'm intrigued, even energized and excited—here's a fresh story overflowing with drama. It will be good to have a book—good for my career. The contract with Simon and Schuster will help pay the bills, to supplement my work in journalism.

Grant and I shake hands and I say "yes," and he says "fine" and we agree to work together. Next Monday, we agree, I'll bring a recorder and tapes to begin, and we'll go from there.

Later that afternoon, I take my daughter Thorina to the white sand beach at Repulse Bay. Sometimes Kay comes too, but today, she just wants to rest. She's still slender—her pregnancy doesn't show yet—and she's not even nauseous. She has a special glow and, every now and then, I see her rubbing her still-flat tummy.

So, today it's just my little girl and me. As we walk onto the sand, with her small hand in mine, she giggles and looks up at me with her big blue eyes. Thorina, at fifteen months old, adores the beach. As soon as we lay out our blanket, she gets busy, carrying buckets of water from the ocean to dump on herself and the sand. She goes back again and again on her sturdy legs. She works like she's putting out a fire.

By the time we get home, Thorina is a little tired. She takes a pillow from the davenport, puts it on the floor, and lays her head on it. With her fanny sticking up in the air, she says "ni, ni." But she's not down for long. Soon she's up, playing with a big doll that used to belong to Lucy. The doll has shiny blond pigtails and a red-aqua checked dress and is bigger than she is. She drags it around the room by its pigtails, with its wooden cheeks scraping the tile floor.

Thorina knows quite a few words; she says "a-lo" into her little green toy telephone, and when our phone rings, she says "a-lo" as we're answering it. She sees a picture of a tomato in a magazine and says "apu"—she thinks it's an apple. "Baba" is her belly button and also a button. She knows all the parts of her face and can say the right words for each. I'm teaching her these words in French. "*Ou est le nez*?" I say and she points to her little nose.

Thorina

When Grant Wolfkill and I begin working on the book, it's as if I'm plunged into a whole different world. Grant's story is frightening and horrific—and also touching. "The guards were vicious and brutal," Grant tells me during one of our afternoon interviews. "But sometimes we met people who were kind to us."

"Were some of the guards kind?"

"Not really—none of them—they were ready to kill us at any moment. But when they marched us by foot through the jungles, I met a man from one of the villages who suddenly appeared and helped me. Afterwards, I thought about this man—what he did for me . . ."

"What happened?"

"I was trying to get water from a bucket in a well. I couldn't do it—I was weak and had a fever and didn't have the strength to pull up the bucket. I tried to force my hands to hold the rope, but it began to slip. Suddenly, a man from the village stepped out of his hut and took the rope from my hands. He quickly pulled the bucket of water from the well and handed it to me."

"Why do you think he did that?

"I don't know. He was kind and he was brave. I was just a stranger, a prisoner from another country. And the soldiers were cruel and taunting us. It took a bold man to do that."

REPORTED TO BE ALIVE

I'm a ghost writer. I'm writing Grant Wolfkill's story, in his voice, with his emotions. It's a gripping story of one man's endurance and courage. I'm writing it as a novel, but it isn't *my* novel.

I'm writing and writing, with sweat, handwringing, and a million cigarettes. I'm the ghost writer and I'm haunted by this story. Sometimes, I feel as if I were the one undergoing imprisonment for months and months.

I've put my own novel, *The Way to the Temple*, aside for now. I don't have time, between writing this book and my work in journalism. But I haven't forgotten my own novel. I'll get back to it soon.

We have a working title for our book, *Reported to Be Alive*. The fate of Wolfkill and the other men who were with him in captivity was unknown for about a month after they had disappeared. Then the United States Embassy in Vientiane, Laos, issued a report: they were "reported to be alive."

Our publisher comes to town—Old Mister Schuster of Simon and Schuster. Max Schuster is stopping in Hong Kong on a tour of Asia.

I want to meet him—this is a chance to talk about my own novel, maybe get a contract.

We meet for coffee in the Peninsula Hotel in Kowloon. It's a large and impressive building, shaped like an H from the outside. Schuster is a man in his mid-60s, with a bald head and a sharp wit. He's about my father's age. He used to be a newsman himself, so I think that's why he took on the Wolfkill book.

We talk about the Wolfkill book and then he says, "I worked in the field myself—not overseas, like you. But I wrote for newspapers and magazines in New York and Boston. I still have an interest in news. I guess you could call me a newsman-publisher."

"I guess you could say I'm a novelist turned newsman." We chat a little more and then I tell him about my novel about Vietnam—*The Way to the Temple*. "It's fiction," I say, "but it tells a lot about what's really happening in Vietnam. I've spent five years living and working in Vietnam and I know the country intimately. My novel has multi-layered stories about both Americans living there and Vietnamese."

Schuster asks me questions and I outline the characters and the plot. He doesn't say a lot, but he nods with each of my descriptions. Finally, he says, "Send us your outline and sample chapters. It sounds like something we might like."

Maybe a contract is forthcoming—maybe.

70

MY SISTER LUCY VISITS

It's late evening. My sister Lucy is here, standing in my study. My little sister who, at age nineteen, is already a young woman. Having Lucy here is like transporting Baker Street to Asia. Everything about her evokes home—her dark hair, her hazel eyes, the little cleft on her chin.

"I can't believe I'm really here," she says. She looks around, wide-eyed, as if she's trying to absorb the room. And in that moment, I see in her the little girl who delighted me with her curiosity and intense way of seeing the world.

"You must be tired," Kay says.

"I guess I am, but I think I'm probably too excited to fall sleep. Do you mind if I look around a bit first?" Kay and I nod.

Lucy wanders around my study. She stands for a while in front of a large painting perched on an easel. "Beautiful," she says.

"A work in progress," I say. The painting is a city scene of tall buildings, almost abstract—Hong Kong. It's five feet wide, and it's always changing, never finished. I work on it in the middle of the night.

Then she stops to look at photos tacked up over my desk. "Oh my god," she says in a low voice, putting her hand on her throat. She's looking at two of my black and white photographs—two halves of the same figure. One image is a man's face, grimacing in pain. The other shows his foot punctured with a thick spike. She turns to me with a question in her eyes.

I explain, "The Viet Cong spread these spikes in the rice fields. The spikes are covered with dung; they're poisonous, horribly painful, and lethal." Lucy looks shocked.

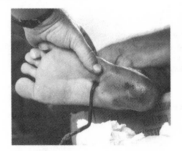 

Man with a spike in his foot

"These photos are not beautiful," I say, "but they're a visceral reminder to me of what this war is about—the pain and brutality. I look at this man's face and every time I share a little of his pain. It's why I'm here—to tell his story."

The next morning, Lucy is up early. She's standing in the doorway of my study. Her long dark hair is disheveled and she's wearing a flowered bathrobe that's a little crumpled from travel. "Can I come in?"

"Of course," I say and get up to give her a kiss on the cheek. "I have a plan for you while you're here—some activities for you. I've hired a tutor from the Art Department at Hong Kong University. He'll give you lessons in Chinese painting and culture. Also, I've contacted the

International Rescue Committee so you can do some volunteer work. What do you think about this educational program?"

Lucy's eyes light up. "When can I start?"

"In a couple days. Let's give you a little time to rest up and recover from jet lag." She's going to be here for at least two months. I want to keep her busy—and for her to learn something while she's here. This is my chance to educate my sister and offer her an extraordinary experience. I'm excited and I'm glad she is too.

Two days later, Mr. Oong shows up at our apartment. He is a calligrapher and a scholar. He's a roundish man, round in his face, his belly and his bald head. A refugee from the mainland, he speaks limited English. But he comes to our house laden with supplies—Chinese brushes, an inkstick, an ink stone, a book of Chinese brush drawings, and rice paper. Kay sets up a card table in the living room for him to work with Lucy.

As I walk by them, I see they're working with inks. Mr. Oong is demonstrating how to hold the brush upright, how to grind the ink. I'm tempted to join them. I would love to paint with his Chinese brushes.

But I must work on the Wolfkill book. So, I go back into my study to tap-tap on my Olivetti. It's coming along, too slowly, but even so, we're making progress.

A few days later, I take Lucy to the Hong Kong office of the International Rescue Committee in a tall tower, where we meet Hallock Rose. The International Rescue Committee helps refugees all over the world—including refugees who have streamed into Hong Kong from mainland Communist China. Hal Rose is a tall, broad, jovial man with a mound of white hair. "What I really want," I tell him, "is for my sister to get an understanding of what conditions are like in Hong Kong."

"I understand," he nods at me. Then shaking hands with Lucy, he says, "So you want to volunteer for us. We have lots of work for you!" He outlines a several "jobs"—interviewing families, visiting children in nursery centers, and teaching English to teenage boys who are training to work as bellhops and busboys in hotels. "Well, which of these jobs do you want?"

"Why can't I do all of them?" she says.

Every day or every other day, Lucy goes on an outing with a translator to interview refugees from mainland China. Her job is to write reports about the children, to be sent to donors in Great Britain and the United States and tell them about the individual children they sponsor. She's using one of our old typewriters. In the afternoons, I see her typing up her notes.

Over dinner one evening, Lucy says, "People are living on rooftops. We saw dozens of tent-like structures crowded on a single roof, one against the other. I saw a child, a little girl no more than five years old, with a bucket that she'd just carried up the stairs to her rooftop home. I wanted to run and take it from her, but Miss Li, my translator, took my arm and stopped me."

"You would have insulted the girl if you took away her job. Miss Li understood that."

"But I felt so helpless. It must be dreadful, living like that. And there was nothing I could do to help," Lucy says. She looks like she's about to cry.

"You are helping them," Kay says, "by writing your reports and getting funds to support these families."

"Can't the government help them? This is a British colony," Lucy says.

"They're all refugees from mainland China," I say. "More than a million people have come to Hong Kong because they don't want to live under the communists. The British government has been building housing, but it takes time, and it's complicated." My sister has impractical ideas about what can be done with a huge influx of refugees. But at least she's getting a taste of the real Asia.

I want to show my sister another side of Hong Kong—the amazing food. We go to the Luk Yee Teahouse on Stanley Street. It's an old and elegant restaurant with two stories and its tables are always full. The walls are covered with ornate dark-wood lattices and masterpieces of Chinese calligraphy. I've invited Bernie Kalb, my colleague and friend, and his wife Phyllis to dine with us. Bernie is always fun to be with and Phyllis is sparkling, with a ready laugh and fish-skeleton earrings. There's always a good conversation with them. Kay likes them too.

We order a banquet of Chinese dishes: char siu, sea cucumber, braised abalone, sea food with bird's nest, spiced chicken, and steamed rock cod—all delicious and traditional Chinese cuisine. Lucy turns to me and whispers, "Is this made with pork? Or this?"

"Just eat it," I tell her. Lucy seems to wilt when I say this. But she stops asking and she eats what she's given.

I wonder—was I too harsh? I want her to taste all of life and be open to new experiences and not be a kosher ghetto Jew. But what can I do? I suppose, it's like my father and me all over again. He had his own ideas for me—different from my ideas. Now my little sister is grown up and, as her big brother and quasi-father, I suppose I'll have to watch from a distance as she goes on with her life.

—

Lucy has been with us in Hong Kong for more than six weeks when I get a cable from Dave Lyle at *The Post*. I need to get back to Saigon.

I've almost finished a story about General William Westmoreland, the head of the American effort, the key American in Vietnam. Suddenly the Americans decide to change their leadership structure. It's not just Westy anymore. Now, there's a triumvirate in charge, with Westy as Commander of the U.S. Military Advisory Group, General Maxwell Taylor as Ambassador, and Alexis Johnson as his Deputy.

Dave Lyle cables, "I'm sorry that extra work results from the timing of the Taylor-Johnson appointment, but that's show biz."

To redo my article, with the new American leadership, I need to do more research—more interviews. I take a plane to Vietnam the next day.

A week later, Lucy follows me to Saigon. She's staying at the home of Huan's brother, Bui Tuong Hy and his wife Simone. When I telephone Simone to ask if it would be convenient for my sister to stay with them, she immediately says, "*Bien sûr*. Of course, it's okay; we're family."

I bring Lucy directly from the airport to Hy and Simone's house. I watch her take in the home, her eyes wide—the red tile floors, white walls, the veranda enveloped by tropical foliage. It's much airier and brighter than our Hong Kong apartment.

I'm staying at the Caravelle. The hotel is new, only a few years old, with an arched entryway, marble floors and columns, modern air conditioning, and bullet proof glass—a sign of the times. It houses several foreign embassies and news agencies and is a favorite hotel for journalists. As I walk in, I'm greeted warmly by old friends— Arthur Dommen, Malcolm Browne, Jim Wilde, who has returned to Vietnam, and several others.

I invite Lucy to come to the hotel on her last afternoon, so we can have a little time alone together. Although she's been in Asia for almost two months, we haven't had enough time to talk, just the two of us.

As we enter the wide lobby, Lucy looks around at the high ceilings and elegant colonial style. "Wow," she says, under her breath. But walking into my hotel room, I notice how disorderly it is. My typewriter is open, with sheets of paper in scattered piles. Housekeeping hasn't made my bed yet. Lucy sits on the only chair and I perch on the edge of the bed.

"Let's sit and talk for a while," I say. I want her to talk about herself. But to open our discussion, I tell her a story about myself, about Dad. "You know, Daddy never wanted me to be a writer or an artist."

"I remember," she says, "when I was a little girl and you came home for the summer, you and Daddy were always arguing."

"You remember that?"

"Sure—but I guess I didn't really understand what it was all about."

"He wanted me to be a scientist, like him. He was disappointed in me. And I guess he was worried that I wouldn't be able to make a living. I'll tell you something I found out when I was home last summer—Daddy really tried to stop me being an artist."

"Really—he tried to stop you! What did he do?"

"He sent a letter to one of my art professors at Johns Hopkins, a man who had been my mentor in painting. He wanted this man to tell me that I had no talent and no hope of being successful as a painter. But my professor wrote: 'I can't do that. Your son has exceptional talent.'"

"How did you happen to find this letter?" Lucy asks.

"Well," I say, "I was snooping in Daddy's desk. I found a file with my name on it."

"I can just picture Daddy doing that. He likes to control things. And I think you're right—he was worried about you. But, really, he's proud of you now."

"Okay," I say, "I've told you about me. I want to know about your life."

"What about my life?"

"Tell me about this boyfriend of yours," I start to say, but Lucy looks wary, as if I'm going to cross-examine her.

"He's nice—he's smart. He's studying chemistry. He's Jewish—you already know that."

"So, are you having sex with this nice, smart Jewish chemistry guy?"

Lucy is quiet for a long time, looking down at her hands, clasped on her lap. "I don't think I want to talk about that," she says finally.

There was a time when she reached out to me. She even asked questions about sex. But those times are over. There's a wall between us. I want her to be my little girl again, but it's not to be, which gives me a deep sense of loss.

Lucy changes the subject. "I like Hy and Simone. They've been kind to me. Are you worried about them? What will happen to them if the Viet Cong win the war?"

"I am concerned. Kay and I talk about this. We're trying to put some money aside for Huan and all of them to help them if they have to leave Vietnam. They're my family."

The next day, I take Lucy to the airport on the outskirts of Saigon. The airport is small, noisy, dark and crowded. I flash my press pass to push our way through the crowds of people.

Then the moment comes when she's about to board the small plane to take her to Cambodia, her next stop. Kay and I had insisted that she visit the ancient Hindu-Buddhist ruins at Angkor Wat.

"Thank you for everything. This trip has been amazing," she says as we hug our good-byes and then she whispers in my ear. "When will I see you again? I worry about you."

Lucy is crying. I am too. How many moons will pass before we see one another again?

My sister Lucy

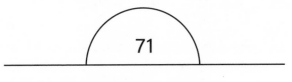

71

COMBAT ZONE

I miss Kay and little Thorina, who are back in Hong Kong. I'm stuck in Saigon with work to finish here—a long story for *The Reporter*, another Vietnam story for *The New York Times*, and two commissions from *The Post*.

The baby is due in two months. I'll be home in plenty of time to greet this one.

Kaynik my love,

How are you feeling? Is our almost-baby inside you giving you some good kicks? I plan to be there to shake hands with this new little one when he arrives in late October. In the meantime, tap an "hello" on your belly from his daddy.

I wish you were here but I'm also glad you're not. The situation in Vietnam is lousy. Saigon is in chaos. Terrorist attacks around the country happen daily. And nothing much has changed with the new military government here under General Khanh. The government is floundering, and the Americans are digging in. Day by day more and more American troops arrive.

Paul was here yesterday wondering if he could earn a living back in the States. When Paul, who loves this country, thinks about leaving Vietnam, you know it's finished here.

I feel stuck here—missing you so much and wanting you in my arms. Kiss our little Thorina for me.

The Post has commissioned two articles from me: a political article about the American leadership triumvirate, Westmoreland-Taylor-Johnson, and another one about American civilians working in Vietnam.

I'm sitting by myself at a café on Rue Catinat, with a cup of coffee in front of me and a cigarette between my thumb and forefinger. I'm reviewing my notes for the political article. The air is steamy and thick—it's one of those hot tropical days in Saigon when the noise and fumes of passing motorcycles and cars crawl under your skin.

Suddenly, Stan Karnow shows up. He's in front of me, blocking my light, and he sits down at my table, scraping the chair along the cement patio. "I've been looking for you," he says. "Friedrich wants us to collaborate on the political story."

I'm jolted. It's as if my story has been ripped out of my hands. This has been my fear and my nightmare—that Karnow would take over my assignments and leave me eating dust.

I look over at Karnow with a sense of shock. "I don't get it," I say. "What do you mean collaborate? Are we expected to split the tri-umvirate in three parts—you take Westy, I'll take Taylor, and we rip Johnson in half so we can share him?" I'm making a joke of this but, inside, I'm fuming. Did Friedrich really suggest this collaboration, or did Karnow insinuate himself onto my turf?

"Look," he says, "it can work out just fine. As we both know, the political situation here in Vietnam is a mess and constantly shifting. I heard about what happened when you were working on the Westy story and it all became beside the point because the leadership turned into a triumvirate. There are bound to be more swings like that, unpredictable and complicated. You and I have different perspectives on Vietnam, so we can work together and help each other."

"Okay," I say, "how do you want to proceed?" I have no choice. But I'm not happy.

Later that same day, I send a cable to Lyle and Friedrich. "I don't understand why Karnow's being brought into my Vietnam story. Do you think I'm incapable of covering the political situation by myself?"

I get Lyle's return cable the next day: "Collaborate with Karnow on the political story and then return to the article on American civilians."

I feel sabotaged by Karnow. I suspect it was his idea to take over my story. I wonder and worry what he's saying about me to the editors at *The Post*. I feel both furious and helpless to do anything but "cooperate."

I count among my good friends many fellow-journalists. In a sense, we're all competing. But there's a special bond among us—we rely on each other. It's different with Karnow. I don't trust him.

After a couple weeks, this supposed collaboration with Karnow is going nowhere. He sends pages to me; I write something and send it to him. And nothing gels. Disaster. Meanwhile, the situation in Vietnam gets more complex and confusing.

Dave Lyle writes that Karnow will take over the political piece by himself and I should concentrate on the American civilian story. In his cable, he says, "I don't deceive myself by thinking that you are going to be overjoyed with our having reached this reluctant decision, but I must do what I can to get these articles produced and into the magazine. The collaboration seems to produce nothing but disorder."

I go back to working on the story about American civilians working in Vietnam. But I've lost my confidence. I'm having the damnedest time with this story. I seem to be in that cruel writer's cycle where one produces 95 different versions of a first paragraph, all of which sound lousy.

It's four in the morning and I wake up from a nightmare. I don't know how else to describe it. It's all about Karnow. I'm running, and I'm drenched in sweat. Above me is an enormous, floating balloon, the kind of figure you see in Macy's Thanksgiving Day parades. It's him. His round head and rounded body fill the sky and hover over me, chasing me. The ballooned Karnow figure grows bigger and bigger, like an eclipse, darkening the sky. I'm dwarfed by this flying balloon. Out of breath, running and getting nowhere, I reach into my pocket, fumble inside the softness of the cotton fabric, thinking, *If only I had something sharp.* I find a small pin and pinch it between my fingers...

Suddenly, I'm awake. It's warm in my room. The air conditioner is off, and my body is damp from sweat. My mind reverberates with the same thoughts which hounded me as I went to sleep. Karnow and more Karnow. My emotions roil like great thunderclouds, violent and dark. Karnow...Karnow...Karnow...

72

A NAME OF STRENGTH AND NOBILITY

It's late in the morning, ten a.m., and I wake up to a loud knocking on the door of my hotel room at the Caravelle. The bed sheet is wound around my legs and it takes me a few moments to untangle myself and stumble over to the door. When I open the door, I find a bellhop standing inches away from me in a crisp red and gold uniform. In his gloved hand, he's holding a cable on a small silver tray.

As I run to my wallet to forage for a tip, I wonder—*Is this more bad news?*

But it isn't bad—just too soon news. "A boy is born to the Roses!" A cable from Kay. It's just the 25th of September. This baby is a month early! *Damn*, I think, *I wanted to be with her for this birth.*

I feel a surge of excitement—we have a boy! Still in my pajamas, I run down the maroon-carpeted hallway, peeking into doorways—many of my journalist friends and colleagues are housed on this floor. I'm jumping, whooping, and shouting, "It's a boy! It's a boy!" Bernie Kalb's door is open. I run into his room and yell, "We have a boy!"

"Mazel tov!" he bellows and claps me on my back. We have a quick glass of whiskey even though it's morning.

Then I run back to my room and call Kay at Canossa Hospital. "Oh Kaynik, my love, I missed the birth again—I'm so sorry. Was it hard? How are you? And the baby?"

Her voice is soft and weak. "I'm fine—the baby is fine." Kay sounds as happy as I am.

"I'll be there as soon as I can hop on a plane." When I hang up the phone, I feel Kay's voice echoing in my heart. I wish I could be there with her.

It takes until early the next morning to get a flight back to Hong Kong, and it seems like hours for the cab to arrive at the Canossa Hospital on Old Peak Road.

But now I'm here in the bright light of her hospital room. Kay looks calm, serene, queen-like, sitting up in her hospital bed, propped by double pillows. The baby is in a basinet by her bed, wrapped in a blue blanket so I only see his gray eyes, plump red cheeks, and shock of very light blond hair.

"He looks like you," Kay says.

A nurse, Miss Chen, who has stopped by her room looks at me and back at the baby and nods, agreeing with her. "Yes, just like you—your face, your chin," she says.

The baby is so tiny. I've forgotten how small a newborn is. I lean over the basinet and the baby and I look each other over—though I'm not sure his eyes really focus. I notice that he has the Rose chin—a cleft chin.

Still looking down at the baby, I ask, "What shall we call you, little one? What name would you like?"

I sit down on a corner of Kay's bed. "Are you still okay with the name Eric?"

"Yes. I love the name. I'm sure some of my Norwegian ancestors must have been called Eric."

"But not with an H." We have a German friend who is Erich with an H—that would be too Germanic for my Jewish taste. "It's a name of strength and nobility."

Then Kay says, "You want his middle name to be Morrow, after your friend, don't you?"

"Yes," I say, and I'm flooded with memories of my school friend Morrow Solomon who died last year. When I visited him in the hospital last summer, his body was ravaged by brain cancer. He didn't want me there, to see him like that.

I think of my friend lying in his tomb under the earth. It's a jarring image; he doesn't belong there. His death so young left me with a bitter sense of tragedy. So, we'll honor my friend by giving our son his name—it's a Jewish tradition.

I turn back to look at our tiny Eric Morrow. I bend over his basinet and put my face close to his. "You have a name now," I whisper to my son, "a good name. How will you carry this name into your life? Who will Eric Morrow Rose be?"

73

CHRISTMAS EVE

'm full of love for our little Thorina, her skin, blonde hair, blue eyes, and mostly her constant discovery of life. She will be two in January. I marvel at how she's learning language. Now she goes around uttering her name without cease. "Torina, Torina do." She counts from one to five and then becomes confused. She says "bye bye" to anyone leaving and has mastered "good night" and "good morning." "Good morning, Thorina," we say. "Good morning, Torina," she says. One can reason with her too, explain why she can't do something or another. I hate saying "no, no" all the time. For example, she loves "by" (beer), and she knows she can't have "whikey." She also likes "Coca." She still sucks milk out of a bottle, though she can use a glass. When she walks, she manages something between a prance and a toddle with a cute wiggle.

Eric is three months old now. I love his tender skin, his efforts to bring up burps, his slow awareness of objects in his blue eyes, his lifting his head, and his sucking desperately on his hands, which are out of control like a spastic's. When he loses his hand, he really gets furious.

—

Kay delights in Christmas. It's part of her Minnesota family tradition. We have a lop-sided pine tree propped up in the corner of our living room with decorations, many of them homemade by Kay and me—little ornaments out of paper and wood popsicle sticks. Kay has arranged colorful wrapped boxes under the tree. The room looks festive but a little out of place in Hong Kong.

Thorina walks around the room scattering the boxes everywhere. "C'istmas present for Torina, C'istmas present for Torina," she says over and over again.

"Some of the presents are for Eric and for Mommy and Daddy," Kay says. She's bouncing Eric on her lap and he bobs his head, his blue eyes following his sister around the room.

"Present for Torina, present for Torina," Thorina says, as she marches around the room dragging a large box behind her that's twice her size.

We open our presents quickly. Thorina gets a Raggedy Ann doll made by Kay's grandmother and sent from Minnesota. But she's more interested in the empty boxes and paper wrappings, which she gathers into a high pile. We have some little gifts for Eric but he's too young to understand. Kay gives me blue silk pajamas. When I open the box, I hold the pajamas next to my cheek and say, "Soft—but not as soft as your skin."

I have a special gift for Kay—a gold necklace with ruby and amethyst stones that I designed and had crafted for her in Vietnam by my favorite jeweler. "Oh Jerry," she says, as she opens the box, "It's exquisite."

Just then the doorbell rings. We've invited our neighbors, the Okas, for Christmas dinner. Kay and I have been working all day with Cheong Jun to prepare stuffed goose, sweet potatoes mashed with pineapple, and all the trimmings, including Cheong Jun's apple pie with a sculpted pie-dough flower.

Takashi Oka writes for the Christian Science Monitor. It was

Takashi who found this apartment for us more than two years ago. He lives down the hall with his wife Hiro and their little girl Mimi, who is five years old. Takashi and Hiro are both American educated. Tak, wearing a charcoal gray suit with a striped tie, is somewhat tall for a Japanese man, with a round face and friendly smile. His wife, Hiro, is petite, gracious, and elegant. Today, in honor of the occasion, she's wearing a silk kimono with lotus flower designs. On ordinary days, I see her in western clothes—usually slacks.

Mimi is slender and tall like a reed and towers over Thorina who follows her around whenever she can. Thorina adores her.

We feed the little ones first while the grownups have hors d'oeuvres and drinks. Kay puts Eric to bed. Mimi and Thorina settle themselves with toys on the living room floor, while we sit down to dinner.

Kay and Eric

The conversation inevitably turns to the situation in Vietnam. "It's chaos there," Tak says. "With General Khanh in charge, the Vietnamese government has gone from cruelty to incompetence. I don't see anything good happening anytime soon."

"I couldn't agree more," I say. "Everyone is glad to be rid of Diệm and Nhu. But there have been two coups so far and there's a sense of profound instability, as if the new government is made from a puff of air, with no substance. I wish it weren't so. I wish I could help."

"What do you know about General Khanh?"

"As far as I can tell, he's just another Vietnamese general. He's a military man with no sense of what his people really need."

We talk a little more about Vietnam and then Tak changes the subject. "There's chaos back in the States too," he says. "Have you been watching news reports about the Civil Rights Movement? "

Kay says, "It's exciting in its way—young people are trying hard to change America—make things better. It brings tears to my eyes. They just gave the Nobel Peace Prize to Martin Luther King. I'm so glad."

Tak is quiet for a moment. "It's not just the Civil Rights Movement. Back in the States, a few anti-war protests are beginning on college campuses. If President Johnson continues to send U.S. troops to Vietnam, there will be a massive draft of young people. There's not much now but if things go wrong in Vietnam, there's going to be an enormous anti-war movement. I can feel it in my bones."

"In the month before he was killed, Kennedy was making plans to turn over the fighting to the Vietnamese and withdraw American soldiers," I say. "But Johnson is doing just the opposite—he's flooding the country with American troops."

We talk a little more about politics and we chat about our children. We have our after-dinner drinks and toast each other for Christmas. Then the Okas take Mimi home, and we tuck little Thorina into bed.

—

The house is quiet. Kay is sitting next to me on the couch, as we sip whiskey, our late-night drinks. The children are in their room, sleeping with baby snores. Cheong Jun is in the kitchen, in the back area of the house. We hear distant sounds of water and clanking dishes. The lights are off, so the room is dark, except for the light of the moon and a few dotted lights in the distance, below our veranda.

"Are you worried, Jerry?" Kay asks.

"A little. This has been a difficult year—especially because of my fight with Karnow. I don't know what will happen with *The Post*. Most likely I won't be getting more assignments from them."

"But there have been some good things too this year," she says.

"It's true. I've gotten assignments from *Time* and my photos in *Life* and *Newsweek*—so I've had breakthroughs in photography. And my book of photos got published—all that is good." I completed a book of photos on Vietnam, with sixty-four full color pages. It's called *The Face of Anguish*. U.S.I.S., the United States Information Service, contracted with me to produce it.

Kay adds, "The Wolfkill book is done. Don't you feel relieved? I know I do—it was so much work."

"Yes, my love, we both put a lot of sweat and tears in that book." I put my arm around Kay and squeeze her shoulder. Kay did all the typing—transcribing tapes and all the many versions of the manuscript. It was a mammoth job for both of us. "It's nice they got Robert Kennedy to write a foreword. It will help sell books. Maybe there'll be a movie." We're quiet for a few moments, and then I ask her, "Are you worried? I haven't earned as much this year as we hoped."

Kay doesn't answer immediately but then she says, "I think we'll be fine. You work so hard and you always have projects. And you're talented. I read your book, every word, every version, as I typed it— and it's good; it's really good."

"But is it good enough? Will it sell? Will anyone want to buy this book about a man imprisoned for fifteen months—even if it's a good book. Will it sell?"

We sip our drinks, look out at the lights in the night sky. "The thing is," I say, after a while, "I really want to write fiction. I need to get back my novel and spend serious time on it. I'm not sure how to do that and still make a living for us. To make this life of mine worthwhile, that's what I need to do."

Kay gently strokes my cheek, "I know, dear, I know," she says.

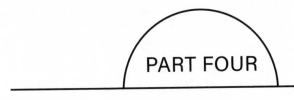

PART FOUR

1965

74

SOMEONE JUST LIKE YOU

Huan, my brother, is Minister of Education in the latest incarnation of the South Vietnamese government. He's on leave from his teaching position at the University of Huế. Huan and I are sitting on the terrace of a small café on Rue Catinat, near the Caravelle Hotel in Saigon. It's late afternoon and the weather is sultry except for a hot breeze that brushes our cheeks and lifts the corners of our napkins.

Huan looks tired and even more gaunt than before, when we were both professors at the university. His hair drifts over his eyes. He has a wife and two babies now—first a daughter and then they had a son, born just a month ago. "Just like you," he said when I called to congratulate him. "Now we both have sons." I suppose he's up at night, like many new fathers.

"Two more *coups d'etat*," I say, shaking my head. "Will there ever be stability? Will this country ever have a decent government?"

Huan says, "Maybe someday we'll have a democracy in Vietnam. It's my dream."

Since the overthrow of the Ngô Đình Diệm regime, Vietnam has been roiled with more *coups d'etat*. In January 1964, General Khanh, a partly bald man with a reputation as a brilliant military commander, took Saigon by surprise with a bloodless *coup*. So General Minh, who had overthrown Diệm only a couple months earlier, was out. But Khanh's tenure as Prime Minister was stormy, with constant bickering and little accomplished. His government lasted less than a year. Now, four junior officers have just deposed Khanh.

Over cigarettes and strong coffee, I ask, "Why did you do it? Why did you join this government?"

He says, "I never imagined such a thing, you know, that I would be on the other side, the government side. But things are different now. I'm not especially close to these military men, but this is just a government in transition. This is my country and I have to do what I can to help."

"I've never had a brother who's a Cabinet Minister," I tease him. "What's it like?"

"What's it like?" he sighs. "Some moments are exciting, even fascinating. There's so much to do, so much to make better. Our children don't know how to read. And it's all up to us, sitting in our little offices, to change that, to bring teachers and books out to the villages. But then most of the time, I'm exasperated. If you can find a little fund to pay for teachers and supplies, suddenly it's gone. And nobody can tell you where. If you try to check it out, somebody will say, it's the war, it's the Viet Cong. But really, it's rampant corruption at every level. I want to scream. But it won't help."

"Why do you stay?"

"Because," he answers slowly, looking down into his cup of coffee, "if the honest people go away, who will be left?" Huan pauses to take a few long drags on his cigarette. "Besides," he continues, "I think pretty soon, it will be much better. We'll have a new government. The military is handing it over to a civilian government. Have you heard who's going to be Prime Minister?"

Actually, I've heard rumors. "Is it true? Is it really going to be Quat?" Huan nods, smiling. Dr. Phan Huy Quat is an old friend of ours from Huế. In fact, he was my doctor when I lived in Huế. He treated me for several bouts of hepatitis. He's a good man, an interesting, intelligent man who is, I believe, incorruptible. Although by profession he's a medical doctor, he's always been involved in politics. He was active in the opposition during the Ngô Đình Diệm regime and was persecuted, thrown in jail more than once. I tell Huan, "If Quat's going to lead the government, there's hope for this country." I really believe that. Having an idealistic and honest man as Prime Minister would be like breathing in fresh air. This could change everything.

Huan suddenly gets up and dashes into the street. In a moment I realize why. He had recognized another mutual friend, Bui Diệm, a man in his mid-forties, dressed in a very neat brown suit. Like Huan, he is a nationalist who fought against the French in the war of independence and was an active opponent against Ngô Đình Diệm. I've known Bui Diem for a long time.

The two of them come back to our table. "I was just about to tell you," Huan says, "this man is going to be Chief of Staff with Quat." Bui Diệm and I shake hands. Huan asks him to join us.

I tell him "Congratulations."

Smiling, he says, "I think it will happen soon."

We chat about this and that. Then, I notice that Bui Diệm is staring at me, through his wide black rimmed glasses. He has a strange, dreamy look on his face. I look down at my shirt, wondering if there's a spot. Huan and I exchange glances. "Is something wrong?" I ask.

Bui Diệm gives me a broad smile. "I was just thinking," he says, "just an idea. We could use an American in our new government, an American who has lived here for a long time and really understands Vietnam. The American would be an advisor or a consultant, not exactly a part of the government, someone who could be a bridge between the Vietnamese government and the Americans. Someone just like you." And then he really does stare at me.

I lean back in my chair, which scrapes against the cement on the terrace. I light another cigarette. "Are you serious?" I ask.

Bui Diệm replies, "I'm absolutely serious." He says this soberly, with no hint of a smile.

"Okay," I say, "if you're serious, I'll consider it."

I'm intrigued. This is what I'm thinking. America is embroiled in Vietnam. There was a time when we just had "advisors," with a small number of American troops. But now the United States is rushing in headlong. You see it in the news—the arrival of troops, not just "advisors"—they're coming now by the thousands. American soldiers are dying here in Vietnam. And the American political leaders back in the States and here don't know what they're doing.

I feel in my gut that I could help. I've been working in and around Vietnam for six years. I know this country intimately and I understand both the politics and the people. For a long time, I've wanted to find a way to help. Maybe everything I've done up until now is just for this—that I can be of service to Vietnam.

Maybe they really do need someone just like me.

75

A QUIET TIME

Dr. Phan Huy Quat is now the Prime Minister of Vietnam. I send him a cable of congratulations. Quat and Bui Diem are men of integrity. There's been so much going wrong in this country, so much corruption and brutality. If anybody could make things better here, it's these good men. I feel a flash of hope for Vietnam.

In my room at the Hotel Continental, I'm composing a brief note to *Time*, at the New York office—a small insert in the international section of the magazine. I write "it's a quiet time in the countryside and the city."

Suddenly I hear a muted explosion.

I grab my camera and race outdoors. Just outside the hotel, on the street corner, I hear a woman saying, "It's the American Embassy." I hail a cab but after a couple blocks, I realize I could get there faster on foot. I hand the driver a few piasters and begin to sprint down the street, with my heart pounding and my camera jouncing against my chest.

When I arrive at Embassy Square, I look up at what used to be the American Embassy. All the windows are shattered; not a single window is left on the Embassy. The street is overflowing with people pushing and crying. Just in front of the Embassy is a car that's mangled, twisted and charred. This must be where the bomb was planted. My hands are shaking so much that I can't open my camera case to take photos.

I wonder—*Is anyone left alive in the building?* My first impression is that everyone inside must have been killed. I don't hear anything from inside the building. But then they start to come out—many are badly maimed. I hear voices shouting, groaning, and moaning and the scrape of equipment along the sidewalk.

A woman emerges from the doorway. She's walking but held up by two medics. Her face is a red bloody pulp. Another man, on a stretcher, has a hole in the center of his chest pumping blood.

With trembling fingers, I manage to take my camera out of its case and snap some pictures. Hot tears stream down my face. I know these people. I've been in this building a million times. My god—this is where Kay used to work.

A Navy medic is helping a woman on a stretcher. For a moment, he stops and feels her heart. He shakes his head. She's dead. He takes off his white jacket and covers her face.

A man wearing a dark blue suit is lying face down on a stretcher. His shoulders are hunched, and his right hand is gripping his left wrist. He has curly hair, just slightly gray. I can't tell if he's alive or dead and just frozen in that position. I hear someone say—"That's Howard Porter." He's the Director of the Asia Foundation in Saigon— the first person I met when I arrived in Vietnam. He's a friend. I feel overwhelmed, drowning in despair, as I watch friends and colleagues emerge, many with horrible wounds.

Another friend, Bill Kohlman, comes out. Bill, who is an operative for the CIA, had polio several years ago, which left him stooped over, needing a cane to walk and unable to use his left hand. As he emerges from the doorway of the embassy, he's covered with blood. But he waves at me. "I'm okay," he says. "I was lucky. Just a nick."

76

GOOD IDEAS

Bui Diệm and I meet for lunch three days after the explosion at the American Embassy. "It's horrible," he says. "Twenty-two people were killed and 200 injured . . .horrible . . .horrible. It was the VC, of course. The military has a team investigating, with American advisors."

"I was there, just after the explosion," I say, "and I saw my friends being taken out. I'm still shaken. I can't stop thinking about it."

"I also had friends who were killed and injured there," Bui Diem says solemnly.

"I suppose the Viet Cong see this as a triumph—a strike against America, their enemy."

Bui Diem shakes his head, "Yes, but the death and destruction happen here, in Vietnam—it's us, in South Vietnam—we are their real enemy."

We're silent for a while—each of us dealing with our own grief and fears.

Then, we turn to the purpose of our meeting—a possible position for me as Advisor to the Vietnamese government. Bui Diệm is a person who gets things done. He's already started making arrangements. He's spoken with Quat, who readily agreed, and with Len Maynard at USOM, the United States Operations Mission. The plan is for USOM to pay for my position—so that technically I'd be employed by the U.S. government.

We're having lunch at the Continental Hotel on Rue Catinet—which is convenient. We have a quiet table in their formal dining room, indoors on the first floor, by a large window. The room is air conditioned and too cold, in contrast to the tropical heat outdoors.

I'm not hired yet, but I've already started my work. As soon as we sit down, I hand him a press statement I wrote in English and French for Quat—to respond to the bombing at the American Embassy. My draft expresses Quat's deep sorrow and his determination to fight terror. Bui Diem holds the paper in his hand, reads it once and then again, nodding silently. He looks up at me and says, "This is good—exactly the right tone." Then he smiles and adds, "It was my idea to hire you, Jerry, and I was right."

"I think I have a lot of good ideas for you," I say. And I start spilling out a series of proposals—about rural electrification and education for village children. As we discuss my ideas, I feel my face flushed with excitement. There's so much to do, so much to be accomplished. Quat and Bui Diem are good men. I want to help them succeed for the sake of their country, for the future of Vietnam.

In the afternoon, I meet Len Maynard, from USOM, on the terrace of the hotel. Len is a tall man in his forties, with dark, slightly receding hair and a deep voice. He's carrying an umbrella and is dressed in a green shirt and white tie with a slight pattern. He shouts for peanuts. The waiter brings some; Len takes a few and says, "Very good, very fresh."

Len knows me as a journalist. We talk about USOM supporting my role as Advisor to the Vietnamese government. If I sign the contract,

I would be employed by USOM. He's friendly, even enthusiastic, about having me ensconced inside the Vietnamese government. My job would be officially Advisor to the Prime Minister. "It would be convenient," he comments wryly, "for us to know what's going on."

They have a budget for this, and the money is good, $20,000. The contract would be for a year or not even that long. Who knows how long this government will last?

But then Maynard turns to me and asks, "What if the U.S. has a policy which you, Jerry Rose, don't like?" That is, they'd want me to push such a policy or program, and I didn't like it.

There's only one answer that he wants to hear. So, I say, "If the U.S. has a policy which I positively cannot recommend to the government, then, of course, I will have to resign."

After I say this, Maynard backs off, saying, "Well, we think you should exercise independent judgments." As for my private opinion, I will remain totally independent in my judgment. The Americans have done enough bungling.

So, today I agree, in principle, to take a job with the Vietnamese government. Len and I shake hands—yes, I'll do it, but only for one year. My motives are complex. But I do think I can accomplish something, serve a function. It's a rare opportunity to do some good. As a writer, I can work on PR—which is not a small matter—to help the leaders have effective communication with their people. And I have ideas about how to improve the lives of the people. I feel a rush of excitement in my blood—I really want to do this.

I haven't signed the contract yet. And I won't until I go back to Hong Kong and talk with Kay.

77

ALL THE HELP HE CAN GET

"Why do you want to take this job?" Kay asks. It's evening. We've just finished our dinner. Our empty plates and the remnants of our meal are scattered around the table, not cleared up yet. The children are tucked in their rooms. We can hear soft baby snores.

"You know how I feel about Vietnam," I say. "It's a unique opportunity. I can accomplish something good for Vietnam."

"What can you really do?"

"We'll see what I can actually accomplish," I admit, "but I have a lot of ideas. I've trekked up and down the country, through villages, jungles, and mountains. I've learned a lot about what the people want and need— like electricity for remote areas and good schools for their children."

Kay looks down at her lap and says very softly, "How long will this government last, anyway?"

"You're right," I sigh. "I don't know how long this government will last. I might be out of a job before it starts."

She's quiet for a few moments and then she says, "But you wanted to have time this year to write fiction, to finish your novel. We talked about that on Christmas Eve."

"Yes," I answer slowly. "I still have that dream—I want to get back to writing my novel. And I will. But working inside the government will give me a lot more material for the novel. I'll keep a journal. And this experience will be part of my novel and make it richer."

Kay is frowning, shaking her head. "I don't like it. I don't have a good feeling about this job."

I'm surprised. "Why?"

"I'm worried—I can't help it. How long before there's another coup? Will they assassinate Quat? And maybe they'll murder everyone in his government. Maybe they'll kill you too."

"I don't think there's a big danger of that, really."

I move my chair next to Kay, put my arm around her and hold her in an embrace. We kiss. But she pulls back and says, "There's something else. If you take this job, you'll have to live in Saigon. Should we all move back there?"

"No," I answer quickly. "I don't want you and the children there. Vietnam is a war zone."

"So, it's safe for you but not for us? You want to leave us for months at a time, me alone with the children . . ." I suddenly realize that she's crying softly, with tears glistening in the corners of her eyes.

"There are planes. It's a short flight and I'll be back here often. It's a steady salary, my love, and I'm only signing for a year. And this government probably won't last that long. I'll be home before you know it."

"I don't like it," she sighs, "but I understand—it's something you need to do. I'll miss you. The children and I will be so lonely without you."

I lift Kay's hand up to my lips and try to kiss her hand. But she pulls her hand away. She's worried and angry—I can see that. She sits upright in her chair, stiffening her spine, as if she wants to harden herself to endure what comes next.

When the official contract from USOM arrives in the mail two days later, I sign it. Kay is standing next to me, holding little Eric who squirms in her arms. "I guess it's for the best," Kay says. She's reconciled but not happy.

A year ago, I had proposed a story to *The Saturday Evening Post* about the American air war in Vietnam. Dave Lyle, my editor at *The Post*, nixed the idea then—telling me that they didn't want to be "Vietnam'd to death." Just recently, I brought the idea up again, arguing that the issue has become even more important—with ever larger numbers of American pilots sent out on dangerous missions. I wrote to him: "Let me try for a cover story. I'd like permission to write a text of 7,000 to 9,000 words. I'd like to do the photography myself, in color."

Now—only one day after I sign the government contract—I get a cable from Lyle: "Proceed with completest blessing."

But I must tell him that I can't do the story, at least not for now. Holding his cable in my hand, I swallow my regret—this is a story I would have loved to do. I send a cable requesting a year's leave from *The Post*, while I take a position as Advisor to the Prime Minister of Vietnam.

Lyle cables back, "I'm duly impressed. I hope you can help the Prime Minister solve his country's problems. From what I've heard, he can use all the help he can get."

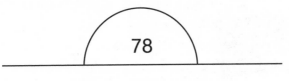

78

THIS IS HOME

I'm home in Hong Kong for two weeks—being with Kay and the children before I start my position in the government. It's a sweet time with my family—strolls around the neighborhood, going to the beach, eating leisurely meals. I don't do much of any work over these two weeks.

This afternoon I take Kay and the children to the PG Farm, which is not really a farm. It's a park and small zoo, with a playground, a few black bears and monkeys in cages, a pond with colorful goldfish, and an assortment of farm-type animals running around the yard. The day is warm but not too hot and the trees and grass make the air sweet and fresh.

We push Eric in his stroller. He's too young, at seven months, to really understand much about the animals or the park. When a small goat comes up to him and nuzzles his face, he starts to giggle and pats the goat on its nose—which makes the goat step backward and look with surprise at this small boy. Kay and I laugh.

Thorina loves the PG farm. I've taken her here many times over the last year. She walks up to each of the animals and talks to them in their own "language"—she says "oink oink" to a family of pigs and "baa baa" to a group of little lambs. Thorina's not afraid of the animals at all. She runs around petting the goats, sheep and even the baby pigs that run loose around the park.

Jerry and Thorina

Dusk fills the sky now. It's early evening. Sibelius' music is playing on the record player. I'm lying on one couch in our living room. Our baby, Eric, is lying on his back on the other couch, which is perpendicular and adjacent to mine. Eric turns his head to the side, and we look over at one another, gazing into each other's eyes.

Thorina is in her highchair and Kay is feeding her. I hear the click-click of the spoon, between dish and teeth, Kay saying "Um, um" with each bite.

I have a profound sense of contentment—a "this is home" feeling.

Eric at seven months is fat and healthy. He begins playing with his toes, gurgling, putting his toes then his fingers into his mouth.

I have a sweet, tender feeling for Eric, so tender for the baby that it's excruciating, and I clench my teeth to contain my emotion. I look at his fat legs and his toothless smile, his pure blonde hair. His blue eyes are full of the morning lake in Upstate New York. His minute but perfect hands are always opening and closing, reaching for life.

Kay puts him on the floor, and he holds himself up on his arms, looking turtle-like. Craning his neck, his oversized head arched back, he smiles.

Then Eric goes off to bed, carried in Kay's arms. He looks back at me, wide-eyed, over her shoulder.

I go to say goodnight to Thorina. She's lying in her crib in the darkness, sucking on her milk bottle. I sing her a song. It's a tuneless song that recounts what she and I did together in the day. "Went to the PG farm, saw animals, a turkey that goes gobble, gobble, gobble. We went for a walk and picked flowers and put them in your hair." Then we start the alphabet song. The final refrain of the song is always the same, to the tune of 'Sweet Chariot'. "Close your eyes very tight and sleep right through the night. Good night, sweet Thorina, don't wake up until the morning."

Tomorrow, early, I leave for Saigon.

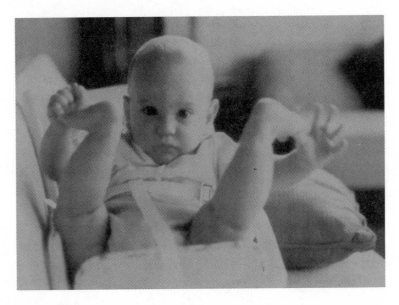

Eric

79

A GOOD BEGINNING

May 1, 1965—my first day. As I enter the three-story government building, I show my pass to the guard who stands stiffly in the oversized doorway. He waves me in with barely a glance at my face. I get on the elevator to go up to the third floor. The elevator is ancient with crisscross metal folding doors and creaking hinges.

As soon as I step off the elevator I'm greeted by Chi, who is Bui Diệm's assistant and will work with me in this new position. His full name is Nguyen Huu Chi. A tall, smiling man, he towers over me; he really is tall, six feet. Chi is twenty-eight, a graduate of Michigan State University. He is friendly and enthusiastic, but he says, "I've been sitting in this office for ten weeks and I haven't had much to do." He brings me into his office, which is small and hot, a cubbyhole, one desk, a white telephone and a shabby typewriter.

"Jerry!" Bui Diệm calls for me. I go into his office, which is next to Chi's cubby and much larger. He tells me they've been very busy with the cabinet reshuffle. "Quat is going to become Minister of Defense as well as Prime Minister," he says quickly. This move worries me. I wonder how effective Quat will be if he juggles a mixture of responsibilities. But I say nothing, at least for now. Bui Diệm asked me to be honest, so later I will comment.

"When can I see Quat?"

"Why not now?" Bui Diệm says. We go one floor down to see the Prime Minister, my old doctor, the man I've known since 1959. I still remember our first meeting. I was a new professor and was quite ill, a throbbing pain in my side. And Quat was wonderful, hardworking and idealistic, refusing to let me pay him.

The last time I was in this office, I had come to interview General Khanh, when he was the Prime Minister. The room looks a little different now. Quat has moved the desk so that it's in the center of the room rather than toward the back end. Being here, not as a journalist but as an advisor, is surreal.

Quat welcomes me warmly, using *"vous"* not *"tu"* as Bui Diệm does with me. Quat is wearing a gray suit with a dotted tie. He's a distinguished looking man in his 50s, with a high forehead and intense dark eyes. We chat briefly. Quat says he wants to form a "good team." But then he shakes his head impatiently. "This business of reshuffling the cabinet takes up all our time. But it will all get settled soon and then we'll work hard."

Bui Diệm and I go together to find an office for me in a building right next to the Prime Ministry. We find a large office with a large wooden desk and paneled walls. It has two air conditioners, three telephones and an intercom system. The office once belonged to a general.

My second day at the Prime Ministry and my office is roaring cold. The air conditioning is on full blast; there's no way to adjust it. Chi comes in. We look out the window and see tanks. Is a *coup* about to happen? I feel my throat constrict, as if I've just swallowed a chicken bone. I turn to Chi and murmur, "Oh no . . ." We call and ask Bui

Diệm. "Don't worry," he says with a laugh, "What you see is just a training exercise."

An hour later, as I sit at my desk, Chi marches into my office with a yellow file folder clutched in his fist. "You really have to see this," he says and throws it on my lap. It's a document in both English and Vietnamese, and it makes my heart jump. A group of people in Binh Thuan Province in Central Vietnam have signed their names on a long list of complaints. They are members of the Animal Husbandry Service. They are filing complaints against the Animal Husbandry Chief. In any province, this is an important man. He's the one who distributes seed and livestock. What their complaints amount to is corruption, a misappropriation of funds—that this Animal Husbandry Chief has been taking illegal profits from his official activities.

What makes this case unusual is that the people signed their names. Because they didn't trust their own provincial officials, they went with their complaints to the American AID representative in their province. AID—the U.S. Agency for International Development—is intended to foster economic growth, civil society, education, health, and social services. The villagers who submitted their petition knew that if they had gone to their regular provincial authorities nothing would happen. I hold the documents in my hand—they burn my fingers. We need to liberate these people from that corrupt chief. And we need to take care of this this now!

Chi and I rush over to Bui Diệm's office. "We have to meet with the Prime Minister," I say, "this is urgent." And so, we go right then.

Prime Minister Quat looks up surprised as the three of us charge into his office. I hand the folder to Quat and Bui Diem. Speaking rapidly, I explain the situation and make a proposal, "We need an immediate private investigation, a real investigation, not a sham. This is your chance to show what your government can and will do." I say this in a loud voice, emphasizing each word.

As Bui Diệm and Quat read over the documents, they both nod. "Yes, yes," they say together. Quat says, "You are right—this needs immediate attention. We will set up a special committee to run the investigation."

Bui Diem adds, "I will call the AID man in Binh Thuan Province and we'll make this happen." As he says these words, I have a sense of exultation. This is what we need to do—we'll have an impact on the lives of real people.

Chi and I return with Bui Diệm to his office. We talk for an hour about the details—how to make the investigation honest and effective, how the central government should be involved, who should be informed in the province and what should be kept confidential. We draft a memo that outlines in detail how to instigate an independent inquiry, to be directed by the provincial American AID office in coordination with the central government.

I walk out of the office with a sense of elation. I've only been in this position for two days—it's a good beginning.

This is why I'm here. This is exactly why I have this role, making a bridge between the Americans and the Vietnamese government. If we can truly help these villagers rid themselves of a corrupt provincial administrator, this will be a major accomplishment for the Quat government.

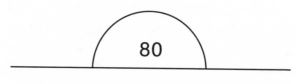

80

EDUCATION IS THE KEY

That night, I can't fall sleep. The windows rattle from a 155-artillery piece in the distance. Somewhere there's fighting; the war is going on around us. After the day's intense work, I feel restless and energized—what can we do next?

I get up and work on a speech for Quat. The theme of the speech is a proposal for a scholarship program for poor children. The idea is for the Prime Minister to make this address on the radio. The speech begins: "Compatriots, Vietnam needs social reform. Today the difference in standard of living is far too great between the poor farmer in the countryside and the rich businessman in the city. . . Equal opportunity for all is the key to social reform. Education is the key to equal opportunity. . ."

The next morning, I have a brief meeting with Bui Diem and Quat and hand them the draft of the radio speech. Quat says he's "extremely interested" in the scholarship program. He will record this speech for a radio broadcast in four days, at the end of the week, on Friday. Chi will translate the speech from French into Vietnamese. I have a sense of excitement—this could be huge.

—

But when I get to the office on Friday, I can't even meet with either Bui Diem or Quat. Their doors are shut, and they're cloistered in a meeting with the Vietnamese generals. I'm not invited to this meeting.

I look out my window late in the afternoon and notice one general riding off in his car, looking glum. *Uh oh*, I think, *trouble*. The meeting is still going on when I leave at 7:00 p.m. So, I still don't know what's going on.

The next morning, Bui Diệm tells me the news: The Armed Forces Council has been dissolved. It gives the authority of government back to civilians, puts it clearly in the hands of Quat. "Felicitations," I say to Bui Diệm. He just nods at me but doesn't particularly smile.

But, later, when I congratulate Quat, he smiles happily, like a cat swallowing a goldfish. For him, I suppose, it's a political *tour de force*.

Quat doesn't get around to recording the speech about the scholarship program.

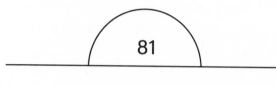

THE BLACK BOX

A few days later, I have a private meeting with Quat. He's wearing a light gray suit. We talk for an hour, ranging over many subjects. We're sitting in two armchairs in front of his large desk. A large window on one wall overlooks the city street below us with its bustle of shops, traffic, and pedestrians. The glass muffles the loud noises of people shouting, the roar of motorcycles, and the honking of horns.

Quat points to the green leather swivel chair behind his desk. "One of the main reasons so many people want this chair," he says, "is because of the huge *caisse noir*, black box." Quat explains that the *caisse noir* is swollen with funds inherited from Ngô Đình Diệm and has been passed down. Various provincial and country leaders have filled their pockets from it, but now he intends to put the whole amount into building houses for soldiers. He has a scheme worked out in some detail.

His hope and dream, he says, is to establish a firm foundation among the people. He notes, wryly, "After all, one day we will have elections."

There never have been free elections in South Vietnam.

—

I've been in my Advisor position for two weeks. On Monday, when I walk into Bui Diem's office, I notice he's wearing the same russet brown suit that he wears every day. It's neatly pressed—but always the same suit. Bui Diem says, "This week is very busy—cabinet reshuffle, clearing the army—then we can get to work." I hear the same old song every day. The days drag on, with little to show. I'm thinking, *Time will tell. And time is also telling . . .*

"It's a mistake," I tell Bui Diem. "You shouldn't neglect the rest of the country."

"I warned you," he says, "you'd lose patience with us before we lost patience with you."

As we're talking, the telephone rings. Bui Diệm is speaking with someone and suddenly, he's furious, shouting into the telephone, picking up a box of matches and slamming it down on his desk over and over.

Finally, he bangs down the phone. He looks up at me and says, "They refuse to resign! We announced the new cabinet two days ago. Duong, the Minister of Economy, and Thuc, the Minister of Interior, are supposed to be replaced. But they refuse to sign the agreement for handing over their ministries. It's infuriating!"

"What are you going to do?"

"I don't know," he sighs. This is a sticky legal problem. Without a popular election, what is the legal authority for this government?

I leave Bui Diệm with his telephones ringing. He's slumped over the telephones, a look of despair on his face. "This is hell," he says as I walk out the door.

82

RUMORS

Huan and I are walking down the Rue Catinat. It's a beautiful street—known as the Champs Elysees of Saigon, with swirls of trees, arched doorways and overhanging balconies. The air is hot and sunny, and everyone seems to be outdoors. The terrace bars and coffee shops are full, and the aromas of coffee, wine and assorted delicacies greet us as we pass. The roads are crowded with pedestrians, bicycles, rumbling motorcycles and cars which miraculously wend their way as through a maze.

"All I hear are rumors," Huan says. "There's going to be another *coup d'etat*—and soon."

"Ah, yes," I sigh, "I hear those rumors too. I've been here almost a month, since the beginning of May, and the Quat government is stuck—nothing gets done. And it's too bad. There are so many things Quat could do to show himself different. But he's playing politics. The old game. The old, fascinating game."

I want to scream. And I know Huan feels the same way.

Huan looks over at me and asks with a grim expression on his face, "What do you think will happen? Do you think Quat is done? Will there be more assassinations?"

"God knows," I say. "It's not good. There's a restlessness in the country. I feel it in my fingertips."

The next day, when I meet with Len Maynard in the USOM office, he says, "The price of rice is skyrocketing. What's to be done about this shortage of rice in Saigon?" Len sits at his desk tapping a pencil nervously. Without giving me a chance to respond, Len goes on, "Okay, there are two solutions—two ways to stabilize the price of rice: either import U.S. rice, or force the peasants in the delta to sell their rice at lower prices."

"You don't really want to advocate gunpoint persuasion, do you?"

But Len quickly says, "Oh yes, that's really what we need."

I wince. "That's not the way to win over the hearts and minds of the people," I say, with some irony. But Len Maynard isn't listening to me.

That evening I'm at dinner at L'Amiral Restaurant with Mal Browne, one of my journalist friends. We order *bisque de crabe, steak au poivre vert, vacherin glacé,* with Pernod to start. We talk about my recent conversation with Maynard. "Gunpoint persuasion," I say, "where will it all end?"

Browne nods grimly. "We're at a dangerous juncture, I think. The Vietnamese already resent the Americans. Now huge numbers of American soldiers are being rushed into Vietnam. What's going to happen when Americans start killing a lot of Vietnamese people?"

"I sense it," I say. "There's an uneasy sense in the Saigon air. The Vietnamese are becoming more and more anti-American."

"And there's going to be a vast increase in Viet Cong terrorism," Browne says. "We all know it's coming. I've been working on a story about pen-assassination guns. A few weeks ago, the police in Saigon uncovered a set of three Parker pens that were really small guns. They were supposed to be mailed as 'presents' to American officials in Saigon."

I say, "I've been carrying a gun, a gat, a small pistol. In the evening, when I enter my apartment, I carefully go through the place: bathrooms, kitchen, and balconies. I sleep with the gun on my bed stand. Yesterday evening, the servant came in late and I almost plugged him. Dangerous business—a gun."

At just that moment, Captain Xuan, who was sitting at the next table with two other men, walks up to us. I know Xuan slightly—he's an officer in the Vietnamese navy. Xuan taps me on the shoulder and announces, "There'll be a coup within two weeks and Vice Premier Tuyen will replace Quat. Quat must fall." He returns to his own place, and the three men sit at their table, huddled like conspirators.

I look over at these men and shudder. *Are they planning a coup?* I wonder and worry. I shake my head and say to Browne, "This is the curse and sickness of Vietnam."

Two days later, when I walk into the office, Bui Diem announces, "Last night—there was an attempted coup!"

"What!"

"It was Colonel Thao again. He had people infiltrating Quat's own bodyguard. They wanted to kill Quat and me and some others." Colonel Thao had tried to oust General Khanh, in another attempted coup, several months ago.

"What happened?"

"The marines and police protected us. They knew about the plan. A marine lieutenant showed up at our office and told us to come with him. We spent the night in marine headquarters. Then the police went looking for the conspirators. I heard they rounded up most of them." Bui Diệm looks keyed up and excited and doesn't seem at all tired even though he was up all night.

"So, it's over and you're okay." I'm shaken. This was a strange and vicious plan.

"Yes, the coup failed."

I congratulate Bui Diệm.

One *coup d'état* has failed. Will there be another?

83

A MISUNDERSTANDING

I miss Kay and the children. I feel adrift without them. We send tapes back and forth as our "letters." When friends travel between Saigon and Hong Kong, they carry our tapes. So, we can hear each other's voices.

I even talk with my little girl on the tapes. "How's my Thorina girl? Get your book, Thorina. A is for apple. B is for ball. C is for Cat. What is D—that's right. D is for Dog. E is what you eat in the morning—an Egg. Daddy loves his Thorina and gives Thorina a kiss. Have you gone to the beach with Mommy? Did you play with a bucket in the sand? Daddy wants to sing you a Nighty Night song... [singing voice] Good night my Thorina and sleep right through the night . . .Good night Thorina . . ."

Kay and Thorina are coming to Saigon—they'll arrive next Thursday. We've talked about this, back and forth. Should they come or not? I miss them terribly. I get this awful yearning to be with them. It's Kay who insists that she come with Thorina, so we'll have a little a little vacation together. Eric will stay back home with Cheong Jun, our number one *amah*. It would be too difficult to manage with the two children and Eric is still very little.

Six weeks have passed since I began my position in the Prime Ministry. This morning, Chi comes into my office with a dark look on his face. "Damn," he says, gritting his teeth. He hands me a long memo—a response to the list of complaints against the Animal Husbandry Chief in Binh Thuan Province. This memo apparently was drafted by officials in the province. The memo describes the issue to be investigated and then goes on: "We investigated the situation thoroughly. We conducted many interviews of the parties involved, including the farmers who registered the complaints and Mr. Nguyen Van Duc, the Animal Husbandry Chief. We also reviewed account records and assessed the distribution of monies. We find no evidence of inappropriate use of funds. We conclude that this was a misunderstanding. The complainants decided to withdraw their complaint."

As I read the report, I look over to Chi. "This has turned into a complete whitewash."

"Of course," he says, "the accused official was alerted and those villagers who made the complaints were cowed into silence."

Gritting my teeth, I say, "They call it a misunderstanding . . ."

I feel the blood rushing from my heart and wonder, *How did this happen? How did all our good plans go awry so quickly?*

I don't say anything to Chi. I just pick up my sport jacket, nothing else, no papers, and I walk out of my office, go out into the street. Holding my jacket flung over my shoulder, I walk past offices, shops and cafés. But nothing looks real to me. I imagine the faces of those brave farmers who signed a complaint, who made the effort to speak to Americans, in whom they placed their hopes.

84

HERE IN NHA TRANG ALL IS PEACEFUL

It's a few evenings later, and I'm having dinner at the My Canh Floating Restaurant with Kay and Thorina. Despite the rumbling rumors of a coup and the guerilla war in the countryside, Kay has come to Saigon with our little girl.

It's early evening and the sky is still bright and fresh, and the water all around us shimmers with multicolored lights from the sky, the boats and the city. The My Canh, overlooking the Saigon River, is the most romantic of restaurants. Our waiter this evening is Phuong, a young man with bright white teeth and straight dark hair falling over his forehead. He brings our little Thorina a "Mickey-Finn"—a ginger ale with a maraschino cherry at the bottom.

Thorina, in her highchair, picks up a single chop stick and tries to stab a chunk of lobster meat, chasing the piece around her plate. She gives up finally, picks it up with her delicate fingers and takes a small bite, making an expression with her nose that combines curiosity, distrust, and the beginnings of pleasure. Kay and I laugh together, as we watch her sweet efforts to explore the world.

As we sit eating our dessert of fried bananas, we see the sun set over the river and the full moon rise up from the water with extraordinary beauty.

After dinner, we go back to Hy and Simone's house where we're staying for now. Kay takes Thorina up to bed. Huan and I step outside into the garden. He's feeling very pushed-to-the-wall because of the continuing cabinet crisis. "The military should just take over and settle the thing," he says, pacing back and forth.

"The military?" I'm surprised that Huan has come to this conclusion.

"At least they're logical. They make sense. I was at a meeting with the generals at the Prime Ministry. General Ky spat at us, 'You politicos in Saigon squabble over nonsense, and my soldiers are dying.' Then he just got up and left, saying 'Now I'm going back to the front.'"

"Is that what you really want—government by the generals, by the military?" I ask.

Huan grimaces. "The politicians are mired in muck. So, the generals should take over and be done with it."

Leaning against the wall of the house, I don't say anything for a while. I don't agree with Huan on this. I don't see that as a solution. I start to say, "What we need, I think, are political institutions." But then I'm silent again. How is this supposed to happen?

Kay comes downstairs and finds us outdoors. In a soft voice, she asks, "Jerry, what's happening?" She doesn't speak French, but I think she intuits that something is wrong.

"It's a mess," I say, "both the Quat government and the country."

She asks, "Is the situation really so bleak?" Truthfully, I don't know how to answer her.

Lying in bed in the evening, we hear artillery, which sounds rather close. Kay wonders, "Should we go to Nha Trang? Is the fighting happening up there? Will we be safe?"

"I think it's okay in that area. I haven't heard reports of battles in that area. And we need this vacation—we badly need this little vacation."

Neither of us sleeps well this night.

In the morning, when I meet with Bui Diệm, the first thing I notice is that he has finally changed suits. For several weeks now, he has been wearing the same brown suit, neat, never mussed, but nevertheless the same one. Today he's in a cream-colored suit. I wonder, briefly, if it might be a sign of better times or better spirit.

"The crisis will be over soon," he says. Bui Diệm has been meeting with the generals. He refuses to give me details about the military's intentions. I suspect he knows. As I walk out of his office, he waves and says, "Maybe I'll join you in Nha Trang."

In the early evening, I get a call from Jim Wilde. "Well, Rose, I hear you're out of a job. Quat just resigned." He sounds serious.

I tell him, "Stop listening to the old rumor mill." But does he know something that I don't?

We've come to the beach in Nha Trang, on the South China Sea. Kay and I met here four years ago. We decided it would be nice to return at least one more time. And besides, we need this vacation, the first real one we've taken in years.

And so, we're here. The sea this morning is calm as a lake; the sky is a gasp of blue. We see Swallow Island, in the mist, out in the sea. But in the surrounding mountains, we hear guns shooting. We're told these are just soldiers training.

Thorina comes up from the sea's edge to lay a red stone on my knee. Now she dashes off again and finds a small fish and a bird's feather.

"A good feather," she says,

And Kay agrees, smiling and nodding, "Yes, it's a good feather."

Elsewhere, throughout Vietnam, the war is raging. But here in Nha Trang all is peaceful. The sun. The sea. In the evening, we eat lobster and drink white wine.

From our hotel, I place a phone call to Bui Diệm. I hear a darkness in his voice as he says, "It's over. Quat resigned. The new Prime Minister is General Ky."

I ask, "Should I hurry back?"

"No, there's nothing for you to do here for now. Just enjoy your family and your vacation."

I ask Bui Diệm, "What are you planning to do?"

"I'm not sure," he says.

My emotions are jumbled—disappointment, confusion, despair. My government job is over, almost before it began. I have a hollow feeling, as if something has been carved out of me—my hopes and dreams for what I might have done, how I might have helped shape Vietnam's future. All this is gone now.

But we're here, on vacation—Kay, Thorina and I. We'll enjoy the sun and the sand, with worries and jobs far away. Nha Trang is lovely.

South China Sea

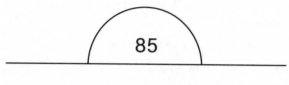

85

FOR A WHILE

Kay and Thorina return to Hong Kong, where it's safe, where it's quiet. They go home earlier than we had planned. We decide it would be best, under the circumstances, both the war and the political situation.

I've been in this position less than six weeks. I assume I'll pack up and be out of a job.

I go to see Bui Diệm. The first thing he says is, "I'm staying in the government. Prime Minister Ky asked me to be Special Assistant for Planning and Foreign Aid. He wants me to help keep good relations with the Americans. So, I'm staying."

"How does Quat feel about your staying on with the new government?"

Bui Diệm smirks and says, "Dr. Quat advised me to take the job. He told me, 'It would be better if we could keep at least some eye on these guys.'"

"Well," I say, "I'll pack up my things."

"Actually, I'd like you to continue in your position as Advisor."

"Really?"

"Just stay on for a while," he says. "I need you. You can help with the transition."

Honestly, I don't know how I feel about this. I answer, "For a while—I guess I could stay on for a while."

It takes a week but finally I get my first meeting with General Ky. We shake hands and go immediately to the far end of the room and sit on a couch. There are no polite phrases of introduction.

I speak quickly, giving him a brief rundown on what I've been doing, what I think I can do, and how I might help him. Then, we talk about general things: education, U.S. aid. All during our twenty minutes, I'm on edge. I sit straight and taut, never really settling into the leather couch. I wonder if Ky is interested at all in what I have to say. He's a military man. Does he care about education and making life better for his people? Or maybe because he's a general and is accustomed to making decisions and giving orders, he could make things happen. Maybe.

We talk in English. His vocabulary is good. He speaks very quietly in articulate English, now and again hesitating to search for the word he wants.

Ky, who is smoking Salem cigarettes, wears his air force uniform, khaki with light green shoulder braids and black epaulettes. He is a cool man. That is the overwhelming impression he gives: cool and clean, perhaps even cold. His eyes are opaque. The appointment lasts all of twenty minutes, beginning at one o'clock and going until 1:20.

Sitting across from this man, whom I really don't know at all, I have the oddest feeling. It's as if I've been on a merry-go-round. I've been spun around and around. When I get off, I'm at the same place where I started—the same government building, the same office with its large, imposing desk—and everything is completely different.

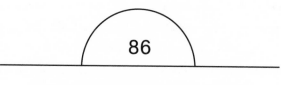

86

A SLEEPING CHILD

Today is hot with heavy rainstorms in the afternoon and then a deluge of sun, and then another rainstorm. By the time I get home in the evening, I feel begrimed with sweat, and slightly claustrophobic from the low-cloud sky and enclosing heat. I shower immediately and the cold water helps; and the cool tiles on my bare feet helps; and drying myself in the wind of the ceiling fan helps. For a moment, then, naked under the ceiling fan, I feel clean, utterly clean, uncluttered and fresh.

Then I hear the first explosion, like an angry uplifting and falling of a stack of lumber. I begin to dress rapidly. Then comes a second explosion. Exactly one minute later. In another minute I'm dressed and on my way out. My heart is galloping and I'm thinking, *Oh no . . . oh no . . .another attack in the city.*

As I run out into the street, I find people rushing toward the river front. I stop an American, walking in the opposite direction, and ask "What happened?"

"A bomb . . .two bombs . . ." He has a look of horror in his eyes.

"Where?"

"It was at the My Canh Floating Restaurant."

Something inside me gasps. *Oh my god, my god, I was there with Kay and Thorina just a few days ago.* It was so lovely, so peaceful, that evening, under the night sky, enjoying our meal, moored along the river at the elegant My Canh Floating Restaurant. And now . . .

I hurry on, wending my way among throngs of people, bicycles and motor bikes. The evening air is hot and heavy. Though I've just showered, my shirt is already damp with sweat. Sirens begin to lift their voices like mourners' wails. A hysteria of sirens.

As I come near to the river, I find a tight line of police and soldiers in crisp uniforms encircling the My Canh. They try to keep the crowd back. All around me, people are yelling and shoving. The scent of smoke, blood, and sweat shimmers in the hot air. I have a crushing sense of déjà vu—it was just a couple of months ago when I stood outside the American Embassy witnessing another scene of horror.

I'm on the opposite side of the street from the My Canh. Headlights from the ambulances illuminate bodies, heaped like mounds of wet red pulp on the gangplank leading up to the floating restaurant. I can barely breathe, and bile rises in my throat as I recognize a waiter from the restaurant—Phuong is his name. He's being hefted into an ambulance. His body is raw and red, as if his skin has been ripped off. Just the other day, Phuong had a bright smile as he sauntered over to our table, holding a small glass of ginger ale with a cherry floating inside and handing it to our little Thorina.

Horst Faas, the German photographer, is taking pictures. His strobe light flashes, flashes, adding to the panic of the scene. It's as if there's a haze in front of my eyes, blurring my vision—my eyes are welling with tears.

On the side of the street where I'm standing, a tall Caucasian man lies on his back, badly bloodied on the left side of his body. One leg is drawn up and he keeps moving it back and forth with a rhythmic groan.

And then there's the child.

She's in the shadows, lying on the pavement. She's about ten years old. She wears black silky pants and a flowered blouse. She lies face down. Her right arm is neatly by her side. Her left arm is extended outward, palm up. She's a sleeping child. She looks like she's sleeping. Except for the already-coagulated streak of blood that has trickled out of her mouth, she seems untouched by the ravage of the explosion.

Perhaps she's just unconscious, I think. I squat next to her and lift her left arm. My hand is trembling. My whole body is quivering. She's not moving. I try her pulse. There is none. I put her arm back into the same position, palm up.

With tears streaming down my face, I stand up. Light, laughter cut short; all the child's glee gone. The girl continues to sleep at my feet. She lies dead in the street.

And the picture continues to burn and hurt. I think she will always remain with me, a sleeping child somewhere within me.

The next morning Bui Diệm tells me, "I was eating dinner in the Club Nautique, next door to the My Canh, when the explosion happened. Five minutes earlier, I had crossed the street exactly where the second bomb went off. I'm alive because of five minutes." He shakes his head. "Fate," he says.

I feel a creeping despair. I desperately miss Kay and the children. What am I doing here? Am I really accomplishing anything with this advisory job? Maybe, if I just make it through this year, I'll pack up the family. We'll leave Asia and never come back.

NO HEROES

I run into Jim Wilde on the street late one evening. He starts waving his hands wildly. "It's all coming," he says, "a quarter of a million American soldiers, a dozen engineering battalions and huge war bases. It's going to be the ruination of this country. And really, for the U.S., it's all about China. That's the whole objective of the buildup. China. No one cares about Vietnam." I hear the panic in his loud voice.

We're both on our way to the Hotel Continental, so we walk side by side, passing bars and restaurants with bright colored lights and the sounds of music and chatter emanating from the doorways.

I share Wilde's sense of impending doom. "The U.S. is sick in its head if it attempts to swamp this country with a huge number of troops," I say with gritted teeth. "The Vietnamese don't trust the Americans. And with good reason. Because the Americans are running this war the way they want, without caring what the Vietnamese think or do. This is a grave mistake and will backfire." I shudder, thinking about what this will mean—a huge war, a disaster.

And what Wilde tells me next leaves me with even more of a sense of anguish and despair. He's just gotten back from working on a med evac story. He says, "Here were Americans supposedly engaged in a lifesaving mission. And the pilot kept referring to the Vietnamese as 'slope heads.' And then this same pilot said he wants to go to the Congo 'to kill niggers.' There are no heroes here."

We stop by a kiosk on the street and buy an evening paper. The lead story: "U.S. Marines kill at least 100 Vietnamese civilians, including many children." As we hold the newsprint in our hands, Wilde and I look at one another and shake our heads in unison. "This is going to be seen here as an American atrocity," I say. "This is exactly what I've feared—that everything the Americans are doing will make matters worse."

The next day, when I walk into Bui Diệm's office, I find him tired and depressed, like me. He's sneezing; he has a mild cold. He says, "We can't talk as frankly to these generals as we did with Quat." A cosmic understatement.

Later, when I'm back in my office, in the adjacent building, I get a phone call from Bui Diệm. With panic in his voice, he says, "Jerry, I need you badly." I go over immediately. Bui Diệm shows me a newspaper report from the *London Daily Worker*. It cites an interview with Ky from several months ago in the *Sunday Mirror*. Ky is quoted as saying "People ask me who my heroes are. I have only one hero—Hitler"!

"What!" I want to laugh—this is like theater of the absurd. But it's not funny, really not funny at all.

A tremendous storm has now broken in London. The British Ambassador pleads with Ky to make some denial. Bui Diệm and I draft a letter and emphasize that what he meant was just the sense of discipline. Even so.

The irony doesn't escape me. A Jewish son, whose mother and father emigrated from Poland just ahead of the Holocaust, is drafting a defense and excuse for a man who idolizes Hitler. I have the bitterest taste in my mouth.

I go back to my office, arrange my papers into neat piles, thinking about packing up. I can't go on with this job. It's time to move on.

88

AN INTERVIEW

Late one afternoon, when I walk into the Prime Ministry, I find Walter Cronkite sitting in the hallway. I know his face, which is larger than life. Walter Cronkite is an American icon. Even though I haven't lived in the States for the past six years, I've seen some of his broadcasts and I know his reputation.

"What's going on?" I ask.

"I'm here to interview Prime Minister Ky. But it seems he doesn't want to talk with me. The manager at CBS arranged this interview and then it was cancelled twice, both at the last moment. So, now I'm here and I've been kept waiting for two days."

I look at my watch. It's six o'clock. "Let's go have some dinner and then I'll get it straightened out for you in the morning."

I take Cronkite to the Guillaume Tell Restaurant. The Guillaume Tell is known for its fine French cuisine. We dine on *escargot, bisque, coquille St Jacque* and *crème brûlée*. But mostly it's a dinner full of Cronkite anecdotes. Cronkite's high forehead, slicked back hair and deep resonating voice are so familiar it's as if I've known him all my life. And although his demeanor is serious, he has a wonderful deep-throated laugh.

"One of my favorite interviews was with a puppet lion named Charlemane," he tells me. "This was for the *Morning Show*. We were talking about the news of the day. The Republican Party had just lost control of Congress, and the puppet said in a simpering-Southern accent, 'We had Congress in our pocket a few minutes ago and where did we put it?' A puppet can say true things that a human commentator would not feel free to utter."

When I ask Cronkite what was the most difficult newscast he ever did, I'm not surprised when he says, "The Kennedy assassination. I tried to control my emotion. But I was crying on national television . . ."

Cronkite and I talk about journalism and war-reporting. We've both followed troops and flown in bomber planes over war zones.

Cronkite stops talking and looks at me, with a sudden intensity. "What's happening here in Vietnam?" he asks. "Jerry, what do you think is really going on here?"

"Off the record," I say, "Truly off the record. In my current position, I can't be quoted with remarks about my bosses—either Vietnamese or American."

"Okay—off the record."

"It's not good. The Vietnamese have their problems. They have a military government now. But even the last civilian government was out of touch with their own people. I agreed to work with the government because I knew Dr. Quat and Bui Diem, and I believe they are good, honest people. But they couldn't get anything done. It was enormously frustrating. But what makes it all much worse is what the Americans are doing—sending masses of soldiers here to take over the war. It's a mess, a disaster in the making."

"So, you are pessimistic." Cronkite takes out a small notebook and pen and quickly jots down a few words.

"Don't quote me!" I say again, this time more loudly.

—

The next morning, I walk into Bui Diệm's office. "It's ridiculous," I say. "It would be good for the Prime Minister, good for Vietnam, and good for you and me, if this interview really happens. Ky speaks English well. This will give him an opportunity to talk with the American audience. And, anyway, it's bad press and embarrassing to ignore this famous newsman from CBS, one of the most watched networks in America."

So, Bui Diệm makes it happen. Cronkite spends more than an hour interviewing Ky. After it's all done, I see his producer, Ron Bond, in the hallway and he says, "I kid you not; it's one of the best interviews I've ever seen." They're planning a special show featuring this interview.

At least I've accomplished something for the new government.

Jim Wilde calls me. "Did you know?" he says. "Karnow has left *The Saturday Evening Post* and has joined the *Washington Post*." Not five minutes later, I get a call from another journalist friend with the same news. And then another journalist calls . . .

Later that same day, I send a cable to Dave Lyle at *The Post*. "I'm still working at the Prime Ministry," I tell him, "but if you want me, I'm ready to return to journalism for *The Post*."

My relationship with *The Post* has been difficult. Although I've published stories and photos over the last year in *The New York Times*, *The Reporter*, *New Republic*, *Life*, *Newsweek*, and *Time*, none of my work has been accepted for *The Post* in a year. They pulled me off the political article and didn't like my story about American civilians in Vietnam. So, I haven't fulfilled my four-article contract with them.

Dave replies, "We are in the business of putting words on otherwise blank pieces of paper, and we haven't gotten many usable ones from you in the last year. The only thing that I can do is propose an arrangement whereby you work off your indebtedness by writing pieces for *The Post* for which we would pay you one-half cash and one-half credit." I write back, accepting his proposal.

What all this means is that my battle with Karnow is over. I'll pick up where I left off. I'll do a story about American pilots and their dangerous missions. It's a story that needs to be told.

89

A LETTER TO MY SISTER

I t's 1:30 a.m. and Saigon is quiet except for the distance-muffled thud-
ding of artillery somewhere in the countryside and the whirring sound
of the ceiling fan just over my head. I'm reading a letter from Nancy—
our middle sister. Nancy is married, lives in Gloversville, and has two
children now. Her letter is full of family news about her children and
about Lucy's wedding. Lucy is getting married in December. As I hold
this flimsy blue aerogram in my hand, images of all of them float before
me—Mother, Daddy, Nancy, Lucy. I've never met Mark, Lucy's Kosher-
Jewish boyfriend and husband-to-be, so I can't imagine him.

My head is whirling slightly like the ceiling fan because *je viens de
chanter la* flute—I've been smoking opium with my good friend Vu
Khoan, Huan's brother-in-law. Smoking opium with Khoan, which
I do from time to time, gives me a sense of tranquility and contentment. We sit for hours over a few pipes and talk. It's a good feeling
and Khoan is a dear friend.

But opium tends to bring on insomnia. I have this tendency without smoking opium, and now *une nuit blanche* stretches before me. I
have an overwhelming impulse to write a long letter to Lucy and send
her my best big-brotherly advice—especially about marriage.

Dear sweet Lucy,

I think of you often. It's almost your birthday—September 15. You'll be 21. And you're getting married soon. I worry that you think I disapprove of your marriage. I don't disapprove—not at all.

You must know how I feel about you, and these feelings have never changed. You were as my own child, and so you remain. The child has grown and has therefore grown apart from the quasi-parent.

I want you to be happy. And I want Mark to be happy with you. If he is happy with you, then there is the greater likelihood that you too will be happy.

Marriage is a whole mountain range of Himalayan molehills. . . and suddenly you recall when you were a child of only eight and you wrote a beautiful poem, several good poems. Jerry said so and he should know because writing is his profession. And you ask yourself: Have I made the best of this world of things, and have I lived up to my potential? And what have I done that a million women and mothers couldn't do equally well?

What I am driving at is the need of the wife to develop herself independently of her husband. Plainly stated I mean: you had better choose an area of intellectual interest and work hard at perfecting that area, work toward professional perfection in that area—whether it's historical studies, or writing or choreography, it doesn't matter. What matters is that you have that serious interest which is independent of Mark.

To prepare yourself, I strongly urge that you continue your schooling for as long as possible. While Mark is still attending university, there is no reason in the world for you not to continue your studies.

Lucy dear, some parts of this letter may sound prophet-like or supercilious. *Please forgive that tone. But I'm deadly seri-ous about the meaning: marriage can be good, but the people involved must be good too, independent of each other.*

Your loving brother,

Jerry

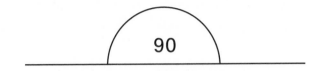

THE MOST COMPLICATED WAR

My father thinks he has a solution to the war in Vietnam. In his latest letter to me, he has a proposal: "to burn down all the jungles in Vietnam to get at the enemy."

I begin a letter to my father. "First, it's not really possible to burn down all the jungles. About 75% of Vietnam is jungle. And secondly, it's not desirable. The jungle is a source of wealth in this country, and if you destroy it, then you destroy much of the country, and if you destroy the country what's the use of fighting to save it?"

What strikes me is that a lot of our top American military men agree with this plan. But, of course, they are not Vietnamese and after they've finished ruining this nation, then they can go back to their nice houses and big cars and golf courses and be happy.

How do I explain this war to my father, who is back in our small quiet town in Upper New York State and who, like most Americans, is impatient for a quick solution? So, I write to my father about the intense political pressures in this country. "Sometimes it reminds me of a steam boiler about to explode because there are too many pressures. But the war is the biggest pressure, the war and the terrible suffering of the people. I think this must be the most complicated war the world has ever seen."

I tell Bui Diem I'm leaving my post as Advisor to the Vietnamese government. "This is not working out for me. I'm going back to journalism."

He nods and says, "You only said you'd stay for a while." Bui Diem is sitting at his desk, tapping his pencil on the scarred and scratched dark wood. "I have one more mission for you. This is important. You know Mr. Ung, the Minister of Rural Construction. He's going with General Hoang to visit refugee camps in and around Quang Ngai Province. I want you to go with him."

I shake my head. "What's the point?" I say. "How would my going there make any difference?"

"We have a severe refugee problem," Bui Diem continues.

"Yes, I know, I know. It's horrible."

"There's another matter," he says, "something you're very familiar with. There's rampant corruption in the provinces. I need you to investigate this—it's a major initiative for us. Help us figure out what to do. Go on this last trip with Minister Ung."

"Okay," I say at last.

Then he adds, "You'll go by plane. It's not safe to travel on the roads."

"When is this trip?"

"You leave on September 13. It'll be a short trip, just a couple days."

So, Ung and I visit a refugee camp in Quang Ngai Province. There are four hundred people stranded here, in a scratched-out field in the middle of a jungle—with straw mats and scraps of cardboard for tents, no running water. The children look thin and hungry. It breaks my heart. A woman comes running up to us and grasps my hand. "Help us!" she cries. I don't need to know very many words in Vietnamese to understand her message.

In my little red notebook, I outline a plan—tents and food, first. And I jot down an additional note—that the supplies need to be delivered directly to the people, out of the hands of corrupt provincial officials.

The people are threatened from all sides, from the Viet Cong who cajole and menace them, from their village officials that steal from them, from the national army which bombards them with bullets, and from the Americans who drop bombs, kill their children and ruin their land. So, they leave their villages to find a place of safety. And what is to be done? And where is a place of safety?

As I walk along the mud paths, I feel outraged—a burning sense of all that has gone wrong. There's a story to write—to tell the world about the suffering of these people. But that's not enough. We visit five camps—all of them grim and lacking in basic provisions for survival. Here is a chance for Americans to do some good—not with bullets and bombs but to bring supplies to help these people.

Our return flight on September 16 is on Air Vietnam, not a military plane. As we walk up the clanking metal stairs, I notice there are bolts missing on the wings. The plane looks battered, grimy and overused. The seats are shabby with holes in the fabric and spongey material popping through the cushions.

As we take our seats, I turn to Ung and remark, "I hope the engine is in better condition than these cushions."

EPILOGUE

LUCY'S STORY

I t was September 15, 1965, my birthday. I had just turned twenty-one. I was at my sister Nancy's home. She had made a birthday dinner in my honor, served on her Rosenthal china with delicate brown flowers. As we ate our slices of birthday cake, we talked about my wedding dress. It was handmade for me by a friend of my new mother-in-law-to-be. It was an unusual dress, Victorian in style, with luscious ivory-colored satin; the bodice was overlaid with lace and had a high ruffled collar and long sleeves. The wedding would be in winter, in December, just three months away.

The dress was hanging in my sister's closet. Everybody was clamoring for me to try it on. "We want to see how you look in your dress."

"Okay," I said and went upstairs, unwrapped my gown with its miles of silky fabric, and gently slipped it over my head.

I was thin in those days, threadlike. I had lost weight on my trip to Asia. Mother remarked if I turned sideways, you couldn't see me. I came down the stairs slowly, careful not to trip. There was no mirror in Nancy's living room, but I could see reflected in everyone's eyes— my dress was lovely.

So, I was standing in my sister's living room, wearing satin and lace, all smiles, anticipating my wedding day.

At just that moment, my brother died.

Or so I imagined. We never knew the exact time, but it was September 16 in Vietnam, across the International Dateline, and that would have been the 15th in our time—my birthday.

The telephone rang early the next morning. It was a sunny, bright day, with a September morning chill. Mother and I had been packing the car. It was my senior year in college, and I was getting ready to leave. Mother was wearing her brown baggy slacks; her hair, not combed yet, was still pinned down with a few bobby pins.

She was on the phone, staring at her own face in the hall mirror. "Oh no. Oh no." Her face was flushed; her blue eyes had a look of horror.

I stood next to her, hovering. "What is it? What's happening?" And then, I just knew. It was about Jerry. Jerry was dead.

The announcer from the local radio station was about to go on the air with a news item, a plane crash in Vietnam. Among those killed were the Vietnamese Minister of Rural Reconstruction, a Vietnamese general, and an American Advisor to the government of Vietnam, Jerry Rose from Gloversville. He called us as a courtesy just before making his public announcement.

The neighbors from Baker Street came first, the women in house dresses. They came to cry with us. Later, my sister Nancy was there with her baby, her son Adam, in his carrying case. The baby, just four months old, was sweet and smiling; we could coddle him and forget for a moment. Kay telephoned from Hong Kong; her voice weak over the long-distance connection. Mother said to her, "I know, darling, I know."

Later that morning, a package came. It was a heavy box, wrapped in brown paper. The return address said Simon and Schuster. Mother laid the box on the dining room table and unwrapped it slowly, her hands trembling. Inside were a dozen books and a card that read, "Courtesy of the author." They were copies of Jerry's just published book—*Reported to be Alive*. Mother, leaning over the dining room table, holding one copy with its red, black and white cover, said, "It should be called 'Reported to be Dead.'"

I had received a five-page letter from Jerry about a week ago. He wrote about my marriage and my future. He wanted me to continue my education and pursue a professional career. His ideas were progressive and feminist, unusual for the time, in 1965. Jerry's letter was full of big-brotherly advice and love—enough to last me a lifetime.

The morning after receiving his letter, I sat down at Mother's little rusted metal typing desk, which was under a window in Jerry's old bedroom. I typed a long letter to him, slowly, with many corrections, on erasable onionskin paper. "I want you to know," I wrote, "I'm planning to get a Masters' Degree in Asian Studies." My husband-to-be was already at the University of California, Berkeley. I would apply for an interdisciplinary program in Southeast Asian Studies at Berkeley. I was following my brother's advice, even before he had given it. I thought he would be pleased.

Jerry never received my letter.

On the day that we received news of the plane crash, my father was in the hospital, recovering from surgery. Walking down the hospital corridor with Mother and my sister Nancy to tell him about his son's death was the longest journey of my life. I can't remember what words we used. He was hard of hearing. I suppose the words had to be repeated. He had been heavily sedated before we gathered around his bed. He looked stunned but he didn't cry much. It was as if he couldn't focus his mind and the medication blurred his understanding.

Two days later, when he was home from the hospital, he opened a letter addressed to him from Jerry. Holding the flimsy aerogram stationery in his trembling hand, he read the letter over and over, and he couldn't stop weeping. It was a loud, weeping howl.

After Jerry died, when I went back to the university, I found a thin package in my mailbox. The address was written in brown ink, in Jerry's handwriting. My hands shook as I undid the clasp, opened the envelope and pulled out Jerry's book of photographs, *Face of Anguish*. He wanted me to have my own copy. Like my father, I cried and cried. I stood among crowds of students picking up their mail, with tears steaming on my cheeks. Someone leaned over to me and asked, "Are you okay?" I shook my head, but I couldn't speak a word.

A couple weeks later, I came home for the memorial service. Kay, Thorina, and Eric had already arrived. Kay looked worn and thin. Her face was pallid and her eyes leaden. When we hugged each other, we were both crying.

We had a full house and had to sort out rooms and beds. The children were in my room. Kay and I shared Jerry's bedroom.

We had a memorial service at the synagogue. One of Jerry's friends from high school gave the eulogy, which no one could hear because he wept throughout his speech. On the sidewalk, just outside the synagogue, we met the parents of Morrow Solomon, Jerry's high school friend who had died two years earlier. Eva Solomon took my mother in her arms, "Both our sons gone," she sobbed. Standing on that sidewalk, we had a duet of grief, theirs and ours.

The Saturday Evening Post published a long obituary in their November 1965 issue, written by Jerry's friend and colleague, Malcolm Browne.

Jerry Rose, who died here September 16 was an exceptional man. Jerry never followed the journalistic herd that gets its news from official briefings and handouts. He liked to work alone and fight his battles alone. He was constantly in the field, generally under fire and in danger.

The last six years of Jerry's life, right up to the plane crash in which he died, were linked to the destiny of Vietnam. In the end, he died not as a correspondent but in the service of the Vietnamese and American governments, on leave from the profession of journalism. He was a civilian soldier.

It takes all kinds of heroes to make a war.

Very few Americans had heard of Vietnam when Jerry first went there in 1959. At the time my brother died, in 1965, the massive influx of American troops was just beginning. Jerry worried about this—he knew it was all wrong.

Over the next ten years, almost sixty thousand young Americans would die in Vietnam and the youth back in the United States exploded with anti-war protests. The war left Vietnam in ruins, both North and South—an estimated three million Vietnamese, soldiers and civilians, were killed. In the United States, Vietnam would become a metaphor in our vocabulary—a term synonymous with failure. Jerry witnessed how this all began. He would have been horrified, but I don't think he would have been entirely surprised at the outcome. He saw the U.S. policy, with the huge influx of American troops, as wrong. "The U.S." he had said, "is sick in its head . . . "

A blizzard battered Upper New York State on the night before my December wedding. Kay and I were sharing Jerry's old room, and we both had trouble sleeping. I heard Kay weeping softly. "I'm sorry," she whispered, "I'm so jealous. You're beginning your life and I feel like mine is over."

Because my brother was neither a soldier nor on anybody's staff, there was no guaranteed pension for Kay and the children. I think it was my parents' lawyer who suggested that something should be done. He contacted Senator Robert Kennedy, who had written the Foreword to *Reported to Be Alive*. Somehow a government pension was arranged.

It was a dozen years after Jerry's death and we were burying Mother in the Jewish cemetery in Gloversville, where she would lie next to her son. We were all there—my sister Nancy and her family, Kay and the children, my parents' friends. We read prayers and poems. Eric was about thirteen, a thin boy with longish blond hair. After our little ceremony was over, I saw Eric leaning on his father's gravestone and sobbing. Neither he nor Thorina grew up with any memory of their father. Even so, there was a large blank place in their lives and in their hearts. At age thirteen, young Eric was crying his heart out for the father he never knew.

Jerry left different legacies for each of his children. Thorina grew up to become an artist and writer. Her art reminds me of Jerry's; her lines are confident and powerful. Eric looks a little like his father and inherited other abilities. Like Jerry, he is athletic and ambitious. He became an entrepreneur and a semiprofessional tennis player.

Bui Tuong Hy and Simone had welcomed me into their home when I visited Saigon in 1964. Many years later, my husband and I moved to Minnesota and discovered that Hy and Simone were living in a Minneapolis suburb. We became good friends. They shared stories about their horrendous experiences. They had been taken hostage at gun point during the early 1970s, had managed to board one of the last planes to leave Saigon, and then had their savings disappear when a Swiss bank failed. Even so, they had survived and Hy was working as an accountant for Republic Airlines. Through them, I met Vu Khoan, his wife, Hua, and other family members who had also come to Minnesota. They welcomed me like a long lost relative. We attended Khoan's funeral, when he died in the early 1980s; it was in a Vietnamese Buddhist temple just outside of Saint Paul.

It was through Hy and Simone that I learned what happened to Huan, Hy's brother and Jerry's "blood brother." Huan's wife and children escaped Saigon on one of those last harried days as the war was lost. But Huan decided to stay behind. It was his choice. He thought he could help with the transition. He believed it was his responsibility. But to the victorious incoming communist government, he was the enemy. They sent him to a "re-education" camp, where the treatment was horrific. When he was finally released from his prison, he was not allowed to work, to earn a living. His family sent him money and tried to arrange for his passage to America. He died in Saigon, from the ravages of his prison life, and never saw his family again.

Jerry's good friend Paul Vogle took a job as a UPI correspondent in Vietnam. He was in Da Nang in 1975 during the final evacuations. His dramatic and vivid story of the frenzied struggle to board the planes was published on page one of newspapers around the world.

I met Isobel (not her real name) only recently—not in person, but we've corresponded via email and had a number of long phone conversations. Actually, it was Thorina who located her, through the magic of Google. Isobel is now in her mid-80s and has been divorced for many years. Isobel told me, "Jerry was the love of my life."

Kay, Jerry's widow, was part of our family. We visited often, and we loved each other. The last time I saw Kay was in 2010; she was dying from cancer and staying with her son Eric at his home in Denver. She was rail thin and had lesions on her chest and down her arm, with cancer in her lymph nodes. I came for a few days to help, to clean and cook a few things for her, even though she had little appetite, and to talk. On the day I left, I was up before the crack of dawn. She was awake, lying there, waiting to say good-bye.

"I thought you would still be asleep," I said.

"So, is this it?" she said as I kissed her good-bye.

Kay died a week later; she was seventy-five.

I began working on this book more than a quarter of a century ago. Jerry had left behind hundreds of pages in journal entries, letters, articles, stories, a partially completed novel, and miscellaneous notes, much of it exquisitely written. He intended to use these materials to craft his fiction. He was meticulous in recording his thoughts and organizing his papers. Kay had stored all his documents, and she worked with me at Kinkos to photocopy page after page.

I pored through my brother's diaries and letters. I located and interviewed—mostly by phone or letter—about two dozen of Jerry's friends and colleagues: Malcolm Browne, Bui Diệm, Daniel Ellsberg, Takashi Oka, Otto Friedrichs, David Lyle, Paul Vogle, and many others.

Many of his fellow journalists were full of praise: "He was very sensitive and absorbed much more of his surroundings than other journalists." "I would include Jerry as among those journalists who had the best grasp of Vietnamese politics." "He was a remarkable man." "He was a writer with a gift for expressing the brutality of combat—graphically and evocatively." "His book—*Reported to be Alive*—was one of the best ever done. It was in a class by itself. And it told a lot about Jerry—about his ability to grasp what was happening in one of the back eddies of the war—in Laos."

I also studied books on Vietnam, as background reading. One of the most famous books was by Stanley Karnow, *Vietnam: A History*, which was turned into a PBS series and received numerous awards. Karnow had been Jerry's boss at *Time*. Something odd happened when I was in the middle of reading that book. I was sitting on a swivel chair in my family room. It was winter and I was facing our backyard, which was blanketed with snow. I was on page 232 when I came upon the sentence, "About that time, accompanied by an interpreter, I wandered into hamlets and villages in the Mekong delta, along the coast of central Vietnam, and in the highlands near the Laotian border." It was as if my breath stopped. I knew those words.

As I read on, I recognized the stories. They were all familiar. I had read them, memorized passages from Jerry's journals, from his hazardous travels through and around the countryside between December 1961 and January of 1962. Of course, Jerry had submitted all these materials to Karnow. They had co-authored articles for *Time* and Jerry had published many of his own articles, based on these materials. Out of Karnow's book of more than 700 pages, three pages are based on these journals, with no attribution, no reference anywhere to Jerry Rose.

I worked intensively on this project, half-time for seven months, while I had a research position for the other half of my time. By the end of seven months, I had completed a draft of a biography of my brother.

Then I returned to my full-time research career and put the manuscript aside. In part, I abandoned this project because I had run out of time. The book needed serious revision and I was immersed in my career. But there was something else. Kay was increasingly uncomfortable with what I was writing. As a very private person, she felt invaded; it wasn't just Jerry's story, it was also hers.

My manuscript draft, my document copies, and all my notes sat sequestered in three drawers of my file cabinet for a quarter of a century.

After Kay died, I began to think again about working on Jerry's book. Thorina wanted to donate his papers to the Hoover Institute at Stanford University. She had boxes of papers, tapes and other materials filling up her garage. She wanted the space back and was worried the documents would be damaged. Before all the boxes were sent off, I spent a week with Thorina at her home in San Francisco making notes and copying more documents.

In the last year of his life, Jerry was a ghost writer. That was what he was when he wrote *Reported to Be Alive*. It was Grant Wolfkill's story. Jerry worked with hours and hours of interviews and Grant's dictations. With these raw materials, he created a book of Grant's story, in Grant's voice. It was a beautifully written book, praised in a review in *The New York Times Book Review*. "The characters stand out as vividly as the events."

But that book was not my brother's dream. He saw himself as a writer of fiction, an artist. He was working on a novel about Vietnam. But he never finished his big novel. His work as a journalist and his many other projects got in the way. Then he died.

Jerry was my mentor, my teacher, in writing and art. It was as if he trained me for a task that neither of us would have anticipated. I am my brother's ghost writer now, charged with drafting the book that he might have written, if only he had lived. As I was working on this book, Jerry was sitting on my shoulder, whispering in my ear.

This memoir is his art, his writing, his story, more than half a century late.

APPENDIX

A Brief Timeline of the Vietnam/American War and Related Events

1887   •   Vietnam becomes a French colony

1923-25   •   Ho Chi Minh trains in the Soviet Union

1930   •   Ho Chi Minh founds the Indochinese Communist Party

1940   •   Japanese troops invade French Indochina

1941   •   Ho Chi Minh establishes the Viet Minh, to fight both French and Japanese

       •   Japanese attack U.S. at Pearl Harbor

1945   •   U.S. drops atomic bombs on Hiroshima and Nagasaki

       •   Japan defeated

       •   Ho Chi Minh models a Vietnamese Declaration of Independence on U.S. declaration

       •   France tries to reassert colonial rule

1947   •   Truman Doctrine: U.S. will assist any country against communism

1949   • French install former Emperor Bao Dai as head of state in Vietnam

       • Soviet Union tests its first atomic bomb

       • Mao Zedong creates the People's Republic of China

1950-54 • U.S. views Viet Minh as a communist threat and supports the French

1954   • French troops defeated by Viet Minh forces at Dien Bien Phu

       • President Eisenhower says the fall of French Indochina to communists could create a "domino" effect, with other countries falling to the communists

       • Geneva Accords establish North and South Vietnam divided at the 17th parallel

1955   • Catholic nationalist Ngô Đình Diệm emerges as the leader of South Vietnam, with U.S. backing

       • Ho Chi Minh leads the communist state in the north.

1959   • North Vietnam begins to build the "Ho Chi Minh trail"—a supply route to support guerrilla attacks against Diệm's government in the south

       • First U.S. casualty in Vietnam

1960   • North Vietnam establishes the National Liberation Front (NLF) as anti-government insurgency in South Vietnam. The US calls the NLF "Viet Cong"– Vietnamese communists

1961 • President Kennedy authorizes secret operations against the Viet Cong and sends helicopters and 400 Green Berets to South Vietnam

1962 • U.S. starts spraying Agent Orange to kill vegetation that gives cover to Viet Cong

1963 • The Ngô Đình Diệm government opens fire on a crowd of Buddhist protestors in Huê, killing 8 people, including children

• A 73-year-old monk, Thich Quang Duc, immolates himself in protest

1963 • A South Vietnam military coup, backed by the U.S., topples the Diệm government

• Diệm and his brother, Ngo Dinh Nhu, head of the secret police, are assassinated

• President Kennedy is assassinated in Dallas, TX

• Lyndon Johnson becomes U.S. President

1963-65 • In South Vietnam, 12 *coups-d'etat* replace one government after another

1964 • *USS Maddox* allegedly is attacked by North Vietnamese torpedo boats in the Gulf of Tonkin.

• The Gulf of Tonkin Resolution authorizes the U.S. President to "take all necessary measures, including the use of armed force"

• President Johnson calls for air strikes on North Vietnamese patrol boat bases

1965
- President Johnson orders the bombing of targets in North Vietnam and the Ho Chi Minh Trail
- U.S. Marines land on beaches near Da Nang, South Vietnam—the first American combat troops
- President Johnson calls for 50,000 more ground troops to be sent to Vietnam
- Nearly 300 Americans are killed and hundreds more injured in the first large-scale battle of the war

1966
- 400,000 U.S. troops in Vietnam
- American aircraft attack targets in Hanoi and Haiphong

1967
- 500,000 U.S. troops in Vietnam
- Massive anti-Vietnam war protests in Washington, D.C., New York City and San Francisco

1968
- Siege of U.S. Marine garrison at Khe Sanh in South Vietnam by North Vietnamese army lasts 77 days.
- Tet Offensive: Viet Minh and North Vietnamese armies carry out attacks in more than 100 cities and outposts across South Vietnam
- In the ancient imperial capital of Hue, communist forces execute at least 2,800 people, mostly South Vietnamese civilians
- Mai Lai: U.S. forces massacre more than 500 civilians in a small village
- Republican Richard M. Nixon wins the U.S. presidential election

1969   • U.S. institutes the first draft lottery since World
              War II

1969-72   • Gradual reduction of U.S. forces in strategy known
              as Vietnamization

            • Secret U.S. bombings in Cambodia against Ho Chi
              Minh trail

1970   • Henry Kissinger begins secret peace negotiations in
              Paris

            • Kent State: National Guardsmen kill 4 students and
              wound 9—all anti-war demonstrators

            • U.S. Congress repeals Gulf of Tonkin Resolution

1971   • The *New York Times* publishes the "Pentagon
              Papers"–documents released by Daniel Ellsberg—
              which reveal how the U.S. government repeatedly
              and secretly increased U.S. involvement in the war

1972   • North Vietnam launches a large Easter Offensive
              against the Army of the Republic of Vietnam and
              U.S. forces

            • U.S. bombers drop 20,000 tons of bombs over
              densely populated regions in Hanoi and Haiphong

1973   • The Selective Service announces the end to the draft
              and institutes an all-volunteer military.

            • President Nixon signs the Paris Peace Accords,
              ending direct U.S. involvement in the Vietnam War.
              The North Vietnamese accept a cease fire

            • North Vietnam returns 591 American prisoners of
              war

1974
- President Nixon resigns after the Watergate scandal
- Gerald R. Ford becomes President

1975
- Saigon falls and the government of South Vietnam surrenders.
- U.S. Marine and Air Force helicopters rescue 1,000 American civilians and 7,000 South Vietnamese refugees in an 18-hour mass evacuation effort
- North and South Vietnam are unified as the Socialist Republic of Vietnam under hardline communist rule

1982
- Vietnam Veterans Memorial opens in Washington, DC

1995
- Under President Bill Clinton, the U.S. normalizes relations with Vietnam

Death Toll from America's Vietnam War:
- 58,000 Americans
- 250,000 South Vietnamese soldiers
- 1.1 million North Vietnamese and Viet Cong fighters
- 2 million civilians on both sides
- 135 journalists

ACKNOWLEDGMENTS

I had the first spark of an idea for a book on my brother sometime in the mid-1980s. I was at a life history conference where an author (it might have been Tim O'Brien) shared his experiences as a soldier in Vietnam. I thought—my brother's story would be different. I knew that Kay, my sister-in-law and Jerry's widow, had saved and carefully stored his papers, published and unpublished.

I had no idea it would take so long to finish and publish this book. The book has morphed, so I have written 100 versions—maybe more. If I had known how long this would take, I wonder if I ever would have started on this journey.

I'm grateful to Kay for her generosity in sharing Jerry's papers and even helping me copy hundreds of pages. So many people helped along the way that it's almost hard to count. Three editors coached me at various points: Marni Freedman, Judy Bernstein and Mary Carroll Moore. Many others served as readers of different versions: Lynn Abrahamsen, Susan Chambers, Father Dave, Melpo Murdakes, Ruth Sloven, Gabrielle Lawrence, Susan Weinberg, Merav Fima, Ted Engelmann, Elizabeth Ensho, Carlo Coppo, and Anna Menniti. Bonnie Blodgett was my agent for a very early version of the book.

Debra Orenstein provided legal counsel. Many thanks to Brooke Warner and Lauren Wise at Spark Press and to Marika Flatt and Leslie Barrett at PR By the Book.

My niece and nephew, Thorina Rose and Eric Rose, have been supportive of this project and granted me permission to use their father's papers and photos. I am especially grateful to my husband, Mark Fischer, who not only read several renderings of the full manuscript, but also has supported me along the bumpy and circuitous path of creating this book.

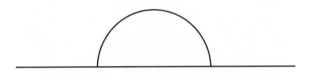

ABOUT THE AUTHORS

Jerry **A. Rose** was a writer, painter, journalist, and photographer. His feature articles and photographs regularly appeared in *Time*, *The New York Times*, *The Saturday Evening Post*, *New Republic*, *The Reporter*, and other news venues. He had an MA in Creative Writing from the Iowa Writers Workshop and published fiction in literary magazines and two books: *Reported to be Alive* and *Face of Anguish*. www.jerryrosevietnam.com

Lucy Rose Fischer is an award-winning Minnesota author, artist, and social scientist. Her previous books include *Linked Lives: Adult Daughters and Their Mothers*, *Older Minnesotans*, *Older Volunteers*, *I'm New at Being Old*, and *Grow Old With Me*. She has an MA in Southeast Asian Studies from the University of California, Berkeley, and a PhD in Sociology from the University of Massachusetts, Amherst. www.lucyrosedesigns.com

SELECTED TITLES FROM SPARKPRESS

SparkPress is an independent boutique publisher delivering high-quality, entertaining, and engaging content that enhances readers' lives, with a special focus on female-driven work. www.gosparkpress.com

*The Restless Hungarian: Modernism, Madness, and The American Dream,*Tom Weidlinger. $16.95, 978-1-943006-96-0.A revolutionary, a genius, and a haunted man . . . The story of the architect-engineer Paul Weidlinger, whose colleagues called him "The Wizard," spans the rise of modern architecture, the Holocaust, and the Cold War. The revelation of hidden Jewish identity propels the author to trace his father's life and adventures across three continents.

Mission Afghanistan: An Army Doctor's Memoir, Elie Cohen, translation by Jessica Levine. $16.95, 978-1-943006-65-6. Decades after evading conscription as a young man, Franco-British doctor Elie Paul Cohen is offered a deal by the French Army: he can settle his accounts by becoming a military doctor and serving at Camp Bastion in Afghanistan.

Engineering a Life: A Memoir, Krishan K. Bedi. $16.95, 978-1-943006-43-4. A memoir of Krishan Bedi's experiences as a young Indian man in the South in the 1960s, this is a story of one man's perseverance and determination to create the life he'd always dreamed for himself and his family, despite his options seeming anything but limitless.

The House that Made Me: Writers Reflect on the Places and People That Defined Them, edited by Grant Jarrett. $17, 978-1-940716-31-2. In this candid, evocative collection of essays, a diverse group of acclaimed authors reflect on the diverse homes, neighborhoods, and experiences that helped shape them—using Google Earth software to revisit the location in the process.

A Story That Matters: A Gratifying Approach to Writing About Your Life, Gina Carroll. $16.95, 9-781-943006-12-0. With each chapter focusing on stories from the seminal periods of a lifetime—motherhood, childhood, relationships, work, and spirit—*A Story That Matters* provides the tools and motivation to craft and complete the stories of your life.

About SparkPress

SparkPress is an independent, hybrid imprint focused on merging the best of the traditional publishing model with new and innovative strategies. We deliver high-quality, entertaining, and engaging content that enhances readers' lives. We are proud to bring to market a list of *New York Times* best-selling, award-winning, and debut authors who represent a wide array of genres, as well as our established, industry-wide reputation for creative, results-driven success in working with authors. SparkPress, a BookSparks imprint, is a division of SparkPoint Studio LLC.

Learn more at GoSparkPress.com